THE SIEGE OF
MASADA

THE SIEGE

OF

MASADA

JODIE LANE

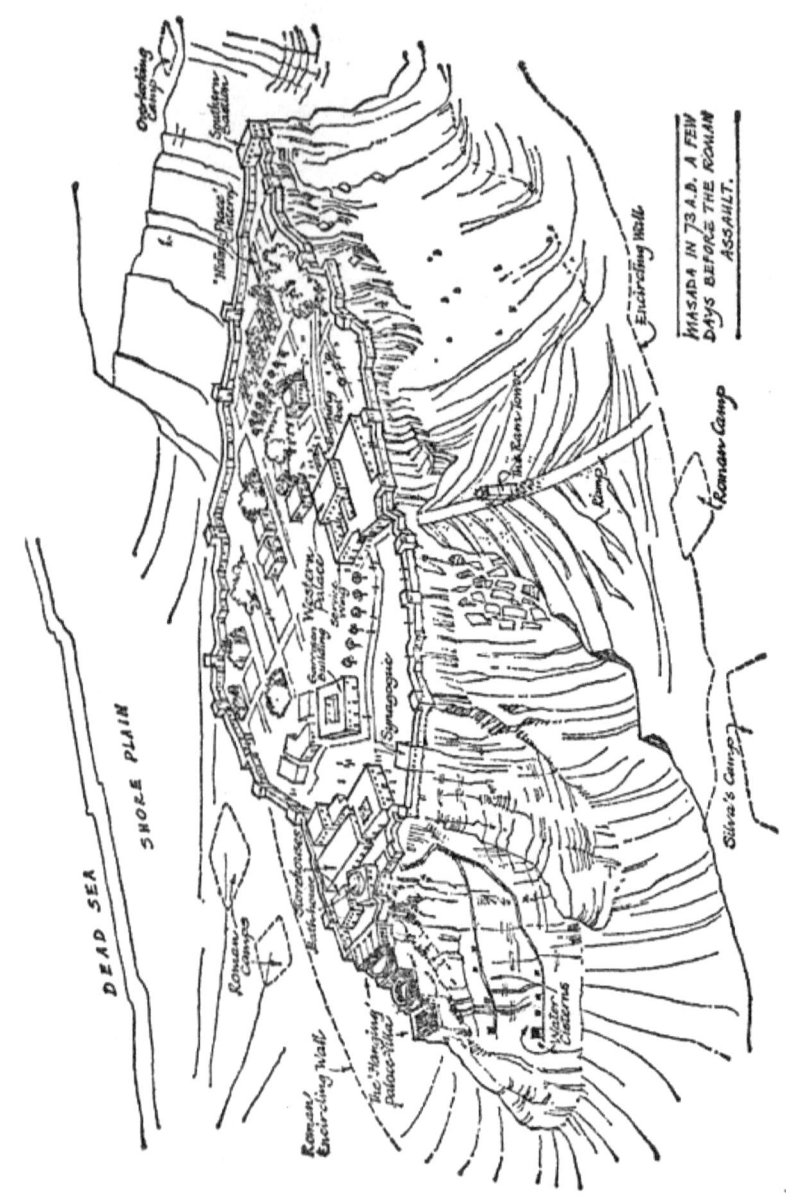

MASADA IN 73 A.D. A FEW DAYS BEFORE THE ROMAN ASSAULT.

ONE

PRESENT DAY

Helicopter gunships patrolled the sky above the beach, the deep whir of blades an ominous reminder that this wasn't a normal family holiday. Gwyn gazed out the hotel window, the Mediterranean deceptively serene beyond the wind stretch of sand below, the city of Tel-Aviv hidden from view behind her.

"Gwyn?" her younger sister, Naomi, called from the living room. "Hurry up and get changed! We're going to the beach!"

"I'm getting there!" Gwyn wished she was as effortlessly unselfconscious in a bikini as Naomi. She wished she could go to the beach by herself but her parents insisted they stick together since they were in a foreign country. She had been so excited to finish the semester and fly over to Israel, but the experience was turning out to be disconcerting. Instead of an exotic land, rich with history, they were staying in a modern city. Stuck with her family for every walk, every meal, Gwyn chafed to go and explore.

Then she would see the soldiers. Young men and women barely older than her old nineteen years toted semi-automatic rifles as they strolled the streets. They were attractive and sophisticated, laughing at each other's joke, at ease with their looks and power.

Gwyn's courage slunk back into a quiet place every time she thought about asking to venture out on her own.

"Come on, Gwyn!" Naomi hassled from the doorway. "Nobody cares what you look like!"

How her younger sister was so much more confident that her, she would never know, but she retorted. "Shut up, or I'll tell Mom and Dad you wandered off at Changi Airport." Gwyn had been frantic—the responsibility of looking after her siblings has been pressed upon her by their parents, but Naomi had reappeared, unflappable after getting lost for half an hour.

With typical arrogance, her sister responded, "And I'll tell Mom and Dad you weren't watching me and Justin properly, you were too busy reading."

Gwyn slammed the bathroom door in her sister's face—or tried to, at least. The soft-close cushioning of the handle ruined the effect. She hauled on her one-piece, glaring at the string bikini lying neglected on her bed, and stormed out of the bathroom, towel wrapped modestly around her waist, joining her family as they exited the suite.

"Finally," Naomi's twin, Justin, muttered. Gwyn glared at him. Her brother was as carefree as his twin—nothing fazed him.

Down on the hot sands, they threaded their way between olive-skinned locals who filled the beach. Gwyn sighed at the gorgeous women and handsome men, sunbathing and playing sport. She felt frumpy and plunged straight into the water, putting distance between herself and her family.

We'll start the tours tomorrow. Then I'll get to see some historical sites and really get a feel for the place. Something a bit more exciting than going to the beach. We can do that at home anytime.

She reminded herself not to be ungrateful. Her parents' contract would finish in a week and the Turners would travel on to Europe for an extended holiday. University didn't start back for two months, but she hoped they might let her defer a semester and stay on by herself.

You can't leave it until the last minute to ask, you know. They'll never say yes if you spring it on them. Besides, they think study is the most important thing in the world, even if you're doing history, not science.

A wave lifted her and Gwyn tried to let the buoyancy soothe her turmoil. *I have to just be brave and ask. Insist even. They can't hold me back forever. I want to travel and see the world, not molder away in suburbia.*

She vowed to spend the next few days showing her parents how sensible and responsible she could be. Getting her siblings over to Israel was just the start. By the end of the week, they would be so impressed that they would be certain to agree to her staying overseas by herself for a few months. She was an adult, after all.

* * *

"I liked the Bahai Gardens," Naomi said. "They were pretty. It's just Jerusalem was boring."

"Except when we saw the beggar dude switching legs near the Wailing Wall!" Justin interjected. "It was like out of *Life of Brian*, Dad!"

Their father laughed.

Gwyn grimaced. How her sister could call one of the most ancient cities in the most boring was insulting. She stared out the window of the minivan—south of Tel Aviv, the bumpy highway was bordered by flat-roofed houses, white and brown and stark in the bright sun. Hills capped with eucalypts gave a strange reminder of home, but as they left the city behind, the road swing east and buildings became few and far between. The hills grew barren and rocky, yellowing grasses and low-lying scrub clusters along invisible underground water sources.

"I liked the gardens too," her mother chimed in. "They were so vibrant and perfect. And seeing Damascus from the Golan Heights was incredible. Looking down into another country. What did you like the most over the last few days, Gwyn?"

She dragged her attention back into the vehicle. Their driver and guide, Benjamin, hummed quietly as he concentrated on driving. Her family looked at Gwyn expectantly.

"The port at Jaffa was cool," she said at last. "I liked imagining the Phoenicians setting sail from there, heading to Egypt, and Greece, and other places."

"Check that out!" exclaimed Justin, gawping at a small Bedouin encampment. In the lee of a small, rocky hill sat a battered old caravan hitched up to a rusty sedan. Beside it stood two camels and a donkey, while a satellite dish perched incongruously atop the van.

He and Naomi spent the next half hour of the drive wondering out loud what TV shows might be watched by the Bedouins. Gwyn returned her attention out of the window. Now and then, acres of date palms sprang up out of nowhere—vivid green oases amidst the stark dryness. But even they petered out as they skirted the northern edge of the stony Negev Desert.

After driving east for well over an hour, the road curved north towards the western shore of the Dead Sea and a small, steep mountain loomed. Benjamin guided the minivan into the gravel car park. Before them, a wide path of white rock slanted up to the ruins perched atop the strange, flat mountain.

"Masada was a palace built upon a natural mesa," Benjamin explained as they looked up at the ruins. "It was fortified by King Herod the Great and other Jewish kings that followed him. But it is most famous for holding out against the Romans who besieged it in 74 AD. The Jews inside refused to capitulate—instead choosing to commit suicide rather than surrender to the Romans."

"Sick," muttered Justin.

Gwyn stuck close to Benjamin, puffing hard as they reached the top. He wiped his brow, sweat dripping into his beard. "The ramp you just climbed was built by the Roman General, Flavius Silva." Benjamin gestured. "Come over into the shade and I will explain how the siege took place."

The Turners gratefully clustered under an archway. Gwyn fanned herself with her hand as she listened.

"The Romans conquered Judea, bringing their own gods, customs and laws. The Jewish people of the time were allowed to continue to govern themselves for the most part, but many, including a group called the Zealots and another called the Sicarii, hated the invaders, and fought for independence. The Romans sacked Jerusalem as punishment, and the survivors fled her, to Masada.

"Less than a thousand men, woman and children were inside when the Romans laid siege, but they had food and water to last them a long time."

"Where did they get water from?" Gwyn piped up. "It's so dry."

Benjamin nodded. "There are great cisterns that collected the winter rains. This building was a Christian church built hundreds of years after the siege, and soon I will take you to Herod's Northern Palace. At the other end of the plateau there was space for fields and gardens, for goats and other animals that were kept for food and wool."

He led them out into the sun again, pointing out the collapsed stone walls that outlined the synagogue to their left. Broken columns bordered bigger ruins ahead.

"This is the Northern Palace," Benjamin announced. "There are bath houses, storerooms, meeting rooms…"

Naomi and Justin wandered off, bored with the history lesson. They began exploring and guessing at the uses of various rooms. While her dad was taking photos, Gwyn and her mother trailed after Benjamin as he described how despite their supplies, once the ramp was built the Sicarii realized the Romans would overcome their defenses and they would be killed or enslaved.

They preferred to die that be a slave. I can't blame them, Gwyn reflected. *Defending their country against the invaders—refusing to give in even though they were the last ones left fighting. They were so brave.*

"Come on, Gwyn," her mother called. "You'll get left behind."

Snapping out of her reverie, she hurried after her mother and they made their way through the ruins of the northern palace down to the lower terraces. Gwyn marveled at the view. The cliffs on the eastern side fell away four hundred meters down towards the Dead Sea. Jordan could be seen clearly on the other side.

The approach on all other sides of the mountain was steep and difficult, if not impossible in most areas. The sun glared down upon the ruins. She tried to imagine the hustle and bustle of people living here, Romans fighting to take the fortress, but the baking heat sapped her imagination and the best she could conjure were faded ghosts and whispered cries of battle.

"I wish the bath houses were operational," Gwyn's mother exclaimed. "I could use the cool down."

Benjamin heard her. "The underground cisterns would have been more to your taste, Mrs. Turner. In fact, the only survivors of the siege hid there when the fortress burned. Two women and some children, by the account of the Jewish historian Josephus.

Gwyn barely heard him. The thought of water taunted her. They had all finished their bottles and the twins harangued their dad, asking if they could catch the cable car down to the visitors' center.

"No, we are all going to walk," he ruled. "It's only two kilometers, and all downhill. It'll be good for you."

"I'd hate to be doing this uphill," Gwyn muttered to herself fifteen minutes later. The Snake Path twisted its way back and forth through the rock, with sharp switchbacks over precipitous cliffs and narrow cuts through looming boulders. Towards the bottom, it flattened out to meet the station of the cable car and the Yigal Yadin Masada Museum, with its restaurant and souvenir shop. Her parents trundled after the twins who were tearing down the hillside faster than the man from Snowy River, albeit without the horse. Halfway down, before the path turned sharply away from the cliff and into a narrow ravine that cut through the rock, Gwyn stopped to take a few photos with her phone of the vista before her—the Dead Sea laid out below, stark desert surrounding.

A clattering of stones and the sound of shouts made her turn. Dust rose, and a figure darted along the path, knocking Gwyn off balance. She tripped and fell—pain and indignation shooting through her.

The figure glanced behind. It was a woman, long hair whipping around her face. Her eyes widened before she took a flying leap off a low outcrop. She hit the ground with a perfect roll and kept running, flinging something into the scrubby bushes that grew on the path edge. A man barreled past Gwyn and chased the woman into a ravine. Another man, burly and thickset, stepped out from behind a rock and tackled the woman. The man in pursuit reached the woman and her assailant seconds later and then, as Gwyn blinked, a blue mist sprang up and when it faded, they were gone.

"What the—?" Baffled, she scrambled up, wincing slightly, as her mother came rushing back up the path.

"Sweetheart! Are you okay? What happened?" she demanded, breathing heavily from her uphill run.

"Uh, uh, I'm fine," Gwyn started to say. "This woman, she …" She trailed off, staring hard at the spot where the people had been. "Where did she go?" She wondered, distracted from her bruised butt and scraped elbow.

"What woman? All I could see was dust and you slipping over! Did you hit your head? How many fingers am I holding up?" her mother grasped Gwyn's shoulders gently, and patted her, testing for any injuries, then waved her digits in front of Gwyn's face.

"I'm fine, Mom. I'm fine!" She rubbed her eyes, the dust making her blink. *Sheesh, overprotective.* "Four fingers! It was just some woman, she ran past and shoved me. I'm sure it was an accident. I didn't see where she went."

Gwyn walked down the path to look for her phone. Scrabbling around in the bushes, a small round metallic object caught her eye. It looked like a small pocket watch, complete with an intricate chain. She picked it up and shoved it into her pocket with her phone, replaying the scene with the woman in her mind. *She threw this.*

"Gwyn?"

Snapping back to the present, Gwyn called, "I'm okay, Mom, just a little winded."

It was tempting to blurt out everything she had seen, from the pursuing men to the disappearing act. Someone had been chased and possibly abducted in front of her. But if her mother hadn't seen it, maybe she imagined it? People didn't just disappear. Was it some Israeli military secret, a new technology to cloak people? That seemed ridiculous. But here was the thing she picked up—the pocket watch, or whatever it was—proof that what she saw had really happened. Her mother would make Gwyn hand it in, and she wanted a chance to look at it herself before that happened.

So she let her mother brush the worst of the dust off her as her dad came huffing and puffing up the hill. He'd seen his wife panic at the commotion, yelled at the twins to stay put and hurried after her. After assuring her parents she was well enough for them to stop fussing, they descended at a statelier pace. No more mention of the mysterious woman was made, and Gwyn decided not to bring it up in case they thought she'd concussed herself. But her thoughts kept drifting back to the strange incident up on the hill.

TWO

2623 AD

"You are under arrest for unauthorized time travel in a restricted period. You are also charged with evading Time Police, resisting arrest, and possession of an unlicensed chronokinetor. You will be remanded in custody until such time as your trial can be held."

Glaring, Michelle snapped back at him, "You're way out of your depth, constable! I'm a special Agent; I have authority for this mission! Check the ID your goons pinched from me, or go straight to Commissioner Hera. She'll clear this up in a second."

"I'm afraid you'll have to go through the proper channels. I can't be bothering the Commissioner with a standard arrest."

His slight smirk made Michelle realize that he knew she was an Agent, and that this was bigger than simple confusion over authorization. Someone had put him up to this. But who? And why?

Her captor must have read the confusion in her face. He hissed. "You don't even remember who I am, do you? Think you're so much better than the rest of us? Agent Michelle, the Commissioner's pet."

Is... is this personal? She wondered. *Surely not. There is too much at stake!*

"Always swanking about, coming and going on your secret missions," he carried on. "While the rest of us do the real work."

Michelle knew not everyone liked her—some people took her being the best as an insult, especially given she was a scholarship nobody. But she wasn't aware she had an enemy in the Agency that had this kind of pull. The fact that they could snatch her from the middle of a classified mission in a restricted time zone was worrying. *I need more information.*

"You're Kenneth, aren't you?" she tried.

"Rickas!" he snarled. "Can't even remember the name of us lowly guards. Too busy fornicating with aliens and ignoring your own kind. Even getting given the best tech—power you don't deserve! Well, you're on your own now, and none of them can save you."

He whirled and disappeared down the corridor. Michelle leaned close to the force field that enclosed the open side of her cell, the proximity of her breath making it hum faintly.

Rickas. I don't recognize the name. But he clearly hates me. Interesting.

As the silence descended, Michelle realized that she was the only one incarcerated on this level.

His words echoed. *The best tech...* He meant her chronokinetor, the one she had thrown away when she knew she was going to get caught.

The one she couldn't afford to return to the Agency without.

* * *

Time passed steadily in Michelle's cell. As one who had spent most of her professional life in time travel, her body was attuned to the passing seconds, minutes, hours—she knew without counting she had been incarcerated for a little over a day, despite having no clock, no visitors, and only one meal.

This frugal fare had been delivered through an electronic opening in her cell wall, removing the need for human contact. It was dull prison food—synthesized protein and carbohydrates with requisite quantities of vitamins and minerals—processed into grey mush. Synth could be made to look like anything you wanted—real meat, fresh vegetables, tasty fruit—but this unappealing pottage was easy, cheap, and reminded inmates that they didn't deserve anything better. Michelle wondered idly if it had sedatives in it (not unheard of in many prisons) but decided that not eating it would result in her weakening regardless. She didn't know exactly where she was anyway—she'd been unconscious from the time of her capture.

She spent her time stretching, meditating, doing various strength and core exercises, and sleeping. The cell provided a narrow bed in one corner, a toilet and sink in the other. Everything was fixed—not that dismantling the furniture would help. Any object thrown at the force field or the food dispenser would immediately set off an alarm and result in nerve gas being released into the cell, incapacitating her in less than ten seconds.

So she bided her time. She assumed she was under observation, but she didn't care. Maintaining mental and physical fitness while imprisoned was part of any agent's training. She wasn't doing anything visible that was out of the norm. But they couldn't see what she was thinking, or planning, and when the time came to act, she would be ready.

THREE

PRESENT DAY

"Check out this mud!" Justin's hands delved deeper into the well and pasted the black sediment all down his arms and legs.

"Gwyn! Do my back please, Gwyn!" Naomi had already covered her face, arms and legs.

Despite herself, Gwyn laughed and compiled. She would never admit she secretly loved it when her sister asked for help. It made her feel needed.

Painting black mud over Naomi's pale skin, the bright rainbow bikini shouted in contrast. Gwyn had inherited their father's tawnier complexion, but the mineral-rich mud put even her tan to shame.

"I'll have to buy some of their skin-care products before we leave En Gedi," her mother mentioned. "It's meant to be full of nutrients. Gwyn, would you like me to get you some too? It's important to have a good skin-care routine."

Gwyn's good mood dissipated, but she forced a smile. "Thanks, Mom, that's really thoughtful of you." *She's being nice, she is. She's not saying you have crap skin, stop thinking like that!*

"Come on, kids!" her dad held up his phone. "Let's take some happy snaps!"

Gwyn maintained her smile for the photos, then rinsed under the sulfurous-smelling outdoor showers at the edge of the Dead Sea. The oasis of En Gedi was one of the few access places that remained after sinkholes threatened many parts of the arid shore.

Unlike swimming in the Mediterranean, the section of the Dead Sea they were allowed to enter was cramped and she couldn't put space between her and everyone else. Gwyn bobbed gently—she couldn't sink even if she tried—and tried to relax, but the scrape on her elbow stung. Her siblings were getting rowdy trying to sink each other and her parents were absorbed in discussion about the level of the water table. It occurred to Gwyn it was the perfect opportunity to examine the pocket watch she had found. The relief in having an excuse to escape flooded her.

"I need some shade."

Her mother nodded understanding and returned to the conversation. Gwyn left her family floating and made her way to the women's change rooms. They were empty apart from her. Once clothed in light cargo pants and button up quick dry shirt, Gwyn pulled out the strange object she'd picked up from the Snake Path at Masada.

It really did look like a pocket watch. Round, with quite a pretty chain of some strange metal. A shiny, brassy look, but somehow not slippery like metal. Not rough either, but it had a textured feel, as opposed to smooth. It was slightly warm in her hand. A spiral symbol, like a sketch of the Milky Way, was etched on the outside. She flipped it over. The same spiral, but reversed in direction, was on the back.

She looked about furtively. She didn't know why, except for that there was something strange about this thing. Maybe it *was* some sort of new Israeli military technology. The circumstances of its discovery, the disappearing act by the woman and her pursuers, intrigued her. *Am I being over-imaginative?*

There was no one else in the change rooms. Gwyn was alone. She rested the pocket watch in her left hand and peered at the device, gently trying to crack the circumference seal with her right thumb.

Whoosh! It was like a window had been opened whilst driving a car at high speed. Air rushed and funneled around her, blasting her ears and forcing her to stumble. For a moment the pocket watch seared hot in her palm, then the pain numbed, but the heaviness of the device remained. Her stomach lurched, a sensation of weightlessness lifted her innards as she was falling ...

Sudden silence. Gravity existed again, but all she could see was a blue haze. She cast about frantically and the haze started to fade. Her surroundings sharpened, and the noise of the world crept back in. At first she couldn't identify the sounds, but then shouting voices and the clash of metal became louder and louder. She was in a room, a small room. *This isn't the women's change rooms!* Clay bowls lay on a rickety wooden table next to her, a woven mat on the floor. It wasn't as hot as before, but she could smell smoke in the air.

"Devil ghost!"

She whirled. A man was half-crouched in the doorway, expression frozen between awe and terror. He was filthy, dark skin smeared with smoke, dirt and ... blood? He held a curved knife in his right hand, blotted with stickiness.

"What?" It was her voice, but the sounds she made weren't English. Higher pitched in panic, she demanded, "Who are you!? Where–?"

A blinding pain shot through her skull and she fell forward. Her hands shot out, but the pocket watch was embedded in her left palm and jabbed into her as she struck the ground. Reflexively, she dragged her hand towards her chest, groaning dully. Swift footsteps echoed in her ear as the second man in the room administered another crack on her head, and she passed out.

* * *

74 AD

"She just appeared! I tell you! We were looking for supplies, the room was empty, then a blue cloud appeared and there she was!"

Gwyn groaned softly, wincing at her headache. The voices in the room were insistent, and she hated them for disturbing her.

"Women don't just appear! Were you drinking?" The second voice challenged, less strident but still demanding.

"Of course I wasn't drinking! We were fighting any who dared to resist us and gathering what we could. Some of the huts caught fire. Joshua was searching this one, I followed him in, then—whoosh! Demon ghost woman appeared!"

"Hmm. Then Joshua knocked her out and brought her back here." The second voice sounded older. Gwyn's brain de-fuzzed enough for her to peer out from under her eyelids at the speakers. The man from the hut—the filthy one with the knife—stood exasperated in front of an older, bearded man in a dark brown robe, who looked skeptical. Her eyes slid carefully about the room. Her attacker was nowhere in sight. This did not reassure her. Her brain, waking up by the second, noticed that no English was being spoken, but she understood every word. *How is that even possible?*

The decor in the room also concerned her. Like the hut where she'd been viciously attacked, it was … well, rustic was the best word she could find for it. Stone, clay, wood—you could sum up the walls and furniture in those three words. Nothing … modern about it.

Her stomach sank, and she began to worry. *Something is very wrong here.*

"She's awake." The voice was deep, but quiet.

Gwyn jolted—he was standing right behind her! No wonder she hadn't seen him. He moved quickly to her side, not touching her but obviously ready to restrain should she demonstrate any demon- or ghost-like abilities. She had been lying on a table, now she shifted so she was half-sitting, half-crouched at one end, eyes darting between the man who'd hit her, knife-man (knife not currently in evidence), and the older, bearded man.

"Well?" Beard raised bushy eyebrows. "Are you a demon or ghost?"

What is he talking about? Her mind began to race. *Where the hell am I? Why on earth is he talking about demons and ghosts? This must be a dream, a really, really weird dream.*

A sterner voice in her head spoke up. *OK, if this is a dream, it is an extremely vivid and painful one. Let's play it safe and avoid getting clocked again.* She straightened and took a deep breath, shaking her head emphatically. Despite the pounding it caused, she managed to assert in a low voice, "I'm not a ghost, *definitely* not a demon."

She paused there—she wanted to find out more before she started volunteering information. She was definitely speaking the same language as them. How this was possible she wasn't sure, but at least it put them on the same playing field for communication.

"How did you come to be in En Gedi?" The bearded man's questions were measured, which reassured her to a certain extent.

Not as panicky as knife-man, who, visibly agitated, said, "She just appeared, Rabbi! Like I told you! Blue cloud, whoosh–"

"Yes, Gad, but I want to hear from her," the Rabbi glanced at Joshua, who stood silently at the end of the table slightly behind her on the right. Gwyn followed his gaze nervously. Deeply tanned and with several vicious scars on his face, Joshua was short but well-muscled and looked as if he'd been in plenty of fights. He'd already proved himself quick and more than capable of acting violently. Her head ached furiously as she concentrated. What should she say? She had no idea where she was, or how she'd gotten here…

The pocket watch! She managed not to glance at her left hand, but a quick exploration of her palm with her thumb told her that it was somehow embedded there. Funny, it didn't hurt anymore, even though she could feel the clear demarcation between metal and skin. The chain had wrapped itself around and *into* her wrist and set there, looking for all the world like a tattoo. Only a close examination would reveal the slight raised bumps it made.

"I don't know," she faced the Rabbi fully. "I don't know where I am, or how I got here. Why was I attacked? Who are you?" She tried to load her tone with confidence, demanding answers, quashing the terror that they would dismiss her as mad and dangerous.

The Rabbi eyed her with interest. He didn't answer for some time, rather he glanced at Joshua, and at Gad, then back to her, and replied slowly. "You are in the fortress of Masada."

Gwyn's heart beat faster.

He continued, "We are the last loyal Jews, fighting against the Roman invaders."

The only change in Gwyn's expression was the slightly stressed tightening of her lips. *Last loyal Jews? Masada? Romans? Either they are mad, or I'm dreaming, or… I've gone back in time.*

* * *

"So you say you have no idea how you came to be in En Gedi?" the Rabbi demanded. "You obviously are not from there, since you look nothing like a villager. Are you a Roman spy?"

He gestured at Gwyn's apparel, ugly suspicion creeping into his expression. She wore dusty cargo shorts and a light collared travel shirt. Her feet were bare—she hadn't yet put her shoes on when she'd examined the pocket watch at En Gedi. Compared to their robes and sandals, she was hideously out of place.

"A spy? Of course not!" Indignant and desperate, inspiration struck, "I remember now. My memory must have been affected when I was hit in the head." She snuck a sideways look at Joshua, hoping she sounded convincing. She went on.

"My name is… Gwyna." It wasn't a Hebrew name, but if she chose a fake name, she might forget to answer to it. "I was visiting my cousins. My family are from Galilee, but my parents were murdered by the Romans, so my uncle sent me to stay with my cousins until he could arrange a marriage for me. My clothes were … sold to buy food, so I dressed in these strange rags …"

She had no idea if they would buy this, but to her surprise the Rabbi was nodding his head, and even Gad, the grubby knife-man, had stopped looking panicked.

"I ran inside my cousin's hut when the village was attacked."

She rapidly dredged up Benjamin's history lessons—was it only a few hours ago? It seemed like—it *was*—centuries ago. Or ahead, if you thought about it. The Jews occupying Masada against the Romans were called the Sicarii—a group of super-extremist rebels.

"*What have the Romans ever done for us?*"

Monty Python rose unbidden in her mind, almost causing her to giggle precipitously. She banished it and concentrated on building a convincing story. If she really were back in time, she didn't fancy her chances as a young woman in a room of suspicious, violent men, let alone one who mysteriously appeared like a witch or a demon.

The Sicarii raided nearby villages, including En Gedi. I must have got caught up in their raid.

"I panicked," she said. "I knocked over a jar trying to find somewhere to hide—there was a cloud of blue dust. Maybe something in the jars smashed." She shrugged, looking puzzled. "Then your men attacked me and I woke up here."

A warm sensation was pulsed faintly in her left hand where the pocket watch was embedded. The back of her mind wondered at it, while the rest of her brain zoomed in overdrive. She needed to distract them from the gaping holes in her tale.

"I had a dream!" she exclaimed. This caught all of their attention. She widened her eyes as if in awe. "While I was unconscious, I dreamt of the Romans attacking this place. It was like ... it was as if God was sending a warning!"

"What?" Joshua spoke abruptly. His was a deep voice—he shifted and her skin crawled as he stared from under thick eyebrows. "God sent you a dream to warn of Titus' scum attacking us?" She couldn't tell from his deadpan tone whether he was being sarcastic or not. She chose to sally forth, showing no hesitation, praying it was the right decision and it wouldn't provoke another attack.

"Yes," she nodded as if remembering. She raised her gaze to the Rabbi. Her voice trembled—no act with Joshua standing so close and threatening. "A siege. A terrible, terrible siege. Fire. And blood. Rivers of blood."

The warm feeling in her palm continued as the Rabbi looked wonderingly at her. The back of her mind clamored for her attention— did she really expect these men to buy her story? But they were buying it. Somehow, incredibly, they believed what she said. Did it have to do with the pocket watch? If this thing had somehow sent her back in time, perhaps it could do other things, like affect the perceptions of those around it.

It would make sense, her mind whispered, *what's the point in time travel if you can't fit in and the locals kill you for being out of place?* But how did it work?

The men were silent for some time. She tried not to hold her breath.

Then, "A message from the Lord," the Rabbi whispered reverently. "A warning. He has seen fit to send you to us, an innocent, with a warning of our greatest enemy! Was there anymore? A time? How many Romans did you see?"

She feigned puzzlement and tried to look as if she were racking her memory. Panic gripped her chest, and she took slow, deep breaths through her nose to stay calm.

Don't be too specific, her brain warned, *string them along. If you are going to pretend to be an amateur prophetess you need to be vague and mysterious.*

"I... It's all blurry. Many soldiers. More men than there were sheep in our village."

Nice touch, her brain smirked, *now you sound like a country bumpkin.*

Better a country bumpkin than a witch, she thought fiercely. She hoped the slight twist in her face conveyed pious resignation, not internal conflict.

"Perhaps if I were to pray, God would see fit to tell me more, and I could tell you, Rabbi."

"An excellent idea! When we know more, you can tell what you know to Eleazar ben Ya'ir. Find a shawl for her, Gad!" The Rabbi nodded violently. Beside him, Gad gaped in awe. Joshua grunted. She hoped like hell he wasn't considering administering another blow to her head in order to induce a dream out of her resulting unconsciousness. And who was Eleazar ben Ya'ir?

FOUR

74 AD

Fiercely isolated, Masada perched atop high, rocky cliffs, just as the ruins Gwyn had seen in the future. Only these weren't ruins. A thick casement wall ran around the perimeter of the plateau. Anyone foolhardy enough to attempt the formidable ascent was under the stern eyes of the men who stood guard in gate towers.

Gwyn didn't have time to glimpse much. Joshua hustled her from the room where she had awoken, past various buildings, into the synagogue. The few people they passed threw her puzzled glances, so she feigned modesty and hid her face under the thin woolen shawl that had been pressed upon her. For the first time in her life, she was glad of her brown eyes and dark hair, not to mention her tan. If she changed clothing, she might have a chance at blending in if no one looked too closely.

"The *Ezrat Nashim* is there," Joshua gestured gruffly towards the women's section. She walked over quickly and knelt, hoping she wasn't doing anything that would give her away as an imposter. She'd been to a Christian private school but her parents were firmly secular, so she was unsure if Jewish people prayed very differently in her own time or now. Sinking her eyes to the floor, Gwyn clasped her hands together.

OK, we are in big trouble, she declared to herself. *This pocket watch* (she could feel it as a faint tingling on her left palm) *has somehow sent me back in time, but not in location. I was at En Gedi. The Sicarii raided En Gedi, captured me and brought me back to Masada. They didn't kill me because they thought I was a demon or a ghost, and they were afraid. Now they think I have been given a message from God to warn them of the Roman attack.*

The Roman attack! *Oh shit.* Siege. Fire. Mass suicide. *Stay calm. I need to stay alive, get out of here and work out how to get this thing to send me back to my own time before the Romans get here and everyone is dead!* She opened her palms and stared at them, her body shielding them from Joshua's view. The pocket watch had faded into her skin somewhat, but the spiral symbol was still clearly marked. It now looked like a temporary henna tattoo, but she could still fell the metal molded into her hand. *How do I make this thing work?*

She tried pressing it. Nothing. She couldn't make it move or open. The edge had vanished into her skin and the chain was as immobile as the watch itself. It was as though her body had simply absorbed it, leaving the appearance of the thing, but not the thing itself. She quelled the rising panic in her gut, breathing deeply through her nose.

Praying. You are meant to be praying. Her brain slapped her panic down. She started to mumble quietly, head bowed, rocking slightly. She tried to itemize everything Benjamin had told them about the siege.

Should she tell them? She sympathized with their fierce independence, hating the foreign invader. But what if she changed history with this knowledge? What if they killed her anyway? She needed to get back to her own time!

She tried tracing the outline of the pocket watch, tried tracing the spiral pattern, tried pressing different points in various orders. Nothing happened. She heard Joshua praying quietly over on the men's side. Her body blocked her hands from his view, but she glanced up guiltily all the same. He caught her looking, and rose, frowning ominously at her under his thick eyebrows. She got to her feet too, and tried to look serene despite her nerves.

"I have been shown another vision." Confidence laced her voice, confidence she didn't truly feel. *Doesn't matter. Walk the walk. Talk the talk. Make them believe you. You know the future, after all!* The thought steeled her. She raised her chin.

"The Lord has sent me another warning. You must take me to Eleazar."

* * *

"The Romans are coming!"

The crowd stirred—some fearfully, some with anger—at Eleazar's words.

"We are the last resistance against the hated invaders. God has seen fit to send us a warning through the words of an innocent girl, whose parents were murdered by Romans!" His voice rang out across the heat of the courtyard.

"The Romans are coming, and they will try to crush us! But we are ready for them! We have food, and water, for many moons! For years, even! We have strong walls, and stronger hearts to defend them! We cannot give in! We shall not give in! Our God is a righteous one! And while He has seen fit to test our faith, to test our hearts, we shall stand strong! And we shall *prevail!*"

His words roared into the hundreds that gathered in the main hall of the palace. The men stomped and cheered, the women ululated, and the children yelled and clapped.

Gwyn stood to the side, eyes downcast, fear and relief fighting for dominance in her stomach. Eleazar had believed her. The Rabbi had spoken quietly and urgently to him when Joshua brought her in, and the leader of the Sicarii had beckoned to her with piercing black eyes and commanded her to speak. She'd begun haltingly, lacing her sentences with "great defender of our people" and "Roman scum" as she started to describe the siege to come. She was deliberately vague, not wanting to get caught out in minutiae; but kept the tale picturesque. Fortified camps and walls surrounding Masada. A ramp built of earth and stones. Romans scurrying about like ants, building and digging. And fire. She told them that they would burn the place, kill the men, and enslave and torture the women and children. She told the Jewish leader that Titus Flavius was determined to stamp out all resistance in Judea. That this was the last stand.

And, like the Rabbi, Eleazar had eaten up her information like a starving man. Fanaticism glinted in his eyes, his grim smile widening.

He looks like this is just the kind of thing he has been waiting to hear. She swallowed quietly. *Good versus evil at the end of the world. I almost feel sorry for him—him and every other doomed soul in this place. They are all going to die, they just don't know it yet.*

"Our true test of faith has come," he declared. "Our mother-city is fallen; our great Temple in ashes, our country, overrun, and God warns us that our oppressors draw near. We are the last to resist. We shall not submit!"

The inhabitants of Masada had been summoned to the main courtyard in the Western Palace. Eleazar was a terrific orator, stirring the hearts of a people primed for a fiery resistance. They had fought and fled the Romans all over Judea—many were survivors of Titus' sack of Jerusalem. They knew the Romans were relentless, grinding down the Jewish defenses under the imperial military machine.

Gwyn recalled from her university studies that Titus' father, Vespasian, had been the commander in Judea during the Year of the Four Emperors. While the lethal political tussling raged back home, his task had been to crush the Jewish Rebellion. When his own troops declared him Emperor, the Sabine general returned to Rome to take control of the Empire, leaving his older son to finish the work. Extremely capable, Titus had besieged Jerusalem, taking the city piece by piece. A number of rebel leaders were captured, however some escaped. One of those must have been Eleazar, she mused.

A few curious glances were sent her way, but she stood back, keen to avoid further attention. It was also to get away from the brooding Joshua, who still stared at her with suspicion. It helped that the leader of the Sicarii was more than happy to dominate the gathering. Certainly God had given her a vision, but only a man as great as he could have deciphered its truth and imminence. He'd dismissed her as carrier, worthy no doubt due to her pure and virginal status, but a woman, no more. That was fine by her—she needed enough special status to keep her somewhat safe, but not so much to draw too much attention and poke holes in her tale. She tried not to meet anyone's eyes—she figured this wouldn't be unusual in a woman in this time anyway. In any case, she didn't want to look too hard at people she knew had only a little time left in this world.

They're already dead, she tried to convince herself. *They've been dead for a couple of thousand years.* She felt sick thinking about it.

After his speech, Eleazar dismissed Gwyn into the care of his old aunt while he set to organizing the citadel's defenses. Cheers roaring behind her, Gwyn was handed over to Sarah, a short, wrinkled woman whose gnarled hands had held surprising strength as she'd gripped Gwyn's wrist and led her into the women's quarters of the palace. In the darkened rooms, she had a chance to bathe and dress in a clean but very second-hand robe, then eat—dried dates, bread and oil, well-watered wine. Exhausted, she fell into a deep sleep, curled up on a mat on the floor.

* * *

She awoke to find the grizzled old woman sitting with another, much younger woman, watching over her. The smell of wood smoke drifted in, voices of other women chattering in nearby rooms. A donkey brayed outside. Gwyn peered at her two companions, sunlight streaming in from a high western window, lighting their laps as they spun wool.

"Awake, I see." Sarah's voice was quiet, with only a hint of a creak in it. She sounded younger than she looked, but it was clear that the years had not been kind to her. She had soft wisps of white hair escaping her head-scarf, and black, piercing dark eyes like her nephew's, set in a heavily lined face. Her hands moved independently, unwatched as she wound yarn using a drop spindle. Gwyn's eyes were caught by the repetitive motion; spin, pull, wind, as Sarah continued to pluck soft tufts of combed wool from the basket next to her.

The younger woman who sat beside her was petite—Gwyn thought her not much more than a child until she spoke. She too, had the dark eyes so typical of many of the people here, but her skin was youthful and smooth. That face had been frowning in concentration as she spun wool onto her spindle—nowhere near as smoothly as Sarah's work.

She stopped to glance up at Gwyn, flicking her long, dark hair behind her ear. Her headscarf sat askew. "They said your name is Gwyna. I've never heard of such a name. Who were your parents? Are you really a messenger?"

"Adi!" The old woman admonished.

"I'm sorry, Sarah, but I want to know!" Adi's voice wasn't at all apologetic, and Gwyn wondered if such boldness in behavior was normal here. Surely people, particularly women, in these times were expected to respect their elders?

She coughed slightly to hide her confusion, sitting up slowly and rolling stiff shoulders. Everything ached. "Uh, yes. My name is Gwyna. I'm... uh, I'm named for my great grandmother who was... from the west."

Adi stared at her, seemingly fascinated. "Hmph. And are you a messenger? Some of the men say God has turned his face from us, that is why Jerusalem fell. But you have come with His warning!"

"Adi, your incessant curiosity will lead to nothing but trouble!" Sarah glared. "Leave the poor girl alone."

Gwyn swallowed. "I don't know about a messenger," she said quietly. "All I know is what I saw in my visions, which is surely what God intended me to see." She sat up slowly and nodded respectfully towards Sarah. "Your nephew interpreted God's warning, so we must be grateful to him and to God."

"Hmmm," Sarah sniffed, unimpressed. "My nephew is very firm in his convictions and his hatred of all foreigners. I do not doubt the Romans will hunt us down and try to finish us off, but surely they cannot begin to believe, in all their arrogance, that they could actually take this fortress?"

"It is a citadel of the utmost strength!" Adi added passionately, "Carved into the rock, we have food and water for months, if not years!"

"This is true," Sarah agreed, still spinning methodically. "They will batter themselves at these walls as the sea batters against the rocks, but they will founder all the same," she finished.

Gwyn did not doubt their belief. Even in her time, the ruins of Masada loomed imposingly; now, intact and heavily guarded, the mountaintop was formidable.

But something else worried her. What if, given her warning, the Sicarii succeeded in resisting the Romans? What if she had upset the whole time-space continuum and changed the course of history completely? She'd seen and read enough science fiction to wonder whether history was immutable or up to chance. The Roman Empire might be completely different without this foothold firmly in the east.

Christianity might never come west to Rome. The whole of Europe, not to mention Africa and the Middle East, could look very different in a few hundred years, not to mention two thousand! As an intellectual exercise it was certainly interesting to wonder at the possibilities, but her most pressing concern at the moment was, *Even if I can get home, will home still be there?*

Never mind that right now! Focus! She realized the two women were staring at her and she hid her distraction by staring at the floor. "I don't know what the Romans think," she mumbled. "They killed my parents, so maybe arrogance is simply another of their many sins."

This stilled the two Jewish women. Then Sarah stopped winding yarn, and put a comforting hand on Gwyn's arm. "I'm sorry, Gwyna, my dear. You have been through a terrible time. If God has sent a warning through you, then we are indeed grateful. I'm just wary of Eleazar's bloodlust. My nephew is prepared to sacrifice everything in fighting the Romans."

"If only they would leave us in peace!" Adi burst out in anger. She threw down her spindle. "They bring their filthy heathen ways, they worship idols, and take our land and taxes. We don't want them here!"

Gwyn looked at her, curious. She felt guilty for eliciting sympathy from her lies, but sticking to her story would likely be the only way she would survive.

"Adi was living in Jerusalem before the Romans came," Sarah saw Gwyn's look and elucidated. "But that was then, and this is now. We must make the best out of what God gives us." She tapped Adi's knuckles pointedly with her spindle.

The young woman frowned. She picked up her work, but continued to mutter, "They are monsters. Boy-loving monsters, and their women are nothing but painted whores." Venom filled her.

"Adi! Such language in this house!" Sarah flicked the girl hard across the ear, and Adi flinched.

Gwyn rocked back at the old woman's sudden fury.

"So, strange girl," Sarah grumbled, clearly cranky now. "You are safe with us now. What else can you do apart from prophesize our doom? Can you spin?"

Gwyn had to quickly confess that no, she could not spin, or weave, or even sew.

"What use am I meant to make of you then?" Sarah demanded. Gwyn kept her head low, in case she too incurred a flick on the ear. Adi shot a sympathetic look, and the girl out of time choked back tears. It was the first truly kind expression anyone had shown her since she had pitched forth into this crazy nightmare.

FIVE

74 AD

The next few days saw Gwyn learn basic living skills that would serve any woman of ancient Judea well. While she was clumsy and slow at first, she concentrated with a fierce terror born out of the fear that she would be found out as an impostor and killed. She attempted spinning wool, learnt how to make unleavened bread, and spent a seemingly inordinate amount of time sweeping and drawing water from the great cisterns. These had been cut into the plateau by King Herod the Great to capture water from the winter rains.

Gwyn's hands blistered from the work, and every night she collapsed on her sleeping mat, fretting over how she was going to return to her own time. Every morning she awoke aching from the hard surface, itching from the fleas, consumed by the burden of surviving another day.

Somehow her poor domestic skills passed with little more than some grumbling and exasperation from Sarah, and vague puzzlement coupled with sympathy from Adi. A warmth in her left palm reminded Gwyn from time to time that the mysterious pocket watch must act in some way to dispel the suspicions of those around her. *Any sufficiently advanced technology is indistinguishable from magic.* Who said that? She couldn't remember, and she was afraid that her memories of the future would fade as at first she stumbled, then began to trudge through the monotonous daily routine.

She was rarely left alone. Always she was accompanied by women, preparing food, mending clothes, caring for snotty-nosed children that scampered or crawled about. The Sicarii who had fled Jerusalem had taken the fortress by surprise a year earlier. Gwyn didn't ask what had happened to the Roman garrison who had been here. She could work it out. No point wasting food on enemy mouths.

"But why bring all of their families here?" she asked Adi.

"And leave hostages outside the fortress for the Romans to capture?" her new friend raised her dark eyebrows.

"Surely they could have been sent somewhere safer?"

"There is nowhere safer!" Adi shot back, emphatic but not angry.

Gwyn looked down, wishing she could tell Adi the truth. That her passion was misplaced. That Masada was a trap, not a haven.

Adi touched Gwyn on the arm. "I know you're frightened, Gwyna," she said softly. "But it is so much more defensible here than Jerusalem. And with men like Joshua fighting for us, we need not fear."

Gwyn frowned at her. "He is definitely a fighter," she said uncertainly. She didn't like to think of the man who had attacked her so viciously.

Adi nodded. "He is harsh, to be sure, but Eleazar says we need harsh men to uphold our freedom." She paused. "I am to marry him once the war is over."

"Oh." Gwyn didn't know what to say. "Congratulations?"

Adi shrugged. "I don't really want to marry just yet, but my father and brothers are dead, so I must. I'm lucky he'll have me. Are you betrothed? You never said."

Gwyn repeated her story about an uncle sending her to live with her cousins until he could arrange a marriage. Adi commiserated, and their conversation turned to other things. Despite their differences, Gwyn found it easy to talk to the Jewish girl. Fierce and quick-witted, Adi disliked chores but went out of her way to help Gwyn with hers.

At first Gwyn couldn't understand why Adi was so helpful and kind. Then she grew to see the importance of family connection and realized her new friend was lonely. The only other women their age were either married or widowed, busy with babies and children and looking after their menfolk. Adi had a nephew, Gwyn learned from Sarah, the son of Adi's much older brother, who had been killed in the siege of Jerusalem. Her friend did not acknowledge the boy and Gwyn didn't have the nerve to ask why, as anger darkened the other girl's face every time she laid eyes on the child.

Other than that, Adi was good company. She laughed when the milking goat kicked over Gwyn's pail but helped straighten it up. She distracted Sarah when Gwyn burnt the bread, or dropped a spindle. Whenever they were sent to feed the doves or fetch water, she insisted they take the long way round so they could talk. If she was another girl, Gwyn might have felt the thrill of attraction, particularly when they hid from Eleazar's wife, Elizabeth, who was often petty and cruel. With Adi, there was only relief and gratitude for the friendship. Gwyn told herself that it was hardly the time or place to develop a crush on someone, even if she had been drawn to Adi in that way.

They inhabited the dwellings on the eastern side of the plateau, closest to the gate at the top of the Snake Path. Many rooms had long since fallen into disuse and disrepair, but the current occupants had cleaned and rearranged a significant section for their uses. Gwyn was absorbed quietly into the household and tried to keep a low profile while she worked out what to do next.

Eleazar did not demand her presence again. Perhaps he had decided he had no need of her now that he had received God's warning, so decided not to attract his attention with more 'visions'. The men of Masada prepared for siege, strengthening gates and walls, arming men and practicing with spears and bows, as well as hand to hand combat. The women cooked and cleaned, checked stores and provisions, prepared medical supplies, and waited.

Not even a week had passed, however, when her prophecy began to come true.

The first warning came on the rising dust of the midday sun. Out of the west, a column of haze snaked its way up into the sky. Then a scout came sprinting up the Snake Path, gasping for breath as he staggered inside the fortress, demanding to see Eleazar.

"They are coming!" he spluttered past the water as he gulped from a goatskin.

Upon hearing this, the rebel leader rushed to the western wall with a number of men. He stared out across the landscape with a hard gaze, jaw set. For a moment, he looked as if he had been carved from stone.

Then his eyes lit up with a fierce fire and he was exultant.

"Our test is at hand!" he bellowed. "Our moment of triumph is near!"

The men around him cheered and scrambled to close and bar the gates.

* * *

Gwyn was sitting in the kitchen shelling peas with Adi and Sarah. A massive pot of soup simmered over the hearth, attended by two gossiping sisters. Almost everyone was related to one degree or another, but since none of the other women were particularly friendly to her, she had not bothered to learn all of their names. They spoke of their husbands, brothers, cousins and uncles, which she ignored, unless the name Eleazar came up, or the name Joshua.

He would come ostensibly to pay his respects to Sarah and Adi, but rarely spoke to his betrothed. His narrowed eyes often landed on Gwyn as he grunted brief responses to Sarah. The old woman seemed to know everyone's business, and while she never spoke against her nephew, Eleazar, a critical air hovered in the room when the rebel leader was discussed.

Mind you, Gwyn's thoughts crept in quietly, *she's pretty critical of just about everyone. She can be a cranky old biddy sometimes.* She did notice Eleazar's wife, Elizabeth, often pursed her lips in disapproval of some of Sarah's comments, but refrained from saying anything. Gwyn sensed tension between the two women, but so far, the elderly matriarch reigned supreme on the domestic front.

This particular day, though, Adi's nephew, the one she never spoke to, toddled in on his chubby legs. He caught everyone's attention when he trundled over to his foster mother and shouted, "Roms! Roms here!"

Gwyn blanched.

Adi dropped the pod of peas she had been handling. Other women gasped and began to wail.

Sarah gripped white knuckles on her cane and rapped it loudly. "Silly hens!" the old woman barked. "You knew this was coming. We were never going to be left alone. Stay calm and get back to work while I go speak with my nephew and see if it is true."

It was true.

Thousands of Roman soldiers poured into the landscape below the plateau like rain gushing into a dry wadi.

Gwyn found out later than Sarah had tried to get Eleazar to discuss the possibility of seeking terms. Despite the old woman's professed convictions that Masada could not be taken by force, she seemed to want to prepare for the remote possibility that something might go wrong. Eleazar turned her away with scornful words not worthy of the respect he should have shown to his elders. She left indignant and upset, his hard words following her out.

"Foolish crone! They cannot starve us out! They cannot make us surrender from thirst! And they will not—will not!—take this fortress by force of arms! God is with us! We cannot fail!"

His determination was forged in the fires of zealous conviction, and he grew more and more fanatical by the day. His confidence spurred the men on as they made the final preparations for the siege. The gates were barred with solid wooden crossbeams, a lookout manned the towers at all hours of the day and night. Spears and swords were sharpened, arrows re-fletched.

As all this took place, thousands of Roman soldiers continued to pour in. Auxiliaries on horseback, slaves, and wagons with siege weapons and supplies in a column that split and spread around the plateau like water lapping around a rock. Busy as ants, they began to dig and build and construct a large military camp west by northwest of Masada. Then the other camps sprang up too, until there were eight sensible, fortified squares joined by a solid circumvallation wall. The sound of thousands of men building busily drifted up the cliffs for days, while Eleazar's men tightened their grips on their weapons and glared.

Any kind of sally would be pointless. The Roman forces were too organized, too alert for a surprise attack, and outnumbered the entire population of Masada, women and children included, by a thousand to one. Gwyn convinced Adi to sneak onto the wall with her the day after the Romans first encamped, and the sight chilled her.

There are so many of them …

Even Adi, ardent in her scorn of the Roman maneuverings in the shadow of the fortress, fell briefly quiet in the face of such numbers.

"Jerusalem was different," she informed Gwyn after some minutes staring down at the milling horde. "Even there, we repelled Titus three times before he overcame us. But it was a city. Too many people to feed. Too many walls to defend. Masada is different. It is impregnable. And God is with us."

Gwyn didn't think she sounded convinced. Her heart sank at the thought of what was to come.

It's not fair. Adi doesn't deserve to die. But there is nothing I can do.

SIX

FOUR YEARS EARLIER

Adi could hear the battle echoing like distant thunder through the quiet streets of the old city. There weren't many people on the street, only an old man shuffling as quickly as he could away down an alleyway. Housewives peered anxiously out of their front doors; children were shushed as they played quietly indoors. Hunger and fear gripped the neighborhood, the latter giving a sharp tang to the former.

Adi wasn't afraid, however. *Her* father and brothers were fighting on the thick outer wall of Jerusalem, defending the holy city from Titus Flavius' army. It had been several weeks since the siege began, and as yet, the walls had not been breached. The Romans suffered loss after loss and Adi had absolute confidence her father and brothers would return triumphant every night.

Normal life was suspended and a surreal world sprang up in its place. Adi idled away the time, her mother too preoccupied with fretting to threaten her into doing household chores. Her sister by marriage, Mary, would find her and chide her into going and drawing water from the well.

"You must help your mother! These are trying times!" Mary scolded. She was heavily pregnant, but that didn't stop her from laboring away every day at housework and (in Adi's opinion) being slightly too good and annoying. Why her favorite brother had married such a pious and boring woman was beyond her.

"Mother just prays," Adi mumbled as she slouched off to obey. "She doesn't do anything."

"She is praying for our victory! And the lives of your father and brothers!"

Most nights, her father and brothers stumbled home from the outer wall, exhausted and filthy, yet elated.

"These Romans!" her father would exclaim, "godless scum! They will never breach our walls! We beat them back day after day until they retreat and lick their wounds!" He would continue to wax prophetic on the future demise of Titus, his army, and the Roman Empire in general, and Adi would listen, enrapt.

She had complete and utter faith in his belief that the Romans would be repulsed. She never questioned that, despite being beat back day after day, they did not desist in their siege.

And this day seemed the same. Skirmishing took place on the walls. Food shortages meant hungry bellies all over the city. Most made do stoically, though some squabbling took place in the marketplace. The shuffling old man was the only soul Adi had seen out for the last hour.

The sound of running feet made her glance up out the window. Two young men, covered in blood and dust, careened out of the alleyway and across the street. She was startled to recognize them as her neighbor's sons.

"Mother! Mother!" they hammered on the door. Adi was perturbed to notice the terror in their voices. Movement appeared in doorways and windows as other neighbors twitched aside drapes to see what the disturbance was.

"*Mother!*" They screamed frantically. Their mother finally pulled open the door and peered out, wide eyed.

"My sons! What is it? Have the—?"

"Come, mother, gather your things! We have to go now!"

More feet sounded in the street. Adi gaped as a handful of men rounded the corner, her older brother amongst them. The air filled with cries for family members to *come, come now!*

Footsteps and yelling grew louder and louder; suddenly the sound of fighting rumbled much closer than usual. Screams began, with terrified children and white-faced women pouring out from their homes, shepherded by the few bloody and panicking men.

"Quickly! Mary! Mother! Adi!" Her brother's normally quiet voice boomed as he burst inside. "We have to go! The Romans are through the wall, we must get you to somewhere safer!"

"Where is your father?" Her mother clutched at him frantically. "Where is your brother?"

He shook his head.

Adi felt as though the world had dropped out from under her feet at the hollow pain in her dear brother's eyes. Her ears roared, and she faltered, steadying herself against the wall. She couldn't hear him say the words. The crumpling of her mother's face told her that her other brother and father were dead.

"We have to go now." It was her sister-in-law, Mary. She was whey-faced, but her hands were firm as she thrust a bag into Adi's arms. Somehow, she and her mother stumbled out the door and they joined the jostling hordes fleeing to the temple. Titus had breached the Outer Wall.

*　*　*

Crying babies and wailing women filled the air with noise; the shouts of men adding to the cacophony. Adi huddled under her shawl as she held her mother's hand, trying not to despair.

If she had thought her mother didn't do anything before, it was nothing compared to the sobbing shell of a woman now crumpled against the temple wall. Not bothering to pray, her eyes stared at nothing, tears welling up and rolling down her suddenly aged cheeks. Adi watched her mother become an old grieving widow in the space of an hour.

They were in the women's section of the Great Temple, her brother having deposited them there. He bid them to stay put.

"You will be safe," he implored. "The walls are thick and strong. I must go help them mount a defense and beat them back, then we will find somewhere for you to stay. I won't be long."

Mary embraced him fiercely, her pregnant belly squished between them.

"Please come back soon," she whispered, gripping his hands as if she'd never let go.

He disentangled himself gently, but Adi could see it breaking his heart. Fear and doubt stabbed her. *Would he even come back? Or would he be killed like the others?* The monotony of the siege had escalated from a dull bad dream into a bloody nightmare. She clutched her mother's hand, but found no comfort there.

The next few days degenerated into an appalling blur. Adi had recently started her monthly bleeding and was still mid-cycle when they crowded into the emergency refuge of the Temple. To her horror, she was forced to break various cleanliness laws because of the lack of hygiene, but could not avoid it. Mary's pregnancy was taking a heavy toll, and Adi's mother was useless—she sat and cried or stared. Adi begged food from neighbors and shamefully prepared it as best she could, but there was little to be had. They huddled in a makeshift encampment, bewildered, frightened, and miserable.

On the third day, word came that Titus had breached the Second Wall. More and more folk crowded into the Temple grounds. Several people died in a crush when someone panicked and screamed that the enemy was at the Temple Gate. Adi's mother refused to eat, and one morning she simply didn't wake up. They had to take her body outside to the join the piles of dead, choking at the stench. The rabbis couldn't perform the necessary rites and disease rioted through the huddled masses. Mary grew haggard, her round belly a pathetic parody of the promise of life. It seemed the end was near.

* * *

"Adi." Mary's voice was quiet. Adi's head snapped up. It had been two days since her mother had died. Her brother had not returned. She couldn't remember the last time she had eaten. Her bleeding had stopped after only a day or so, and her scrawny frame and sunken cheeks were further evidence of her deteriorating physical state.

"Adi," Mary repeated. Adi stared unseeing at her sister-in-law, who said, "We have to leave this place. He is not coming back."

The words registered slowly in her brain. Adi's mouth hung open slackly, and she shook her head.

"He is dead, Adi," Mary repeated. "My cousin saw him fall. My husband, your brother, is dead. We cannot stay here anymore. There is nothing for us here."

What did she mean? They couldn't just walk out of here. Titus' army had flooded the main city, they were battering at the Citadel and the walls of the Temple. They were trapped, like rats in a barrel, waiting for slaughter.

"Adi, there is a plan to help us escape. My cousin said we must meet him at the small gate at before nightfall."

The sun was already lowering in the sky. Smoke haze filled the air, casting a baleful red light down onto the desperate and defiant alike. She stared at Mary in confusion.

"What—?"

"Shh," Mary shushed her. "Just save your strength, and be ready."

Even in her pitiful state, her sister-in-law was still calm and level-headed in the face of crisis. As the afternoon drew to a close, Adi wondered at Mary's strength of character—she'd always dismissed her sister-in-law as nice but dull. They didn't have much in common. But now she respected that stolidness—Mary had every right to degenerate into hysterics and collapse in a weeping fit, or give up and die like Adi's mother. Her husband dead, her baby starving inside her, yet still she planned, holding on to hope, to survive somehow.

* * *

As the sun lowered itself gently past the Fortress of Antonia Tower, Adi surreptitiously bundled her things together in a spare shawl and pulled a scarf tighter over her head. Mary took her hand, and they drifted past the groups of women filling the space. Shuffling carefully so as not to stumble on anyone, they reached the outer courtyard and crept around the edge to the small gate. A cloaked man awaited them there, looking anxious.

"Cousin, we must hurry," he hissed. "Praise God you are alright. I will take you out of the city. Who is this?" He spotted Adi. She stopped, stricken. Was he going to refuse to take her with him?

But Mary spoke authoritatively. "She is the sister to my dear husband. Her mother and father and brothers are dead. I am the only one who can help her now. I cannot leave her here." Mary touched her cousin's arm gently, her other hand cradling her swollen belly. It seemed even larger now, distorted by the dim light and shadows as the sun set.

"Very well," he muttered. "Though I know your husband did not hold with our views, so why should we save any family of his?"

"She is my family now," her voice was firm but with an edge of pain to it. "Therefore she is yours, cousin."

"Hmph. Let us go." With not another word, he herded them down various alleyways, the shadows creeping after them.

Adi was frightened and confused; she did not understand what was going on. What did Mary's cousin mean about views? How were they going to get out of the city without being captured and killed—or worse—by the Romans?

The man turned into a dark doorway. The last vestiges of daylight glimmered into nothingness and stars crept into the growing indigo sky, serenely unaware of the chaos that rocked the world below.

"Here." He tapped a sequence on the door three times. It opened. He hustled them inside and passed the silent doorkeeper, down a set of stairs into a cellar. An old woman and several others waited down there.

"Sarah!" Mary lost her composure and rushed to the old lady, hugging her tightly.

"There, there, my child," Sarah soothed. "It's alright. Time to be gone from this place, I think." She patted Mary's stomach. "You are quite near your time? This journey will not be easy, but you are strong and God is with us. But who is this?"

Adi was swiftly introduced as Mary's sister-in-law, then two men in the group shifted a set of large wooden shelves to reveal an opening in the wall beyond. They crept into the tunnel single file, tripping occasionally in the dark. Several candles were held, but the light they cast was poor, and. Mary stumbled several times. Adi was there immediately to assist her. It was difficult, though, in the narrow tunnel with an uneven floor and damp walls. She wondered if it had been an underground stream, working its way through the mountainside, discovered and enlarged by these men and others.

It seemed like hours, but probably was only one, before they finally emerged into open air. The sky was dark, with no moon, only the light of the stars, and the gully where they stood was overgrown with juniper bushes. A terrible reek assaulted her nostrils. They were near one of the refuse pits wherein rubbish and waste from the city was dumped and burned. A place no sensible Roman would choose to come. *Or Jew, unless they are desperate.*

The long night continued as they allowed themselves little rest. The tail end of a group that had begun the exodus several nights previously, they could not afford to fall behind the others fleeing Jerusalem under the cover of nightfall. Slipping through enemy lines and making their way in a circuitous route south and east, they walked for days. The countryside lay half-abandoned, generally subdued, but for pockets of resistance to the Romans that existed the further south they marched.

The march was torture for Mary, Adi could see. Her pregnancy weighed her down, and each step was a burden to take. They fell further and further back in the line each day, walking for longer to catch up and collapsing every night into a restless sleep, disturbing Adi who slept beside her. Several days after they had escaped Jerusalem, she noticed Mary's sandals were wet, yet the road upon which they walked was dry and dusty.

"Sister," she began tentatively. "Your feet … your sandals are wet."

Mary offered her a wry smile even as her shuffle slowed. "The baby is coming, Adi."

"What? Now?"

"Soon." Mary paused and gasped quietly, a shudder wracking her body. Adi rushed to support her. "Go and tell Sarah, she'll know what to do."

Lowering her sister-in-law to the side of the path, she barreled past others in the train to find Sarah, hobbling with stoic determination. Upon being informed of the imminent arrive of her great niece or nephew, the matriarch swiftly directed various members to carry on and find shelter and others to come with her and assist. A small group clustered around Mary, managing to get her up and walking but falling further and further behind the convoy.

Time began an excruciating crawl. The day inched on as Mary's contractions drew closer together. Many times she had to stop and rest, clutching at Adi's hand and breathing in great gasps, then groaning like a cow in pain. Finally, they reached the camp that the other members of the group had gone ahead and set up. Gentle hands ushered Mary off the path to a grove of olive trees on the hill, Adi trailing helplessly. It was slow going, but once in the shade women buzzed about, settling the soon-to-be mother, washing hands and preparing cloths. The sun set, and still Mary labored on.

"It's taking a long time," muttered a woman helping.

"Many babes do, the first time," Sarah snapped back, but her lips were pursed with worry.

Well into the night, the baby's head emerged. Adi was in tears; she could see Mary was exhausted, but she tried to be encouraging.

"Almost there!" she whispered in Mary's ear. Mary pushed again, and the women cheered as a baby boy slid out, squalling and bloody. They lifted him to her breast.

"Well done, my child," Sarah wiped the sweat from Mary's brow. "A fine baby boy."

"Call him Joel, for his father." Mary's eyes started to flutter and baby Joel screamed all the louder, he wasn't latching on.

"Quick, girl! Move out of the way," Sarah pushed Adi back, but Adi glimpsed a great gush of blood pooling between Mary's legs. Mary's head lolled back, and the baby continued to scream, and scream, and scream.

* * *

They buried Mary's body beneath a cairn of stones to stop wild animals from eating it. Adi's newborn nephew was handed to a cousin who still had milk for her own, toddling child. Words of sympathy tapped gently at Adi's ear, but she felt hollow. If Sarah hadn't ordered her to get up, she might have stayed at Mary's grave forever. It was the last connection she had with her family. The baby did not count. She hated the small, squalling thing, refused to be aunt to it. It had murdered her good, kind, brave sister-in-law.

"It was too much for her." Sarah's face crinkled in grief, even as she gently tugged Adi to her feet. "The siege, the death of her husband, the escape, the march. She was so very strong to have made it this far in her condition. Just not quite strong enough. She is with God now."

Adi didn't reply, but silently raged. Everyone else had left her, why Mary too? If she was so strong, why couldn't she have lasted another few days until they reached safety? For she knew now where they were going; as the morning sun crept over the River Jordan, the light struck a strange, flat-topped mountain rising in the south.

By evening, they had toiled their way up a steep and winding path and reached the fortress of Masada.

SEVEN

2623 AD

"Stand to attention!"

Michelle jerked from her meditative state. She blinked and rose languidly, taking care to project stupor. Eyes dull, lids half-lowered, hands listless and mouth slack, she stared as if unable to focus on Rickas in his smart gray uniform, smirking at her from the other side of the forcefield.

"Hands!" he demanded.

Michelle turned her empty palms out slowly.

As if I could have hidden or manufactured a weapon in here, she thought. She had been fully scanned and physically searched when she entered the prison. Rickas was following protocol, but he did not seem wary of her in any way. And there was only one of him.

Good.

Placing her wrists into the small opening that appeared in the force field, Rickas electro-cuffed her. In front. Clearly, she didn't even pose enough of a threat to cuff her hands behind her, nor did he shackle her feet.

Even better.

The force-field deactivated and Rickas prodded her with his shock-baton, current not on, she noted thankfully. Michelle shuffled along compliantly. Noting the corridor signage she determined he was taking her from a holding cell level to an interrogation level, though it didn't illuminate her as to whether she was on Earth or otherwise.

They passed empty cells. *That's why it's been so quiet. We must be in a low crime area or… they've deliberately kept the level clear so no one else comes near me.*

They reached a lift and Rickas scanned his authorization crystal. There was no one in sight.

As he turned to punch the level into the computer, Michelle coughed and made a dreadful hoicking noise, like she was about to vomit. She sank to her knees as Rickas turned back, pudgy face pulled into a grimace of disgust and she puked up the contents of her last meal. *Funny, it looks pretty much the same coming out as it had going in.*

"Oh, yuc—!" He didn't even finish when Michelle rose faster than her breakfast, smashing her cuffed hands under his chin. His head snapped back as his hands flailed for his baton. Michelle snatched it, flicking the safety off and tasing his crotch before administering a sharp nap-tap to his head. Rickas' eyes rolled back, and he slumped, unconscious, to the lift floor.

Michelle helped herself to his authorization crystal, releasing her wrists from their cuffs. She scooped up a handful of her vomit to smear over the cameras in the top rear corner and outside the lift. Using the unconscious guard's body as a step so she could reach the ceiling, she smashed out a panel. She then used the crystal to select a floor and send the lift on its way as she skipped out of the way of the closing doors.

Standing in the silent corridor outside the lift, she judged herself out of the way of the next camera. Carefully, she opened the panel beside the rubbish chute opening and squeezed herself into the maintenance access way, gently bringing the panel to a close behind her. The chutes were small, but she hadn't lost any flexibility during her time in the cell. *Time for all that stretching to pay off,* she thought as she wriggled her way along. She hoped she wouldn't run into any cleaning or repair bots, but it was the best way to stay out of the way of motion sensors and cameras that guarded the prison hallways.

She hoped the lift with its smashed-out ceiling panel would buy her a little time. She wasn't naive enough to think she could escape with the refuse—she would be incinerated—so she needed to make her way to a level where she could either transmit a message for help, or find some other way out.

Michelle wiggled through the maintenance shaft up three levels, pushing away the claustrophobia that clawed at her. When she would take no more, she stopped to regroup and hoped like hell three levels would be enough. Punching open an access panel, she reached above her head and propelled herself out of the shaft, just in time to see a male and female security guard stroll around the corner and gape at her in astonishment.

She kept the momentum of her roll and sprang at them, decking the female officer and kicking the man in the groin. His hands fell away from his mouth where he had been about to activate his wrist com and clutched at his groin. A blow to the head rendered him unconscious, and she turned to the woman. She had also been knocked out.

Michelle tugged off the woman's uniform and swiped both their shock-batons, com units, and authorization crystals. Straightening her newly-acquired jacket and tucking her hair into the hat, she lay the man half over the woman. From a distance, it might appear as if they were embracing passionately on the floor. An onlooker wouldn't be fooled after a second glance, but she hoped a few seconds bought now might pay off later.

Using the woman's crystal, Michelle accessed the lift around the corner. Her ascent through the maintenance shafts had been enough to get her above the long-term detainment levels. By the options that flashed up on the screen when she scanned the crystal, this guard wasn't permitted access to any level below this one, which appeared to consist of temporary holding cells. She thought it strange that no alarm had sounded. Surely an escape of a prisoner would set off some sort of klaxons?

Unless my captors don't want it known that I'm here ... I could have been incarcerated under a false name. She frowned. That might explain the total isolation. *If Commissioner Hera caught wind that I'm being kept here, she'd break balls and walls to get me out.*

That constable had been taking her to the interrogation cells. She might never have been heard from again. Sure, torture was illegal, but so was unauthorized tampering with timelines, and that hadn't stopped someone from sending those guys after her.

What exactly are they after? My chronokinetor? Or me? She wondered, as the lift took her six more levels up to one of the office floors. She exited and nodded briefly to the Rilan clerk who oozed past her, arranging a bored expression on her face. It didn't give her a second glance. She strolled past and along several office corridors. Administrative staff ambled in and out of doors, and she held the door politely for a young man talking animatedly on his com.

"Sure, I'll be there, honey. I'm leaving right now! Order me a pep-juice, won't you? I really need one—" His voice cut off as the door swung shut. She glanced about the office quickly; no one else was left in there. She used the crystal to log into a work station. The logo on the screen told her she was in the Vivaldis Central Detention Centre, and that it was late afternoon, local time.

Huh, she thought. So she was in the capital. Whoever was trying to keep her out of the picture was trying to hide her in plain sight, not on some backwater prison moon. So many criminals, petty and serious, transferred in and out of VCDC one more would have been easily lost in the data chips. The arrival of a new inmate on somewhere isolated would have been cause for note, no matter how many palms were greased. Someone, somewhere, might have asked questions.

She accessed the internal network and logged an "Improvement Opportunity" with a code that should flag and be re-routed to Commissioner Hera. To the observer, she merely detailed:

VCDC Level 3 Hygiene Facilities missed by cleaner-bots. Time to seek new cleaning contractor perhaps?

'Time to seek' was a clue that an agent was in trouble and couldn't contact the Agency directly. She had flagged where she was, and hoped that the Commissioner would start looking for her soon, if she hadn't already. But she couldn't stay where she was, and she couldn't approach Hera directly—they'd be watching and waiting for that (whoever exactly "they" were, she still wasn't sure). The Commissioner wasn't the only one who was looking for her, and she didn't intend to be caught again.

EIGHT

74 AD

In the next week, Gwyn learned what Adi had discovered in Jerusalem. *Sieges are boring most of the time.* They took to peeking over the wall more and more, watching the Romans send out parties to cut wood and dig haul stone, building the wall that would join their camps and encircle the plateau. Gwyn would have admired the organization if her own impending death hadn't preoccupied her instead.

She tried to question Adi about the siege of Jerusalem.

The Hebrew girl only frowned and refused to discuss it beyond, "My father said they kept beating the Romans back. But they just kept coming. Now they are here, and he is dead. All of my family is dead."

Gwyn left it alone after that.

The bigger concern she had was that the pocket watch proved to be stubbornly resistant to any of her attempts to make it work. *Maybe it was pre-set, and I triggered it? Does it need to be reset?* Nothing she tried worked. It remained firmly inside her skin, and did nothing when she pressed it, stroked it, or even slapped it on the ground in frustration. *Stupid thing!* She fought the urge to cry. *I just want to go home, dammit!*

After a few days, she noticed that the outer lines on the spiral pattern that decorated her palm seemed to be shrinking. Watching it carefully, she realized with trepidation that every day the lines grew shorter, retreating back towards its center. Was it a countdown? A draining of battery? What would happen when it ran out?

If it's a countdown, it might not matter where I am when it runs out. That reassured her. If she zapped back to her time at Masada, she could at least get help from other tourist, or the visitors' center.

But what if it does matter where I am? The safest bet would be to return to En Gedi in case that's where it needs to be to make the damn thing work. And if the spiral is a battery indicator, I need to get there before it runs out.

"Gwyna!" Sarah's voice sent her scrambling to her feet. "Go and get some more water for this garden before the poor vegetables wither in the sun!"

Gwyn hastened to the garden courtyard—she had learned to jump at the matriarch's command. *I can see why she gets frustrated with me and Adi compared to the other women here.* The endless toil of the household astounded her. Dawn to dusk they spun and wove, gardened and cooked, cared for children and the injured. *And some of them still find energy to sing and joke, even when they were trapped in a fortress surrounded by their enemies. It isn't fair what is going to happen to them.* Her heart wrenched.

You can't save them, she told herself sadly. *You have to be practical. You need to concentrate on saving yourself.*

Coward, part of her whispered. *Surely there is something you could do.*

She quashed the thought. Making her way into the building that housed the closest cistern, Gwyn idled another escape plan. Somehow she had to evade the guards, get out the gate, sneak down the Snake Path in the dark and… then what? Steal a mule, evade the legion of Romans that stood between her and En Gedi?

Mind occupied, she turned a corner into a narrow gap between two buildings and collided with Joshua.

Her empty buckets clattered to the ground and rolled. Joshua reached out and steadied Gwyn.

"Sorry!" she exclaimed. His hands remained gripped around her biceps and he frowned at her with dark eyes and heavy brows, saying nothing.

"Pardon me," she tried again. "I didn't see you coming." The Hebrew no longer sounded strange to her ears, though it still baffled her as to how it was possible that she could speak it. *Another mystery of the pocket watch.*

His hold on her increased, and he glared. Gwyn stiffened, swallowing, wishing she was strong enough to break free and hit him.

"Had any more visions, girl?" he demanded, his breath rank on her face. "Any answers as to how long these parasite-ridden, boy-loving scum remain encamped at our door? Why do they not simply attack, as is honorable? They are cowards! When will they leave us?"

"Uhh…" She forced herself to remain calm and still. Nothing she knew about the future would make this man happy. "Nothing has been revealed to me as yet," she whispered. "But surely the Lord will defend His most loyal followers. The Romans will be cast out." *Let go of me, you deranged prick!* Anger and fear rose in her throat, and she tried not to panic.

"Hmmph." He looked at her now with a combination of resentment and growing speculation. "Maybe you really are a witch, as Gad said, if you can only foretell evil befalling us."

"I not a witch! And I—I'll be sure to go straight to the Rabbi if God gifts me with any more dreams or messages," she stuttered. "Adi and Sarah must be wondering where I am with the water. I must go."

At the mention of his betrothed and the formidable matriarch Joshua released her, watching silently as she retrieved the fallen buckets. He didn't move, forcing her to brush against him as she stepped past. She shuddered internally and hated him.

* * *

Gwyn said nothing to Adi when she returned with the water. Sarah scolded her for being a lazy girl and taking so long. She flicked Gwyn's ear sharply and ordered her to clean out the clay chamber pots. Gagging at the smell, Gwyn completed the task as quickly as possible before scrubbing her hands and arms clean and seeking out her friend. Adi was in a small barn which constituted one of the many service buildings of Herod's great palace. There she was milking the goats, encased in the warm animal fug. The smell was strong, but better than Joshua's rancid breath. Soft bleats punctuated the squirts of milk—the nanny goat threw her head up, listening for her kids.

"Help me, Gwyna," Adi was struggling to keep the nanny from kicking the bucket over. Gwyn quickly moved to grasp the hind legs, holding her face well back from the flicking tail.

"Adi," she began, "how well do you know your betrothed, Joshua?"

Adi squeezed and released, squeezed and released with firm strokes, finishing the nanny and nodding for Gwyn to let go.

"What do you mean?" Adi frowned as she rose from the milking stool and led another goat over from the pen.

Gwyn rubbed the embedded pocket watch nervously with her left thumb. "Well, when did you meet him? Have you spent much time together?" This goat was much more sedate, Gwyn didn't have to fight it to keep the legs still.

Adi kept milking, nudging the little black kid that butted her and nibbled on her clothes.

"I met him when I came here," she stated. "I had no one; my family was all killed in Jerusalem. Sarah took responsibility for me, but her son Eleazar said I should be married as soon as possible, that it wasn't good for a girl to be unmarried for too long. Elizabeth suggested Joshua, but Sarah insisted they wait until I'm a year older. I'm surprised they haven't arranged something for you yet. I suppose they will. They are just waiting for a suitable period of mourning to pass for your family."

Gwyn stared at Adi, her stomach clenching. They might try to marry her off? *Not cool!* Her mind clamored. *And so not fair that they picked that jerk Joshua for Adi! That Elizabeth needs a serious wakeup call if she thinks he's good husband material.*

She probably doesn't care, her brain whispered back. *She doesn't even like Adi, you've seen how rude she is when Sarah isn't looking.*

"Oh," she managed to say. "So you didn't really get a whole lot of choice in the matter?"

"No." Adi looked at Gwyn as if she were crazy. "I always expected my father would arrange something. I hope he would be happy in the choice that has been made for me. Joshua seems to be a good man. He is very passionate about the cause."

A good man? He's a bastard! She wanted to warn her friend, but what was the point? She thought miserably, *we're all going to be dead in a few weeks anyway. How long is this bloody siege going to take?* She couldn't recall the guide telling her family anything about how long the Romans took to build a ramp and storm the walls. Obviously, she didn't expect it to happen overnight, but it was inevitable.

I have to get out of here. She was not going to wait for terrible things to happen to her. If she stayed here, she faced the unwelcome attentions of her friend's violent fiancé, the gloomy prospect of an arranged marriage, and finally fire from the Romans and certain death at the hands of the fanatical Eleazar.

But there has to be something I can do for Adi.

A memory struck her. "Adi," she began offhandedly. "Obviously it won't actually, um… It's possible, you know… Um, well, the water cisterns would make an excellent hiding place… In case of fire… You know… on the tiniest off-chance the Romans were to break through the defenses…" Her voice trailed off as her friend glared.

"Don't say that, Gwyna!" the Hebrew girl admonished. "Masada is impregnable! They can't possibly break through! This isn't Jerusalem!"

Gwyn muttered an apology and helped Adi finishing the milking. Her friend took to bucket to the kitchen and Gwyn stayed in the barn, absently patting the kid that now nibbled on her own dress.

Great, she thought, *Adi is in denial, Eleazar is a fanatical nutter, Joshua is a violent creep, and I'm stuck here awaiting a quick trip to the altar and even quicker trip to the grave!*

The impossible plan to escape was looking more and more appealing.

NINE

2623 AD

Michelle didn't have much time. Either the security guards she'd attacked would wake or someone would find them. Luckily, it was the end of the working day and most people were leaving. There was little reason for anyone to descend to the cells until later in the evening, when the detainment of nocturnal criminals would start to take place. Michelle figured that the sheer number of cameras in the complex meant there was no way they could be actively monitored all the time, so the odds of the incident being seen electronically were slim. At some point these guards would be expected to check in on their coms, and she needed to make good her escape before then, or their non-responsiveness might send the facility into lockdown. Tugging her hat low, she exited the office to join the shuffle of people crowding onto the ramps that took workers up to the entrance. She edged behind a larger gentleman, and, as soon as he was through the checkpoint, swiped the stolen authorization crystal, surrendering one shock-baton and a pair of electro-cuffs with a bored expression on her face. The second baton was shoved down one trouser leg. As long as the crystal cleared, the checkout staff didn't look hard at material exiting the detention center. They were usually more concerned with people trying to smuggle illicit objects in.

She breathed easier once she was outside the building, but while appearing relaxed she did not lower her vigilance, watching and listening for any sign of alarm.

The guard's crystal took her onto a transport that stopped near one of the main stations of Vivaldis City. She caught a suburban line, changing twice and doubling back several times before alighting in a poorer neighborhood, leaving the crystal on the carriage. This outlet was poorly maintained, and it was easy enough to skip over the exit gate without getting busted for it. A prison guard's authorization crystal would be trackable. She wanted it to be far from her when that guard woke up and reported it missing, if they hadn't already.

She dumped the hat in a rubbish receptacle, scuffed her hair over her face and turned the jacket inside out—she recalled a current fashion for inverting one's clothes. She hadn't sensed or seen anyone following her, but that didn't mean she shouldn't take every precaution.

Was I getting lazy when those pricks starting chasing me down? Is that why they got the jump on me? She shook her head. She had sensed the attack, jumped in time to get away, but they had followed her! Even then, Michelle had stayed calm, skipping through several time zones, certain that would take care of them.

It hadn't. Michelle would never admit to panic (a good Agent never panicked, and wasn't she the best?) But when she realized capture was imminent she ditched her special model chronokinetor. A lot of people would pay big money to possess a timepiece with such range—as valuable as she was as an Agent, the tech was worth more.

They had knocked her out with a sleeper jab, which would have given them plenty of time to search her. Had they sent people back to the twenty-first century to look for the chronokinetor yet? Most likely, but she had run a fair distance through those ruins, skipping through broken doorways and crumbled rooms, over walls and down that treacherous path. There were many places she could have dropped, thrown or hidden it—a systematic search would be required and they couldn't risk being spotted in such a paranoid military post-industrial state.

If I can get back there, I have a chance of finding it before they do, especially if I time it right.

The sky overhead darkened as night crept in, punctuated by the lights of atmospheric aircraft and space shuttles. Vivaldis Prime Space Station was easily the brightest star in the heavens, its geostationary orbit making it a constant feature above the planet's capital.

Michelle slouched along the grubby street. Graffiti and rubbish littered the gloom. Several youths on the corner stopped kicking a broken holocaster and stared at her, looking poised to say something. Michelle sneered, and they decided she was not worth their while.

A hover-car passed, its engine grumbling quietly. Michelle casually turned her face away. Two more blocks and she turned into a dark apartment building. The faint smell of urine lurked near the wall computer; Michelle breathed through her mouth and pressed the door alert for one of the units.

No answer. She rolled her eyes and hit the screen again.

At last a sleepy voice responded, "Stacey, if that's you I haven't finished it yet. Come back tomorrow."

She lifted her face so the camera could see her clearly.

"It's not Stacey, Owen. Let me in."

Muffled swearing took place, and she narrowed her eyes. *Be patient*, she cautioned. *It's been a long time.*

The outer door slid back. Michelle glanced backwards once more to check no one had followed her, then entered.

The lift shuddered its way up to the third level and she buzzed the alert for the first door on the left. A skinny, lank-haired young man looked at her apprehensively as she entered the tiny apartment.

"Shit, Michelle, what do you want? Why are you here?"

"Need your help, Owen. Don't worry, I don't plan on staying here long."

"*I* don't plan on you staying here long," he muttered.

Michelle frowned at him. "Quit your whining. I'm in a spot of trouble. I need a timepiece, something that will move."

He scowled at her. "I don't do that sort of shit anymore. The Agency comes down really hard on people who tinker with their precious timepieces, remember? Being able to see back in time is one thing! Being able to go there, well, they don't want just anyone doing that!"

She raised a skeptical eyebrow. "You've thrown it all out then? Dismantled everything? Funny, I could've sworn someone like you would always have backup, some insurance if they needed to get out of here in a hurry."

They stared at each other for several long seconds. Owen broke the deadlock, muttering, "I might have something. Sit down and don't touch anything!"

Michelle ignored him and went straight to his kitchenette dispenser, punching in a request for some protein and carbohydrates. She helped herself to a long drink of water, and then proceeded to demolish the meal, trying to take small bites and chew each mouthful.

"Thanks," she said as she tipped the empty dish back into the cleaning slot, feeling slightly ashamed for being so rude and helping herself. "Was starving. Had a rough few days. Going to use the hygiene facilities, if you don't mind."

He glared at her from his seat at his workstation but didn't say anything. An array of computers, crystals and wiring framed the large bench, taking up half the living area, which was cramped to begin with. Owen ferreted through storage compartments as he assembled components on the bench.

Michelle made use of the hygiene facilities, relieving herself and washing her neck and face. The mirror screen showed dark circles under her eyes and a grim mouth. She worked on relaxing it, taking several deep breaths, then poking through the cupboards in a quick search.

Returning to the main room, she watched silently as Owen continued to open drawers and compartments. Some were locked, she noted, and he opened several twice but didn't take anything out. The sequence seemed random, but then final drawer popped out from a previously opened space. It required thumbprint and eye scan verification to unlock, and he took out two unprepossessing wire coils.

Michelle took the time to observe the rest of the small room, which was filled with assorted computers, screens and little holograms of characters from a late twentieth century Earth fictional movie.

"Can't believe you collect this stuff—it's ancient." She examined one image, a white-clad helmeted soldier. "This a main character?"

"No! Don't touch anything!" Owen snapped, assembling components. Tiny crystals joined thin mesh, encased in plastic insulation and seated in a round metal case.

Michelle fell silent and stretched quietly for several minutes before listening at the door and checking the one window. Had she ever lived like this? One main room with miniscule hygiene facilities through one doorway and a sleeping alcove next to that. No kitchen for independent cooking, just the meals dispenser. Despite the clutter, however, it was clean. Owen had always been finicky about dirt. *Comes of being space-born.*

She hovered over his shoulder for several minutes, despite his growing annoyance, then shot out a hand and said, "That's enough, I'll take it from here."

"But it's not finished!"

She smiled humorlessly. "I can finish it."

"But—" He looked at her closely. She knew he wasn't seeing the same young woman he'd known at university. The mirror had shown hardness in her face and the beginnings of crow's feet at her eyes.

"Michelle… How long have you been working for the Agency?" he asked hesitantly.

Michelle studied him, then picked up a tweezer-shaped tool and began to twist and connect several components. Concentrating on her work, she replied, "For some time."

He watched silently as she finished the homemade chronokinetor, then asked, "And how did you know where to find me? I haven't been here that long. I'm not listed on any contacts; the apartment is in a friend's name. I haven't seen you since…"

They both knew what he meant. He'd been expelled from the university in disgrace just days after she'd been accepted into a traineeship with the Time & Space Agency. The engineering faculty had discovered his experimental timepieces, devices that would not only allow the user to see back in time, but actually move than the person in time as well. They charged him with unethical activities, confiscated all the materials, but he'd fled before the hearing took place and disappeared.

This time, she looked up with genuine amusement as she clicked the last piece into place.

"Why, *you* told me where to find you, Owen. Or you will. If I need to reach you again, I'll send a message to this address." She typed a secure, non-trackable com link that would bounce through a dozen different satellites each time it was used. It could be accessed from anywhere public, but shifted hosting frequently and was not one of the Agency-issued ones that would be monitored. "However, I suggest that now would be a good time to disappear again. Sorry to be a hassle."

She smiled at him, twisted the chronokinetor into her left palm and disappeared.

TEN

74 AD

Gwyn deliberated hard that night over the best way to make her exodus from Masada. She wanted to escape as soon as possible, before the Romans could finish circumvallation of the plateau and leave her doubly trapped.

Triply trapped, if you count trapped in the fortress and trapped in this time, she thought glumly.

The next day she filched food and a water skin, and stashed them in a disused cupboard. Adi chattered as they completed their chores, oblivious to Gwyn's guilty silence. She was a coward trying to save herself from the death she knew awaited everyone else atop this mountain. Apart from Joshua, no one had been cruel or threatened her. She'd had nothing to do with any other men since her initial encounter with Gad, the Rabbi, and Eleazar. Sure, Sarah had dished out a number of whacks with her cane and flicks over the ear, but given the situation, Gwyn could forgive her that. The old woman was impatient and generous in the same breath, exasperated by Gwyn and Adi's poor domestic skills, yet she fussed over them eating enough. Gwyn knew Sarah thought often about what would befall the two girls should the Romans prevail. She was kinder than the cold-mannered Elizabeth, who sneered at Gwyn's attempts to spin, and talked over Adi.

But Gwyn couldn't save them, any of them. She'd warned the resisting Jews of the Roman attack, so at least they hadn't been caught unawares. If there had been men out of the fortress, conducting a raid like the one at En Gedi, they might have been slaughtered by the

Romans and leaving the fortress with ever fewer defenders.

She wondered if things would have been different if that had been the case. The small Roman garrison stationed at Masada had fallen prey to the Sicarii's stealth attack. While it might be a little trickier to sneak up with a whole legion, having everyone inside the fortress versus some of the best fighters stuck outside might have skewed things. Gwyn did not actually know how many people were inside Masada now—was it more or less than the historical thousand?

A chill sent a shiver through her spine, and Adi looked at her, concerned. "Are you alright, Gwyna?" she touched Gwyn gently on the arm.

The girl out of time gave a half-hearted smile, even as she felt sick to her stomach. *What if I've changed it from how it's supposed to be?*

* * *

Dusk dragged itself into the air. Impatient, Gwyn forced herself to tuck into the evening meal despite her lack of appetite. She'd need all the sustenance she could get for the night ahead. An hour later, she complained of stomach pains and excused herself to go to the latrine. She reassured Adi she'd be alright, but with a bashful look she indicated she might be awhile. And could she borrow Adi's shawl? She was feeling quite cold. Sarah's scolding about gluttony followed her out the room.

She left the other women and walked gingerly through the kitchen and past the small herb garden that occupied the courtyard outside. She stopped and hunched over as if her stomach was in pain, using the movement to sweep up a coil of rope she'd dropped carefully by the garden hoe earlier. Half bent, she jammed the rope down the front of her dress. It itched her skin madly. As soon as she re-entered the building on the opposite side, she straightened from clutching her belly and accelerated into a brisk walk. Down one passageway, taking herself past the disused cupboard to collect her food and water stash, she wrapped the supplies in Adi's shawl, slinging it over her shoulder.

The living quarters where she had been staying were on the eastern side of the plateau, which meant she was already on the right side for the gate she wanted. While guarded, it was common opinion that the path was too steep and narrow. Any Romans fool enough to try that approach would be too strung out to mount a proper assault.

Creeping quietly with her own shawl pulled over her head to cover her features, Gwyn hastened between the buildings until she sighted the gate. It was opposite to the path she'd taken with her mother, back in the future, where they'd approached from the direction of the northern palace after visiting the ruins there.

It was this next part that she feared most. If there was a vigilant guard standing watch on the gate, she was screwed. She had not had the opportunity to watch the guards—not when there were chores to be done! Only in her brief explorations with Adi of the palace grounds had she cast her eye on the gate, daydreaming idly of escape, remembering the dusty ruins she'd walked through, almost two thousand years from now.

Now she peered intently around the wall of the last building before the small gatehouse. The four meter thick casemate wall which bound Masada had a small tower built over the gate for defense and lookouts.

Luck was with her so far. Two guards sat inside the gate-room eating their supper. They didn't even glance up as she slipped silently up the outer stairs onto the wall, passing their doorway like a shadow. Shedding her subdued persona, Gwyn cast about, selecting a suitable defensive protrusion in the wall and made a loop of the rope. She fumbled as the rough fibers twisted in her hand. Cursing silently, she prayed this would work. *If you can't do knots, do lots,* she thought, frustrated by her own ineptness as she tried several times to form a decent loop that would tighten as her weight went on it. *Why didn't I ever do anything useful, like girl guides or cadets? Reading adventure novels doesn't exactly prepare you for adventures.* After five tries, she deemed it adequate, and worked it over the outcrop with the loose end dangling over the outside of the wall.

Gulping with nerves, she paused and rearranged Adi's shawl with its purloined goods over her left shoulder and under her right underarm, pulling it tight against her back and tying it firmly across her front. This left her right arm—her dominant arm—free from constraint. She clambered over the edge of the wall, shooting a look back at the guardhouse in the tower. There was no sign they had heard anything, no challenge or cry of outrage. Yet.

She scooted her legs out from under her to dangle over the wall and looked down. *Oh man.* Her heart faltered as she peered into the darkness below. Praying to whatever good fortune had kept her alive up until this point, she grasped the rope firmly in both hands and eased herself around until she faced the wall. Carefully, she began to lower herself, wrapping feet and legs around the rope to take her weight as she walked her hands down. The rope burned her hands. A blister broke, and she winced, struggling not to cry.

Then her feet dangled into free air and her hands clenched, desperately holding on. She had reached the bottom of the rope. But how far was the ground? Gwyn peered awkwardly into the shadows, but couldn't judge it. She hadn't measured the rope, hadn't really any idea how high the wall was, and she fought not to panic or despair as her arms tired.

It can't be that far, she told herself. As her eyes adjusted, she made out scrubby bushes and hoped there weren't too many sharp rocks. *Either way, I can't hang here forever, and I doubt I could manage the climb back up, so I need to get as low as I can and drop. Maybe I'll just twist an ankle instead of plunging to my death. Mind you, death from a broken neck would be fast at least. Maybe...*

She didn't plunge to her death, but she came close. Her stomach barely had time to lurch before she smacked the ground. Gwyn rolled, and became tangled in a spiny bush. Lying still and wheezing, she mustered the strength to sit up, shoving back from the bush, then stopping as she started to slide. Moving with caution, she crawled back to the wall and took stock. She would have some terrific bruises, but she could still move.

A breeze wafted up the Snake Path, beckoning with the scent of juniper and cold stone. Clouds above drifted and a crescent moon emerged. Jarred, but not yet broken, Gwyn started down the mountainside with the thin light of the moon as her guide.

ELEVEN

2573 AD

Flick. Flick. Flick. Fl–

Michelle halted her time jumps and glanced around, the sound of time receding in her ears. It was night, and she stood in a vacant block, but glowing signage advertised *NEW APARTMENT BLOCK COMING SOON! CLOSE TO CITY, SHOPS AND ENTERTAINMENT! BUY NOW!* There was, however, no one but a stray Vivaldan cat to witness her sudden appearance out of thin air. The cat hissed and skulked off into the shadows, its neon eyes glaring balefully at her, both tails flicking with disdain. There were far fewer lights in the sky now. Vivaldis' moons dominated the heavens, a treat to see all three risen at once. The Space Station glowed brightly in the sky too; she hadn't gone back too far, only fifty years, so it was operational but not quite complete. She was amazed at how half a century could turn this hopeful new suburb into the dingy slum that she had walked into less than an hour before.

She pulled out the knife she had stolen from Owen's hygiene room. Rolling up her left sleeve, she dug the tip of the knife into her bicep. Hissing at the pain, she forced herself to push the blade in until it levered behind a small object, which she flicked out. Sitting down hard, she dropped the knife and pressed her fingers over the wound, fighting nausea. Teeth grit, she applied pressure to slow the bleeding and sprayed antiseptic sealer (also stolen from the hygiene room). Thankfully, the sealer had numbing properties, so after a few minutes of throbbing, it reduced to a point where she could push it out of her mind.

She had an edge now. If indeed whoever had ordered her capture had been using this device to track her, she was leaving it behind now. While she hadn't detected immediate pursuit after her escape from Vivaldis Prime Detention Centre, she suspected they might trail her to see if she would go after the chronokinetor. Access to her tracking device seemed the only feasible explanation given those goons' ability to follow her quick time jumps when she was trying to escape. Again, this made her suspect that someone within the Agency was attempting to steal the specialized chronokinetor for themselves.

Michelle had to keep moving. It wouldn't take them long to mobilize and come after her once they'd realized she'd dumped the tracker. She jumped forward in time a month (construction of the apartment block had just begun) and began walking.

This timepiece she acquired from Owen wasn't a fleck of space dust on the one she lost. It had the safety feature of stabilizing the time traveler onto solid ground, however it only allowed two-year jumps, maximum, so it would be slow going. But she didn't know anyone at the Agency who could set times and jump as fast as she could. Even if her enemies worked out when and where she was going, she had the head start, and she wasn't going to hang about in one place or time long enough for them to catch her again.

Once she had her chronokinetor back, she was going straight to the Commissioner. She didn't dare show up without it—it was the most advanced timepiece the Agency possessed. It had been tuned specifically to her, but that could be adjusted. It would mean her career to have lost it, not to mention her pride.

Who wanted it? That was for the Commissioner to work out. Michelle was good at following orders and her orders were to use her chronokinetor to fix the turning point at Masada. She would do this and good luck to anyone trying to stop her.

A spring entered Michelle's step as she walked the few blocks to the brand new shuttle stop. She kept an eye out, and didn't have to wait too long before a late night shuttle stopped there, smelling of fresh plastic spray-coat. She boarded in the direction of Vivaldis Prime Spaceport.

* * *

Spaceflight was much the same, even fifty years prior to Michelle's present. She had deliberately stopped in a year not long after the hyperspace drive breakthrough, an advance that removed the need for cryo-sleep on journeys of more than a few light years.

Nerida's Wormhole Principle had been realized in a new style of hyper drive developed by a group of Shanista scientists, the founding species of the Allied Planets. The Principle had predicted that a suspension of the normal space-time constriction would enable an object within the suspended field, i.e. a spaceship, to slip through 'soft' spots in space and emerge elsewhere. Simply put, the ship traveled through a wormhole, making long distance space voyages much, much quicker.

Interestingly enough, Nerida's Wormhole Principle was also the basis for time travel. The Agency was still in its infant days in the year that she was currently in now: a largely secretive government organization exploring the theory of seeing back along the fourth dimension. Owen's illegal work had taken that exploration further and sought to create wormholes in time, which was why her lost chronokinetor was so valuable.

The original timepieces could project the user back to view the past only. Five decades on from 'now' and the hops of two years maximum enabled actual time travel. But the one she'd been chased for, well, that was a game changer, wasn't it? With its ability to project longer wormholes, she could make massive jumps. There were extra features, but one of her mission objectives had been to test out the simple mechanics of the device by making a series of those massive jumps on Earth, logging scientific observations and running atmospheric and geological tests in every time and place she stopped.

Earth had been selected because humans had only started proper intra-stellar travel in the year 2020, and only achieved extra-stellar travel by the twenty-second century. So most of human history took place on its planet of origin, even though the Allied Planets were expanding rapidly now.

She mused on this as she affected the slightly annoying excitement of a tourist going to space for the first time. The memorized details of various bank accounts in various recent time zones allowed her to book an express trip in the Spaceport. She gushed to the booking agent how a surprise inheritance from a distant aunt allowed her to make this trip of a lifetime to Earth. The agent smiled blandly and didn't bother to meet her eyes as he pushed the ticket towards her and called for the next customer.

She scanned the screen of the ticket. Three hours till boarding. A little long for her taste. It was possible her enemies were reviewing camera footage or financial records from the Space Station in the last fifty years, and would try to intercept her.

Michelle had had to guess the timetable—the route to Earth was only done once a week from Vivaldis—but memorizing small details in history had always been a specialty of hers. You never knew when they would be needed.

She took the next shuttle up to the Space Station and continued to play the cashed-up tourist; strolling through duty-free shops, purchasing a ship suit and some other articles of clothing in a casual manner. She picked a multi-entrance hygiene facility, showered and changed into the ship suit—a discreet grey and blue—and left from a different exit, proceeding swiftly to her gate.

She boarded with no dramas, made her way to her allotted bunk (tourist class, no sense drawing more attention that she had to) and lay down, ignoring the other passengers. She accepted the dispensed anti-nausea medication but stuffed it into a pocket rather than take it. The same advantage she had in being able to time-jump quickly meant that wormhole travel did not bother her with any ill-effects either.

As the ship cruised out of the solar system, Michelle permitted herself to catch up on some much required sleep. She did not even notice the lurch several hours later as the ship 'fell' through the wormhole and emerged some distance from Pluto's orbit.

As Michelle woke and consumed some light refreshments, they were passing Saturn. She joined the other tourists on the viewing deck to gawk at the gas giants incredible ring system. The sight cheered her up.

Despite the danger of her mission, her capture by as-yet-unknown but decidedly unfriendly assailants and possible pursuit even now, she was confident that she would be back on Earth soon and skipping through time to retrieve her lost timepiece.

Then she would return to Commissioner Hera and resolve this.

TWELVE

74 AD

Gwyn stumbled and clambered her way down the Snake Path, stopping often to rest her shaking legs, or wait as clouds passed over the moon, blocking its feeble light. She proceeded slowly, painfully; fearful of breaking an ankle or tripping over a precipice.

The rocks were sharper than their modern counterparts—patiently awaiting two thousand years of erosion to soften their edges. A slip into bushes wrought scratches all over her legs—Gwyn grit her teeth and wished she wore trousers instead of an inadequate dress which tore as she yanked it from the vicious juniper.

Two kilometers of hairpin bends and rough ground took what felt like hours. Disoriented by the twists and turns, Gwyn paused as the path began to level out. Where had the moon been when she had started? She couldn't remember, wished she had thought to pay attention.

I'm not cut out for this. People who have adventures know how to navigate by the stars, or hunt for food. She chewed gloomily on date and sipped from her water skin, then re-tied the stolen shawl and continued in what she hoped was a north-easterly direction, away from the main Roman camp and towards the gap in the not-yet complete wall. No mule conveniently wandered across her path, ready to carry her to En Gedi. Footstep after footstep, legs settling down now the steep descent was done, she walked.

Trudge, trudge, trudge. The moon edged towards the horizon. *At least I'm a bit tougher after several weeks' manual work,* she consoled herself. *I'd kill for a real bed and a hot shower, though. I even miss Naomi and Justin's stupid bickering. I miss Dad's stupid jokes. I miss Mom.*

In the wavering moonlight and under the bright stars, tears welled up. All the fear and homesickness of the last few weeks bubbled up and Gwyn sat down abruptly, great, heaving sobs bursting from her.

No comfort came. The cool desert air absorbed her misery without giving anything back, and after a while, the tears faltered, seeming to realize their futility. Soon all that remained was a sniffling nose and a heartsick soul. Possessing nothing that resembled a handkerchief, Gwyn blew her nose into her right hand and flicked the mucus away.

"Yuck," she muttered as she wiped her hand on her dress. "I'm sick of this filth. I want a bath. I want to go home!" This last was uttered half at a plaintive wail.

She almost choked in fright when a deep voice spoke out of the darkness. "Well, you certainly are a long way from home, girl!"

She leapt into a defensive crouch, panic clutching her insides. *Why did you stop, you pathetic whimpering idiot!? Stupid! Stupid! Stupid! Someone's followed you and you're as good as caught!*

But another part of her brain whispered, *That didn't sound like the same language as what you've been speaking these past few weeks. I don't think one this is one of the Sicarii.*

The first part of her brain, the panicking part, yelled back, *How the hell would you know if it sounds different or not? Joshua has tracked you somehow. You're dead!*

Forcing the panic down, Gwyn demanded aggressively, "Who's there? What do you want?"

A shadow moved in front of her, and she tensed to either fight or flee. But it stopped and her eyes gradually made out the figure of a man in the starlight. Whether young or old she couldn't tell, but he appeared to be wearing a short tunic, cloak, and helmet and carrying a spear. A solider.

"You're a Roman!" she blurted.

He cocked his head sideways and peered at her in the darkness, "So are you, by your accent. What the Pluto's name are you doing inside enemy lines? Are you a whore? You're a long way from the camp."

"What? No!" she was indignant. *Think fast, talk fast,* the calm part of her mind urged. *You must be speaking Latin. The pocket watch is doing its thing again. Convince this soldier to help you. You can do it.*

She straightened her shoulders. *Act Roman.* "I was trapped in Masada, captured by the Sicarii," she declared. "I managed to escape. I need to get away from here before they come after me!" She tried not to let her voice shake.

"Calm down, calm down. Those fanatics won't dare stir from their hill." He took her left arm, not roughly, like Joshua had done, but in a firm manner that brooked no opposition.

She resisted the urge to shake him off. She had had a gutful of people who saw fit to manhandle her, but she ground her teeth in silence.

The Roman soldier said, "If you really have come from inside the fortress, I'm thinking you need to speak to my commander. Come on, this way." They started walking, not northeast as she'd hoped, but north and then west back around towards the main Roman army camp.

Her heart sank in a resigned fashion. Yet again, she was a prisoner

* * *

Lucius Flavius Silva had been looking forward to a quiet night. The building of the circumvallation wall was proceeding well. Once it was complete, he would proceed with the next stage of the campaign: to test Masada's defenses and attempt to breach the fortress. An experienced campaigner, he was patient and prepared to do things one step at a time. He knew much of war was simply sheer bloody boredom, and had long ago learned to make the most of opportunities to rest.

So he was irritated when one of his centurions, Aelius Drusus, disturbed him not long after he'd finished his evening meal. Silva had already dismissed his attendant and settled onto his couch to read when the centurion appeared in his tent.

"General."

Taciturn and of a melancholic disposition, Drusus was nonetheless one of Silva's most reliable and capable officers. Sighing, the general put down his scroll and ran fingers through his thinning hair.

"What is it, Drusus?"

"I'm sorry to disturb you, sir. One of my scouts captured a young woman at the base of the mountain's eastern side. She appears to be

Roman, sir, and claims to have escaped from the Jews hiding in the fortress. She may be able to tell us something useful."

Silva raised thick eyebrows. Drusus had little time for women, but his diligence as a professional soldier insisted that even an apparently fugitive female could be useful. No stone would be left unturned if it could gain them an advantage in the war.

Not that it was really a war anymore. Titus had put paid to that. No, this was merely the final clean up exercise for the Procurator of Judea, and Silva was determined to see it through in the most efficient manner possible. And if that meant taking five minutes to question a woman when he'd rather go to bed, well, that was simply one of his duties as a commander.

He sighed, then ordered, "Bring her in."

Waiting, he wondered how did a Roman woman came to be a prisoner of the rebel Jews. Perhaps she had served the soldiers who had been garrisoned there, though whores were usually locals.

His interest deepened when Drusus' scout marched in the woman. Dark hair framed a thin face with eyes that at him with barely concealed suspicion and not a small amount of apprehension. It put him in mind of his daughter, Flavia, when she knew she was in trouble. But Flavia's cheeks would have been plump and glowing. This girl knew hunger, and hardship.

Silva stood, considering the best approach. Thinking of Flavia had him wondering where this girl's father or husband was, who was responsible for her.

"What is your name, young lady?" He peered down his patrician nose. "How did you come to be here?"

For her part, Gwyn saw a stern middle-aged man, thickening in the waist but still hard in the shoulders, with receding fair hair and a prominent patrician nose. A powerful man—she had heard her captors call him 'general'. He looked too young to be the emperor's son, Titus, so who was he?

Doesn't matter. Gwyn took a deep breath. *You've done this before, you can do it again. Make it good, make it believable.*

"Sir," she began casting about for the first Roman sounding name she could think of. *Um, Julius Caesar. Mark Antony. Those are men's names!*

Antony … Antonia! "My name is Gwynia Antonia. My father was a merchant here in Judea, trading goods with the Roman garrison at Masada, but he was killed by the Sicarii when they attacked and captured the fortress. They didn't kill me, though. They took me as a captive, and held me as a slave."

She felt guilty at the lie, slandering Adi and Sarah like that. Sure, the taking captive part was accurate, but she had been worked no harder than anyone else living in Masada, and certainly not treated like a slave.

"Gwynia Antonia …" Silva rolled the name around in his mouth. Her heart beat loudly in her chest. Would he believe her? The pocket watch felt warm in her palm, and she prayed it was doing its thing.

He nodded. "You're a very brave girl, Gwynia," he said kindly, reseating himself on his couch. "How in Jupiter's name did you manage to escape?"

Gwyn answered honestly, figuring the fewer lies she told the easier it would be to keep her story straight. "I was quiet and did as I was told. A strict watch wasn't kept on me—I don't think anyone imagined I would try to escape. I stole a rope from the kitchen garden and climbed over the wall near the east gate. I came down the Snake Path, and your soldier found me there. It was not easy." She trembled as if recounting the deeds forced her to relive the exertions. Living on edge for weeks, trying to blend in and stay out of trouble had taken its toll. Joshua's threats may have given her the nerve to escape, but the harrowing descent from the mountain and the long walk around the base of the plateau had exhausted her. Gwyn wobbled. Running the gauntlet and failing was the biggest blow of all.

Silva noticed her shakiness and motioned the scout to bring a stool. "Fetch some wine," he ordered.

Handed the wooden cup, Gwyn's nostrils flared at the smell—sharp red wine. She managed a few sips as Silva asked the scout questions about where he had found her.

You can do this. The wine was awful, but had a relaxing effect. She concentrated on deep breathing and kept control of her feelings.

"Can you tell me anything about how many Jews are holed up there in the fortress?" Silva's tone seemed to indicate he doubted she could provide any useful information, but would go through the motions anyway.

"Several hundred men," she answered. It was a guess. "Not more than a thousand all told, including women and children."

Silva exchanged looks with the centurion, then asked. "It seems they took the place by stealth from the garrison there—are there any other Romans still alive up there?"

Gwyn shook her head. "I do not believe so. I did not see any, and while I could not go everywhere, there was no sign of them that I could see. I believe they were all killed by the Sicarii."

Silva leaned forward. "But not you?"

"I hid." Rubbing her eyes and yawning, she elaborated. "The water cisterns are extensive. I wasn't discovered for several days, but when I tried to steal food, they caught me."

He nodded acceptance of this. "A few hundred men. A pittance," he mused. "Drusus, if we were on an open field we would crush them like a beetle."

Gwyn watched the Romans, thinking. How much of the truth should she tell? Was she influencing events in such a way as to change the course of history? Or would it simply happen anyway?

"Excuse me, General," she piped up, "they are determined. They have plenty of food and water, and are fanatical about holding Masada against you. They'll die before they surrender."

Surely when Silva realized his enemy was so pitifully small, and bolstered only by non-combatants, it would convince him that a long siege was not worthwhile. Starvation would not wear down these rebels. Yes, she was afraid that she would be changing the past, but then, as she blundered about in this time, almost anything she did might have an effect. She would never know how fragile or robust history was if she didn't get back to her own time!

Weariness swept over her. *I'm sorry, Adi,* she thought guiltily. *I was never meant to be there.*

Drusus and Silva exchanged a look. Gwyn gazed up at the general dully, stifling another yawn. Whatever he was going to decide to do with her, she hoped he would just let her sleep first. Physically and emotionally, she was exhausted.

"We will speak more in the morning, Gwynia Antonia," he declared.

"You have had a grueling ordeal, and it is very late."

"Where would you have me put her, general?" Drusus asked.

Silva knocked back his own wine and considered. "She will need to stay in here—I cannot have her wandering amongst the men. Gwynia, you are under my protection but this is a camp of soldiers. Do not leave this tent."

Gwyn nodded, glad she did not need to walk further that night.

"Drusus, send in Gaius, and see you scout is discreet about what has taken place here tonight. I will decide how I want to disseminate this information."

"Very good, General," the centurion replied. "I'll see he stays quiet. Soldiers gossip like fishwives if you aren't careful."

Silva chuckled and nodded his dismissal. Drusus turned on his heel and exited the tent.

The general rose. "You may sleep on the couch, young lady. My servant, Gaius will be assigned to you to watch over you and keep you safe."

And keep me from escaping. But she bowed her thanks and, as soon as Silva had seated himself over at a small but sturdy desk, she lay down and closed her eyes gratefully.

Drifting off, she was vaguely aware of someone entering the tent and speaking quietly to the general. She did not see the look of astonishment from Gaius, when Silva informed his servant that the grubby young woman on the reading couch was Roman and needed to be kept under close watch, for her own safety but also because she had information about the rebels inside Masada.

Silva watched as Gaius located blankets and tentatively covered the sleeping girl, then sharpened his quill, crushed and mixed fresh ink, and began composing a letter to his wife.

While he used a scribe for official communications, he found the act of writing as excellent way to arrange his thoughts. His wife was his primary correspondent—unusual in many Roman marriages, but by no means unique. Despite the distance between them and time apart, he always found her advice and opinions measured and intelligent. The fact that he would not receive her reply for many weeks did not bother him. As he outlined the situation, her melodic voice sounded in his head, asking questions and proposing solutions. It cleared his mind.

He glanced over at the sleeping girl, whose face was still tense and troubled despite her unconscious state. Her lips twitched and fists clenched as if she dreamed, and he wondered if her appearance was a blessing or a curse.

THIRTEEN

74 AD

Gwyn awoke slowly, her mouth furry and her body aching. Eyes still closed, she waited for Adi's grumble or Sarah's poke with her walking stick. When neither came, she sighed in relief and decided it must still be before dawn.

Rolling over to settle back to sleep, Gwyn came up against something hard. She opened her eyes and frowned.

"Excuse me, mistress?"

Jerking up, Gwyn quickly took in the couch upon which she had slept, the tent in which the couch sat, and the young Roman man hovering by the partly open tent flap. The events of the previous night rushed back to her. The mad scramble down the mountainside. Recapture, this time by Romans. Giving information to the general and then falling asleep in exhaustion.

A soft woolen blanket covered her. Gwyn smoothed it out onto her lap as she straightened to a sitting position, endeavoring to stay composed. *Stay calm. Remember your story.* Her eyes adjusted as the light from outside brought detail to her surroundings.

The Roman watching her carefully must have been about her age, deeply tanned skin and dark, thick hair cut short. Unlike the centurion of the night before, he wasn't scowling, and unlike the general, he didn't look harassed. This young man was not dressed as a legionary. He wore a plain brown tunic and dust-covered sandals, but spoke politely.

"Mistress, the general sent me to see if you were awake? He would like to speak with you."

Gwyn cleared her throat as she lined up the details she had created for her new identity. Fortunately, like the Sicarii, these Romans had seemed less interested in her than what she could tell them of their enemy. Hopefully once they had what they wanted, she could slip away unnoticed.

"Yes. Forgive me—I hadn't realized quite where I was." *Better keep the general happy. He seemed a lot nicer than that centurion.* "Can I...? Is there some way I can clean up or... or, um...?" She shifted uncomfortably. She needed really needed to go to the toilet. *If there is one,* her brain chimed glumly. She was too grateful to be embarrassed much when young man blushed red and pointed towards a bucket in the corner.

"You can use that. There is a pitcher of water there as well," he indicated a small stand, upon which also rested a basin. "I'll just be just outside." He coughed and bowed.

Despite his apparent decorum, Gwyn was as quick as she could be without splashing. *No underwear to trip over at least,* she thought wryly.

She had been bizarrely lucky to have not had to deal with the problem of no underwear and menstruation as of yet. She should have had her period the first week she was in Masada but it never came. At first she had panicked, thinking she had been raped while she was unconscious—Joshua creeped her out for more than just his violence. But she had not felt like she had been touched anywhere private and suffered no other symptoms of pregnancy. After several weeks she wondered if it was another attribute of the pocket watch. Suppressing some normal bodily cycles would be handy for time travel, she supposed. Not that it would stop her from getting a full check up at the doctor *and* dentist when she returned home. She hadn't suffered anything worse than a mild diarrhea from eating too many dates the first week she and fleabites from the clothes and blankets, but who knew what ancient bacteria or virus had invaded her body?

That's a Future Gwyn problem. You need to focus on now.

A tiny bronze mirror rested upon the stand which bore the water. Gwyn sniffed the jug of water, deciding a few mouthfuls were destined for her furry tongue and parched throat. Only after splashing some handfuls on her face and hair did she dare to peer at the disk of metal.

A blurred, thin face peered back at her with large eyes. A stranger.

The mirror was nowhere near clear enough to inspect her skin for blemishes or imperfections like she would have done in a modern glass. She looked at her hands, roughened by weeks of manual work, scraped by her escape of the night before, and suspected her face bore similar wear and tear. *Silly to even worry about such things—pimples and dark circles under the eyes. As if anyone here cares. Why did I ever care?*

Upon glancing at the mirror again, the stranger's jaw was set and the eyes bespoke a determination that made her straighten her spine.

I had my cry last night. That's okay, but now I will continue to survive in this time and do whatever it takes to get back home.

Her fists clenched and she could feel the embedded pocket watch heat slightly in her palm. *Take me home,* she wished with all her heart, not daring to hope.

Nothing happened. Deflated, she pulled a face, took one last look at her dull, blurry reflection, and walked out of the tent.

* * *

Gaius was permitted to remain during Silva's questioning of the mysterious girl in the tent he used for official audiences. Although Gaius wasn't a slave, rather an indentured servant, his obedience and silence was taken for granted just the same. He watched her discreetly while she answered the general. *Quiet, succinct, but confident without being arrogant.* If she didn't know the answer to a question, she stated so, but presented an opinion based on what she did know. She qualified it by stating that was just based on her what she had seen or heard, so she might be wrong.

They are sound observations, though. He was impressed. So was Drusus, though the crusty old centurion gave no clear sign of it. *You can tell by the way he shifts his weight and grunts softly at her details. He stays stone-faced if he doesn't like what he hears.*

Gaius continue to watch the girl. Skinny and not pale enough to be beautiful, but with clear eyes and a quiet strength. As the general continued his questioning, Gaius realized he was staring and altered his gaze to take in the tent wall instead. *Focus on her words, not her looks. She seems to think the siege is a waste of time.* It was incredible that a girl dared to

76

voice an opinion on military matters, and his respect for her grew.

"They're isolated, weak and outnumbered," the strange female insisted. "What further harm can they do? Most of them are women and children who had no choice but to be dragged along by their fathers and husbands. Do they deserve to die?"

"We do not wish to kill women and children," the General ignored her agitation. "But my orders are clear. This is the last pocket of resistance in this Jewish Revolt, and it must be crushed in order to subdue any future uprising." He cleared his throat and straightened in his backless chair. "However, if all you say is true, then a normal siege would indeed be useless. We will run out of food before them, and they will outlast us comfortably housed in stone palaces, while we will suffer the winter rains under nothing but tents and wooden barricades."

Good point. Let's finish up here and get back to somewhere more civilized. Somewhere with bathhouses. Gaius was lucky to serve the general, but he missed Rome, missed his sister. It had been years.

Silva continued. "I will think on it. Thank you for help, young Gwynia. Hopefully have saved us all from wasting a great deal of time."

The girl nodded politely, but Gaius could see she was trying not to grimace. "Forgive me, General," she asked, voice tense, "but what is to become of me now then? I have no family here, only cousins back in Rome. But how will I return there?"

Silva returned his attention to her and considered briefly. "We can write to your cousins. I will send your letter with my official dispatches. But I cannot send you alone back to Jaffa or Rome, and I am not reassigning imperial soldiers to accompany you." He stroked his freshly shaved chin. "I will assign young Gaius here to be your protector in camp, but you must stay in and around my tent. My men are disciplined but they are still men. You sound as if you were raised by a good family. I must care for you in place of your father""

Gwyn heard Drusus snort quietly and flicked him a look. The centurion's face was impassive, but Gaius wondered if he also thought their commander sounded a little pompous.

"Your safety and virtue are in my hands," Silva carried on, oblivious. "As a father of a young lady I know that women can be curious and excitable, but if you do as you are told I will see you home safely."

The girl stared at him with raised eyebrows. Her lips quirked. "Why, thank you, General," a hint of amusement in her voice, which dissipated as she continued. "Trust me, I don't want any excitement. I'd just like to go home."

* * *

Gwyn was escorted back to the General's tent by the servant, Gaius. As they walked out she heard Drusus and Silva converse quietly but with intent. As soon as they were clear, Gaius asked, "So, uh, what did your father trade in?"

Gwyn shot him a surprised look. She had been contemplating escape from her current dilemma and not paying attention to her guard, though a frivolous part of her declared he was nice to look at.

At least now I'm on the outside of Masada and slightly *less likely to be doomed to mass suicide and burning,* she thought cynically. Inveigling herself with the winning side had placed her in yet another cage, however, and she needed to think how she was going to get from here to En Gedi. She was convinced now that the pocket watch needed to return to the same location for it to work, since it continued to do nothing even when she had tried here in the Roman camp. Perhaps if she hadn't been attacked and carried off by Joshua and Gad she might have worked it out there and then. *No point dwelling on that now. At least you're one step closer to getting back there.*

She realized the Roman was waiting for her answer. "My father?" she asked. "Uh, he traded in spices. From, uh, the Far East." *Sufficiently vague, I hope. No one seems to be questioning my story so far. It's incredible how this thing affects people's perceptions. I wonder how far I could push it...*

"Indeed." Gaius fell silent. She wondered what he thought of her.

They didn't have far to go, just back from the parade ground a dozen yards. Silva's command tent was large and presided over the square. It was surrounded by other tents, including his personal quarters and those of his tribunes. The camp stretched out in row after row. Gwyn looked about, observing as much of her surroundings as possible. *Who knows when I'll get the chance again?* She glanced up and down the main Via which ran north-south. Horses were picketed in one section, mules in another.

Men bustled about—weapons practice was taking place in one corner of the parade ground—gladius clanged against gladius and a centurion shouted orders. Everything was regimented and tidy.

A number of Roman soldiers turned to stare. The dusty, dark-haired girl in a grubby brown dress, accompanied by the upright young attendant; hair neat, tunic perfectly in place, an air of eagerness about him. As Gaius ushered her back to the general's private tent, Gwyn wondered sourly what conclusion they drew. Probably thought she was a badly-dressed whore. *Well, stuff them.* Hopefully respect for their commander would translate into the soldiers leaving her alone. So far Silva had seemed fatherly rather than lecherous, and she intended that attitude should continue, even if it was irritating. She would need to keep her wits about her.

I just need to survive here for now and then work out how to get away. They entered the tent.

"Excuse me." It was Gaius, hovering at her elbow. This close she observed he was not much taller than her, but strongly built. She supposed keeping up with the legion involved as much marching and manual labor as the soldiers.

"Would you like something to eat?" he asked. "I know the General would prefer you stay in here so I can arrange to bring something from the officers' mess. I often do that for him anyway. You look like you could use some food."

She gazed up at him, then her face relaxed and broke into a smile. "That would be wonderful, actually. I thought their questions would go on forever. I'm so hungry!"

He beamed back at her. "I'll get bread and olives and cheese and some wine."

"Wine? This early?" She had managed to get by on rainwater from the various cisterns at Masada, sipping wine only at Sabbath meals. *How on earth did the Romans conquer an empire if all they did was drink wine all day?*

Gaius' brows furrowed. "Early?"

"Ah, never mind," she smiled tiredly and patted his forearm to apologize for confusing him. "If there was any clean water, I'd drink that over wine."

"Oh, I was going to water the wine, don't worry!" he jerked at her touch. "I'll be right back!" he half-turned, then faced her again. Don't go anywhere, just stay here. It's not safe for you out there."

Slightly bemused, Gwyn, nodded and watched him exit with alacrity. *What did I say?* she wondered.

* * *

Jupiter, she must have thought I was going to try to get her drunk. Gaius blushed as he hustled into the officers' mess tent. "I need food for a guest of the general!" he called to the nearest cook.

He tapped his foot as the slave assembled bread, cheese and a selection of snacks: olives, dried meat slices and nuts. *Not a classic beauty by any means, but pretty,* he thought. *Somehow soft, too, though she must be tough to have survived being captured by the Jews.* He grinned. He knew better than to judge a woman solely by her looks. His sister had taught him that. His smile faded. *I hope she didn't go do what Junilla had to...* Gaius pushed that thought away as the tray was handed over. Either the slave had not heard the rumors or was too dull to be curious, and no questions were asked. Gaius hurried back.

His charge perched awkwardly on the couch, and Gaius set down the tray on the low table in front of her. He ducked into the general's personal stores and brought out a skin of wine—not the finest, but a respectable red suited for every day. He poured it into a wooden cup and watered it down well from the pitcher, placing it beside the tray.

She hesitated. "Would you like some?" she offered, seemingly unsure of the etiquette.

"Oh no!" he bowed and stepped back. "I ate already this morning." *Does she not have slaves or servants at home? But she sounds so refined.*

"Please," she gestured, "I couldn't possibly eat all this. I mean, I'll have a shot," she grinned and scooped up some olives with her right hand. "I'm pretty hungry, but I'd feel better if you had some too."

He hesitated momentarily before seating himself on the adjacent couch and daring a piece of cured sausage. Extra food was never something to say no to, though he kept one eye on the entrance of the tent in case someone came in and saw him breaking protocol.

The girl slowed her eating and sipped her wine. Gaius forgot the tent and gazed at her lips, then remembered himself and concentrated on eating. After a while, he ventured, "So... did they treat you badly up there? The rebels?"

She glanced at him and appeared to ponder her answer, chewing slowly on a crust of bread. "Not really," came her reply. "I mean, apart from taking me prisoner in the first place. The women I met there were alright." *Most of them.* "I was worked just as hard as them, but they didn't beat me or anything." *Just flicked me over the ear.* But that was easier to forgive now that she was away from it. "I feel frightened for them, actually, knowing what will... what might happen to them." Her tone turned glum, her jaw set. "Hopefully your General will see it's a pointless task and leave them be."

Gaius looked surprised and paused halfway through a mouthful. "Choo fink ...?" He gulped and swallowed. "You think so? I'd be surprised. Flavius Silva is a most determined man. He was given this task by Titus himself, and I don't doubt that he'll see it through."

Her response was a deep frown. "I can only hope. Those women and children certainly don't deserve to die. Would it make such a difference if he left them be?" she wondered, half out loud, half to herself.

It is as if she actually cares about them, Gaius mused. He wondered if she was not all she seemed to be.

FOURTEEN

74 AD

"Have you heard, Marcus?"

"Heard what? No one hears anything in this stinking desert."

"Oh stop moaning, it could be worse."

"How? How could anything possibly be any worse than quelling bloodthirsty Jews in this festering pile of rock and sand?" Marcus sounded resigned rather than bitter, focusing more on darning the hole in his tunic.

His friend considered. "Well," he finally replied, "we could be quelling bloodthirsty Celts in Britannia. At least it's sunny here."

Marcus rolled his eyes.

His friend continued. "Anyway, so you haven't heard then?"

"Heard what, Lucretius? What in Hades is it that I'm supposed to have heard?" Marcus growled, exasperated.

"About the general," said Lucretius, smug at provoking his friend into asking. Marcus rolled his eyes again. *Never so chuffed as when he gets to break a story.*

"What about the sodding general?" Marcus grumbled and continued to darn, swearing as he accidentally stabbed his thumb with the bone needle.

Lucretius beamed with self-importance. "He's got some secret plan to winkle out these rebel Jews and kick their backsides without us even lifting a finger to fight! A sorceress is helping him."

"You idiot." Putting down his needle and thread, Marcus glared at his comrade. "It's just some floozy he picked up from the camp followers. I heard it from Festus."

"What?" his friend retorted. "Festus wouldn't know if his arse was on fire."

"Ha! Well, he had it from Antonius—the cook, not the tribune—who chats with Gaius, the general's servant. And as if we're going to march all the way out here and not get a fight! You saw how they fought for Jerusalem. Tenacious bastards, I'll give them that."

"Whatever." Lucretius clung sulkily to his version of events.

Marcus shook his head. His friend wasn't a coward, but his service was due to be up soon and nobody want to fight more than he had to. Lucretius preferred to run petty gambling rings and was notorious for filching valuables from the deceased after a battle (*enemies only, of course, legate!*).

They had been friends since childhood, growing up on the Aventine, enduring military service together. They had been to the rain-blasted island of Britannia, marched through the haunted forests of Germania. Lucretius teased Marcus for being gloomy but Marcus, built like an ox, provided the muscle when their fellow soldiers decided that Lucretius had rigged dice and needed a seeing to.

Now they sat in the rocky desert of Judea, Marcus admiring his finished darning, when the centurion Drusus rounded the corner.

Marcus leapt to his feet, an impressive achievement for such a big man, while Lucretius and the other soldiers in their contubernium hauled themselves to attention.

Drusus cast a disapproving eye over his men. "Form up. The general has work for you."

He moved onto the next group, snapping out orders until the whole century had assembled itself and started marching. Legionary after legionary tromped down the main via, away from the fortress that loomed above.

Lucretius whined, but Marcus ignored him and wondered glumly what was in store for them now. The circumvallation wall was effectively finished; another century was set to complete the ring of palisade on the northern side of the plateau. *Doesn't look like we're launching an attack yet.*

But he hadn't joined the army in order to think. Following orders was easier. So when they reached the sparse woodland some distance from the plateau, he did as he was told and felled trees, split wood and bound it in heavy bundles to be dragged back to camp by men and mules.

Two days later their century was reassigned to the western spur, where the timber they had cut was being used as bracing. He and his fellow soldiers followed orders to dig and build, dig and build, dig and build.

FIFTEEN

2573 AD

Earth. The original planet of humanity. Once isolated by the extremes of space, this species had nevertheless clawed its way out of the primordial soup and up the evolutionary ladder, barely avoiding self-destruction from war, epidemic, and environmental disaster. Technology and pollution had almost choked the small blue sphere—indeed it had wiped out multitudes of plant and other animal species. But finally that same technology advanced sufficiently enough and humanity endeavored to slow, halt, and reverse the damage inflicted on this world. Some of it was irreparable, though, and humans knew that to survive, they would have to reach out.

Escaping the gravitational pull of their home world, explorers began to shift excess population into intra-stellar colonies, starting with the Moon and Mars. They mined for resources, energy and new materials that lessened the burden on the severely depleted Earth. Light relays from Mercury stored phenomenal amounts of solar energy in giant crystal batteries, replacing the rather inefficient and feeble solar panels that had previously powered spacecraft built in orbit. With faster ships and the power to terraform various other satellites in the solar system (starting with Calisto, Europa, and Ganymede) whole new worlds were opened up, literally, for humans to reach out into the stars. Concentrated efforts to rehabilitate the Terran environment and rescue many species from extinction saw a re-greening of some of the planet, and an improvement in the quality of life of those humans who did not venture space-wards, but many sections remained wastelands—refuge for criminals and the desperate alike.

Michelle pondered this as the passenger ship began docking procedures at one of Earth's many, many space stations. History had been her major at university, and her line of work meant that she was far more familiar with the story of humanity than most people. She knew how close humans had come to wiping themselves out. She also knew that she was about to venture back through some of the more violent episodes of the Earth's history. But if she kept her wits about her she should be able to make her way back in time inconspicuously, locate the special timepiece, and zip back to the future without too much hassle. *I might even be able to complete my primary mission objective.*

Earth's current batch of humans weren't particularly warlike, however. They benefitted from 'origin tourism'—an industry driven by the descendants of those who had left and set out to colonize the galaxy, but were curious to visit the home world.

Tourists weren't limited to extra-terrestrial humans either. Encounters with alien species had varied from benign and even friendly, to wary and, at the worst, hostile. The last few hundred years had seen humans join a rough alliance of several intelligent life forms. The Allied Planets sought to protect and enhance the lives of its like-minded members. Other aliens were out there, and not all species were communicative, nor friendly. The Shanista were at the core of the Allied Planets, seeking not power but harmonious and sustainable growth. Humans had been a recent, but useful, addition to the alliance, with their ability to adapt to a variety of living conditions and innovate under pressure. There were still some xenophobes, Michelle thought bitterly, but several generations of integration with Shanista, Mayash, Rilans, and Nolii, and dependence on each other for technology, trade, and defense, meant that so-called "Purity Politics" were generally considered short-sighted and distasteful.

"Welcome to Earth! Humanity's home world!" The announcement boomed out in cheery tones as passengers shuffled off the transport. Reminders not to leave any personal belongings chimed overhead as pleasant music began to play and a soft scent filled the air, contributing to the welcoming atmosphere. It tried, Michelle had once been told, to capture the essence of twentieth century Hawaii, a series of tropical islands in Earth's largest ocean. With friendly faces and relaxed auras, Earth stood testament to a species that never, ever wanted to return to its dark days.

* * *

Several hours later Michelle was several shuttle flights on, standing in a beautiful green field in the Province of Scandinavia. She planned to rest, gather some supplies, and prepare in a location far from where any pursuers might expect her. She knew that while she might not be being tracked at the moment, her pursuers might wait for her to find the timepiece then waylay her on her way back into the future. She snorted quietly. They had taken her by surprise once. They wouldn't do so again. She intended to travel to the Province of Greater Arabia, and then time-hop back to the day she had lost the timepiece.

It would be an extremely time-consuming process, but if anyone could stand so many repetitive time jumps, it was her.

Flick. Flick. Flick.

SIXTEEN

74 AD

Unlike with Adi, Gwyn did not feel an immediate camaraderie with Gaius. He was the enemy, after all, of her friend stuck up the mountainside.

But she found it hard to dislike the young Roman. He was amicable, thoughtful and polite. His duties included caring for the general's person and his effects, so he was often present; tidying, cleaning, and mending when he wasn't running other errands. The first of these was finding her something more appropriate to wear than her filthy homespun dress.

Chests of booty from the sack of Jerusalem were part of Silva's luggage, including dresses, shawls and scarves to take home to his wife and daughter. The general had given Gaius permission to rifle (*carefully*) through one of the chests, where he found a blue linen dress, the color of which suited her well, even if it hung loose on her frame. Gwyn had been so grateful to wear something clean she didn't care.

Getting clean had been another this entirely. When Gaius appeared with dress, bucket, sponge, oil and strigil he had cleared his throat.

"Would you like me to bathe you, mistress?"

Gwyn stared at him speechlessly. "I beg your pardon?"

A dull red crept up his neck. "I can probably find one of the camp followers if you prefer a woman," he ventured. "But the general doesn't like them in the actual camp.

Gwyn swallowed, feeling herself flush. *Normal. Slaves and servants do this sort of thing. It's normal.* "I can manage myself. Thank you, though."

Gaius nodded, not meeting her eyes, then laid out the bathing implements and gave her privacy, guarding the tent from the outside.

A cold sponge bath, quick towel off onto linens and a splash of oil onto dry skin. She had no idea how to wield the strigil, so avoided it, but the result was a clean, if somewhat flustered Gwyn. Her brain teased her with thoughts of a hot shower, then threw in intrusive thoughts of Gaius offering to bathe her there as well. She thrust those thoughts out as she cinched the blue dress tight with a corded belt, relieved to be dressed again.

"Mistress?" Gaius called.

"Come in!"

He waited a few moments before entering the tent. Instead of tidying the bathing things, he opened a small bag and produced a fine-toothed comb carved from bone along with a smaller flask of oil.

"If you sit here, I can brush your hair." He indicated a stool.

Not wanting to seem churlish after refusing the earlier assistance, Gwyn sat. Gaius splashed a few drops of oil on his palms and worked it through her tangled hair, using the comb to gentle tease out the knots.

Gwyn sat rigid. She couldn't remember the last time someone else had brushed her hair. She and Naomi used to do it when they were younger; practicing braids, yanking ponytails. Gaius' hands were tentative. Gwyn shivered.

"Did I hurt you?" he asked.

"I'm fine," she hastened to reassure him. "What's that oil—it smells amazing."

"Rose oil." He sounded pleased. "I'm taking some home for my sister, but she won't mind if I spare a few drops."

They fell silent, and once he was done, Gwyn retreated to the couch, sneaking glances at Gaius as he tidied everything away.

After the constant chores of Masada, Gwyn was relieved to rest for a few days. Left to her own devices in between Gaius' provision of meals, she recovered her strength and explored her new enclosure.

Silva's private tent was not cluttered, neither was it austere. There was the bronze mirror on the stand with the pitcher and basin. The couch she'd slept upon was not the only one—clearly Silva could entertain small groups in here should he wish. A scroll-covered writing desk with ink and quills was surrounded by various chests over to her right. The back opened led to Silva's sleeping quarters.

She barely saw the great man after those first encounters. He was an often out, inspecting the other camps and issuing orders to his centurions and tribunes. Gwyn understood that as long as she kept out of trouble, he would be far too busy to worry about her. She hoped that his travels to the other camps and survey of the area would convince him of the futility of the siege.

Confined to the relative luxury of the tent, Gwyn tried not to become impatient. A discovery that helped was realizing she could read the scrolls left on his desk. An official document told her that the general was Lucius Flavius Silva, Procurator of the Roman province of Judea. The army with which he was conducting this siege was called the Tenth Legion of the Sea Strait.

She took to perusing whatever unsealed scrolls she could find. Silva kept many letters and official dispatches locked in a small chest, but she discovered a dusty copy of Herodotus that kept her occupied in between Gaius' visits.

When he was present, Gwyn asked first about his time in the army, and then about the sister he had mentioned. Guarded at first, Gaius slowly opened up as he polished a pair of the general's boots.

"My sister and I lived with our uncle in Ostia, but he—he was something of a nasty bastard. Sorry—man." Gaius cleared his throat. "So we ran away to Rome. Junilla worked and looked after me, but we couldn't always afford food and lodgings. She borrowed money, ended up not being able to pay it back, so we agreed to sell me to cover the debt. We were lucky—we found a good place for me in the General's household. I worked my way up to look after him personally, so he brought me with him to Judea. Another few years, and the debt will be cleared, and I'll go back to Rome to look after her."

Gwyn was speechless. *Lucky? To be sold to cover a debt?*

"Aren't you angry?" she finally managed. "I mean, selling yourself to cover your sister's debt! That's…" *Barbaric,* she wanted to say, but she didn't want to offend. The concept was so alien to her it defied understanding.

Gaius shook his head. "She did everything for me—fed and clothed me; sent me to school. I would have died in a gutter but for her."

She must mean a great deal to him. Gwyn's heart wrung in pity. *Even in this day and age, it seems extreme.* She recalled a university lecture that mentioned debt slavery in Ancient Rome, but the details had been fleeting and she wasn't sure how common it was.

"Anyway," Gaius continued brightly, "you remind me of her. Not in looks—she was fair." He gazed at her. Gwyn looked away before she blushed. "But she had a determination about her, and she didn't get flustered easily. What you've been through can't have been easy, but you don't show it. You're very composed."

She raised her eyebrows. *Composed? Guess I hide my agitation well. Speaking of which...* She coughed and tried to sound... well, composed. "Um, thank you. So... what are they doing out there, do you suppose? It's been a week since I told the General how pointless this siege was. I was really hoping we'd up sticks and head back to Jerusalem." En Gedi was on the road north, and she hoped that in a moving column of soldiers she'd find a way to slip off unnoticed. *There's no way I want to get sent back to a cousin in Rome who doesn't actually exist.*

The young man frowned. "You know, I'm not actually sure. I've heard rumors from the cook, that they are building something." He hesitated for a moment. "We could walk down the main Via and see? You'd have to wear a cloak. The General doesn't want you to gain the attention of the men."

It's always about that, isn't it? "Won't a cloak be more conspicuous in this heat?" Her tone was dry.

He considered. "Perhaps. Still better than having every man stop their duties and stare at you. The General would kill me if I let anything happen to you! I think you remind him of his daughter. You look a little like her."

"Fair enough," Gwyn stretched and rose, trying to seem casual as she rolled up Herodotus. "Let's go then. You find a cloak, I'll wear it." *Anything to get me out of this damn tent.*

He leapt to his feet, still clutching a polishing rag.

"Oh, finish the boots first," she yawned, flopping back to the couch. "I don't want to get you in trouble. Can I help?"

Gaius considered her for a second, then hesitantly passed one boot over with another rag. He watched her as he polished the first quickly and diligently. Gwyn hid a smile as she copied him. *I'm not afraid to get my hands dirty, boy.*

He caught her eye, and they smiled at each other. "You're more than a posh accent and a pretty face, you know."

Gwyn suddenly found polishing required all her concentration.

* * *

Half an hour later, a gray woolen cloak was procured. Gaius had obviously thought of this when he had first been ordered to source garments, and she appreciated his conservative taste. No attention-grabbing damasks or silks for her.

Thus cloaked and in the fading evening light, the girl out of time and the young Roman strolled south along the Via and climbed the palisade to bear witness to the busy efforts from the legion over the last few days.

Gaius gazed about, as if puzzled at the earthworks and constructions. Gwyn, a sinking feeling in her heart, could see clearing despite the dimming twilight. A mound of earth began to form a great ramp. It rose slowly, but its direction was clear. It was aimed squarely at the western wall of Masada.

SEVENTEEN

74 AD

The ramp was typical of good Roman engineering. Silva had directed his efforts at a natural spur that jutted out from the western side of the plateau, known as the White Cliff, and the results were promising.

No prolonged siege for the Legio X Fretensis. No attempting to starve out their enemy, while disease and hunger took their toll on his own men. He would take the fight up to them, and finish the Jewish Rebellion once and for all. Masada stood as a symbol of defiance against the Roman Empire, and Rome would not, could not, permit that to continue.

The backs of soldiers were put to cutting wood and hauling rock. The dry river bed that wound its way west of the spur was filled and packed to form a secure base. Engineers calculated the height of the cliff and determined the maximum angle that could be tolerated by a siege tower as it was pushed up on wheels. The rest was simple mathematics, an exercise in triangles, thus determining the length and overall size of the ramp.

Watching from the walls, Adi felt familiar dread wash over her. These invaders were like swarming, scurrying ants—swat one and more crept up to take their place.

She had felt sick with fear since the night her new friend had disappeared. They had not taken much notice at first, but finally Sarah grumbled that, sick or no, that girl must have fallen in the latrine because she was taking a blessed amount of time.

Adi had searched the latrines, the sleeping chamber, many other rooms and courtyards of the palace, growing more and more worried. Reporting to Sarah that she couldn't find the other girl anywhere, the old woman had been at first irritated as she had been ready to retire for the night, and then grumpily anxious as she enlisted various other women and children to search.

Nothing. It was as if the strange girl had vanished. Hearing the disturbance, the old Rabbi had ordered them to rest as they had more important things to worry about than a foolish chit who would receive a thrashing for inconveniencing them all so. Joshua stood nearby, saying nothing, but disappearing to search on his own, suspicious of the disappearance. Eleazar's wife Elizabeth frowned disapprovingly at the disturbance, pursing her thin lips and muttering that Sarah was wasting everybody's time.

That had been over two weeks ago. The only trace had been an abandoned rope tied around the wall on the eastern gatehouse. Adi couldn't believe that her friend would have run off like that. *Gwyna hated the Romans. They killed her family! Why would she leave us to join them? She was the one who warned us they were coming.*

"I knew there was something wrong with her." Joshua's voice was quietly vicious. "She was a Roman sympathizer! That is how she knew of their coming! She blasphemed against the Lord with her lies of visions and warnings!".

"But why?" Adi entreated her betrothed, fearful of this sudden, violent mood. "If she was a sympathizer, why tell us anything? Why not let them take us by surprise?" *It doesn't make sense!*

He rounded on her and slapped her hard. She gasped and fell back, hand cradling her stinging cheek.

"She would have said anything to save her own skin! She sold her people! Now she has scuttled off back to her Roman masters to whore for them!" He stormed out of the courtyard, leaving shocked tears rolling down her face and the other women staring in fright, except for Elizabeth, who was po-faced. None of them moved to help her, and when Sarah returned from the kitchen the old woman was for once protective and kind, admonishing the other women fiercely for not interfering.

"He is not her husband yet! She does not have to endure his temper and beatings!" Cool water was drawn to bathe her face while Sarah scolded those around her. Despite her pain and bewilderment, however, Adi noticed that the others, while looking abashed, gathered closer to Elizabeth, who ignored Sarah's admonishments.

Why would any woman ever get married if she has to endure a man's temper and beatings? She had never seen that side of her betrothed before. *Was that why Gwyna asked me about him? Did she… know? Is that why she ran away?*

None of it made any sense, she miserably gazed down from the western wall upon the impending hordes. All the defiance and confidence she had felt for her people holding out against the Romans had fallen away since her friend had seemingly abandoned them.

"What are you doing up here, girl?"

She turned slowly, trying to formulate a reply to their illustrious leader. Eleazar peered at her in consternation. Several men flanked him. Joshua was not amongst them, thankfully.

"I said, what are you doing up here? It's not safe! And it is most unseemly for a young lady such as yourself to be unaccompanied! Who is your father?" he demanded.

He doesn't know who I am. She felt relieved, then irritated. *There are less than a thousand people up on this rock, and he doesn't even know who I am.* She hid her anger below a respectfully ducked head and meek voice. "I am sorry, sir. I was looking for my betrothed. Sarah sent me with a message for him. But he is not here, I see. I will search for him elsewhere."

Dismissive, Eleazar flapped a hand. "Be gone from here. As I said, it is not safe and most unseemly. Send a lad to find him if you need to. You are better off staying by Sarah's side."

"Thank you, sir," she scuttled down off the wall. Would he question Sarah about this? Probably not. The old woman and her nephew were not on good terms anymore. He refused to see her, too busy "mounting the defense of God's loyal people" to listen to "a nattering old crone," as he said. *I can't believe how disrespectful he is being to her. No wonder Sarah is so irritable and withdrawn.* Since Gwyna's disappearance and the incident with Joshua, Elizabeth's voice was heard more and more often. Eleazar's defiant mood had infected and galvanized almost all who inhabited the mountaintop, so any who felt dissent kept it to themselves, None of the women dared complain about anything in front of his wife. Adi herself was too frightened and distraught to talk to anyone, and a tiny part of her wished that she had escaped with Gwyna. She knew she was betraying the memory of her dead parents and brothers and even Mary, but she had no true ties here, despite these being her people. What was a 'people' anyway, if not a group with like-minded ideas? She didn't like the minds or ideas of any of those around her these days—hysteric defiance choked the air.

She must be a coward and a traitor for feeling so.

EIGHTEEN

74 AD

"But why? They're holed up in there with no way of getting out and causing trouble! What's the point of going after them?" Gwyn's voice was hushed but intense.

"You can't question the General!" Gaius defended Silva. He hurried her past the curious glances of soldiers lighting torches along the Via. The sun set quickly in the desert.

Gwyn fumed, anger not helped by hunger as she smelled roast meat from cooking fires. She jerked out of Gaius' guiding hand and stormed towards the tent.

It was all going wrong. Despite her efforts, the ramp was going ahead. A half-constructed siege tower squatted at the base, surrounded by hammered iron sheets and wooden spikes.

"Slow down!" He trailed in her wake. "What did you expect? This is war. The General would be a laughing stock if he retreated from such a tiny force. The Emperor would order him to fall on his sword!"

"War," she spat, whirling on him. "Against women and children and a handful of religious lunatics. That's the stuff of legends, for sure."

They faced each other in the growing darkness. Gwyn growled and pulled her cloak tighter. "Come on," she snapped. "Don't want to get you in trouble for letting me out."

No other words were exchanged until they were back inside. Gaius lit several candles while Gwyn threw herself on a couch, vibrating with anger.

Gaius poured a cup of wine and approached cautiously. "The

Rebellion must be completely annihilated, or the seeds will grow for future dissent and destroy the peace. I don't expect you to understand, but that's the way things are."

She threw him a withering look. "I understand better than you could possibly imagine. Career building, regional stabilization, gaining resources. The rise and fall of the great Roman Empire, just like every other empire before and after it. Sure it's all conquering and triumphs now, but wait till you've all gone mad from drinking water out of lead pipes!"

Open-mouthed, Gaius stared at her as drew her knees up to her chest, glaring at her feet.

"I'm sorry," she went on after quite a few moments of silence. "I don't think anyone really goes mad from drinking water out of lead pipes. You say I'm composed! You'd think me crazy if I tried to explain. I'm just sick of this place, the dust and heat, the lack of sanitation, the food, this damn war. I don't belong here. I want to go home. And I hate hearing myself whine like this! Who would have thought history would be so damned irritating?"

Wordlessly, he crossed the tent slowly and sank down to sit next to her on the couch. Gently, he took her hand and rubbed his thumb over it.

She tried to ignore the distracting tingle it sent up her arm.

"I'm sorry it's so horrible here for you," he said, his voice low. "I hope it will all be over soon and we can all go home." He gave a small smile and with his other hand brushed her jaw. "But I'm glad I've met you."

His hazel eyes locked with her and for a moment, Gwyn forgot to breathe. Very slowly, Gaius leaned over to kiss her.

She was too astonished to even close her eyes. He pulled back and they stared at each other for a second. She raised her fingertips to her mouth and brushed them gently against her bottom lip, as if to convince herself the sensation was real. His hand caught hers, and he leaned in again, slowly, whether to give her the chance to pull away or out of his own hesitation she didn't know, but her breath caught and her eyes closed...

Gaius rubbed his thumb against her right palm, then slid it slowly up onto her wrist and arm. Gwyn shivered with excitement or nerves—she wasn't sure. She hadn't kissed many boys before, and only one girl; her social awkwardness in high school had resulted in only two dates. *No idea if I'm doing this right!* She let her mouth open slightly, and he seemed to take that as encouragement, placing his other hand on her leg.

Woah! Don't start something you can't finish, girl! As that thought struck, the knowledge that he was virtually a slave crashed into her and she tensed, pushing his hand firmly off her leg and sitting up straight.

Gaius stared at her, confused, then the look on her face made him turn a beet red. "I shouldn't have done that," he muttered. I'm sorry." He looked mortified, but disappointed.

She coughed to cover her embarrassment. *Dammit I've gone bright red too, I can feel it!* "I don't think the general would think too well on it!" *Please let that be enough.* She was acutely aware how vulnerable she was. It wasn't exciting in a good way like romance novels made out.

"Of course!" He leapt up. "Please don't report me."

Guilt warred with justification that she was only protecting herself, woven with visceral dismay at having stopped when they did. "I won't," she replied stiffly. "Just ask me if you want to kiss me next time."

Gaius bowed deeply and strode to the tent entrance. He paused, turning slowly.

Gwyn tensed, wary.

Gaius bowed again. "Gwynia," he began formally.

"Yes?" she put steel in her voice, endeavoring to warn him that bad things would happen should he make one wrong move.

"Gwynia," he repeated, more quietly this time, face serious. "May I... May I kiss you?"

Oh man, what have I got myself into? she wondered. *I really would like to, but ... what if he doesn't stop?*

Do you want him to stop? You have to find out sooner or later ...

Yes, but I want that to be up to me ... And seriously girl, there's enough bullshit in your own time about how and when women have sex. You really think that experimenting in this time is a good idea? Plus, you might get pregnant or bloody well catch something!

"Perhaps later," she tried to sound aloof and disinterested, as though she were merely declining another glass of wine.

To her surprise, he smiled and blushed.

"I look forward to it," he said, and left.

Surprised, she lay back on the couch and stared at the tent ceiling for some time.

I certainly didn't expect that.

* * *

"Sarah?"

"What!" the old woman snapped irritably. Adi shrank back into the doorway.

Sighing, Sarah turned and gestured the girl in impatiently. "Come now, I won't bite. What is it you want?"

Slowly, Adi entered, bearing a bowl of soup. "I brought you something to eat, Sarah. You didn't eat at breakfast, nor noon. You need to eat." Even as she spoke the words, she wondered why she bothered. She knew as well as the old lady that eating was pointless. The Romans had started their barrage with siege machinery, and despite the arrows, spears and rocks of the defenders, the invaders were relentless. Every day they battered the walls, spreading their ballistics as if they knew how few men stood to fight and protect each section of the wall. The attack ramp built of earth and stones was almost finished, and the target was clear: the western wall. It wouldn't be long until the Romans gained enough height to assault it directly.

Eleazar laughed in the face of the Roman assault. He mocked their efforts and exhorted the men to fight harder.

"Soon they'll be scurrying back to their soft couches and gilded whores! Like waves breaking on a rock, they will founder and melt away. God is with us, brothers!"

One or two men had muttered, concerned that Jewish prisoners of war were being used to construct the ramp through slave labor. They suggested care should be taken when launching missiles from the walls, but their illustrious leader scoffed and decreed that any Jew who chose to assist their enemy was as good as dead. That they should have chosen death before allowing themselves to be Roman pawns.

His theme of death before defeat resounded again and again, though he still promised victory.

Sarah, on the other hand, had retreated into herself, not daring to undermine her nephew's authority. *She is no longer convinced we can ride out this storm.*

Secretly, Adi shared her doubts. She remembered Jerusalem. The similarities in situations began to seem more pronounced that the differences. But the other women in the household cast scornful looks and frowned disapprovingly if she dared voice any thoughts in that direction. Since Eleazar had ostracized his aging Aunt it had discredited her as matriarch, and gradually Elizabeth's rise could not be stopped until all of the others followed suit. *They ignore her as a panicky old woman, losing her wits.*

Now she sat alone in a dark room. Adi pitied her—despite her fierceness, the old woman was genuinely caring.

"Sarah, what's wrong?" she blurted out. "I mean, apart from the Romans and the siege and—" she felt too disrespectful bringing up Eleazar and Elizabeth's behaviour. She didn't want to rub Sarah's face in her loss of place in the household hierarchy.

"Apart from that? Oh, nothing." The sarcasm dripped in the dark room, but her tone softened as she took the soup and began to slurp away quietly. "My girl, you have seen some terrible things in this war, and lost your entire family. I fear we have been a poor substitute in caring for you."

"Oh, no!" She didn't want herself to add to Sarah's burdens. "You've been kind to me! You made them wait when they wanted me to marry. You have looked out for me."

"Hmph. I fear kindness is not enough. You should not marry Joshua, he is not a good man. He will hit you and demand your obedience. A true marriage is built on respect, not blind deference. But I fear also that your wedding might never take place, if Masada falls."

"You think the Romans will defeat us here too," Adi said flatly.

There. It was out in the open now.

"I pray to God they won't," Sarah's voice was suddenly tired and creaky. "But do you remember your young friend, who so mysteriously appeared to us with a vision."

"Joshua thinks she was a spy for the Romans," Adi mumbled. No one else had dared to mention Gwyna since the rope was discovered at the eastern gate.

"Humph. Perhaps. But why warn us of their coming? It only gave Eleazar time to prepare. And do you remember she spoke of fire and rivers of blood. Whose blood? The Romans? Perhaps. But fire—fire would undo us. Yes, the walls are made of stone, but so many of the buildings and made of wood. The roofs are made of wood. Wood will burn and we will burn with it." Her rambling mesmerized Adi. "What if her vision merely forewarned us of our end, and there is nothing we can do to stop it? If it is God's Will, then we shall indeed perish. Perhaps I am damned for thinking it, but maybe God will find it in his wisdom to forgive a frightened old woman."

Adi shivered. "It might not happen ..." she whispered.

Sarah stared at her soup. "I hope not, but I am old and I worry. Time will soon come where I place myself fully in God's hands and be judged. Until then I must do what I think is right, even if others do not want to hear it. Your young life is still in my protection, as are the other women in this household and their children, even Elizabeth. I do not think God would wish us to waste our lives needlessly."

But what other fate might await us? Adi wondered. *Perhaps it would be better to die than be enslaved?* She didn't really know.

Still, at the bottom of all her fear, a spark of anger lit. She wasn't ready to die just yet.

NINETEEN

74 AD

Trumpets blew; short, sharp blasts that indicated another attack. While the Sicarii defended fiercely, as had the Jews in Jerusalem, they fell fast and hard, and no one stepped up to replace them. The ramp had reached its full height now, over seventy meters high. Silva's cleverness lay in listening to his engineers, then deciding on how best to take advantage of the natural layout of the land. A rocky spur had formed the spine of an artificial incline, wide enough and of steady elevation. The well-shielded siege tower could now be hauled and pushed to the top. With that achieved, and shrugging off any missiles from above, the soldiers concentrated their battering ram on the main western wall, pounding day after day.

All the women and children had been completely moved from their living quarters on the eastern side up into the northern palace, slightly closer to the fighting but more defensible. The men had begun to construct an internal wall around the western palace, cutting that area off from the rest of the fortress. It was built from wood butchered from the surrounding buildings, then they heaped earth on it to compact and solidify their next line of defense.

Crash!

Marcus was up there, grunting with effort as he pulled on a rope to swing back the ram again. He had to watch Lucretius be carried off screaming, an arrow in his arm—a lucky shot by a defender on the wall. It reminded everyone working on the ram to stay under the fire- and missile-proof ceiling of the siege tower.

Crash!

Marcus hoped Lucretius' injury wasn't fatal. They were so close to being able to go home. Just this last wasps' nest to smoke out.

Crash!

The problem with trying to kill wasps was that they still could sting you.

Crash!

"Smoke the bastards out!" he swore in his deep voice and the ram was swung back again.

Crash!

"You fuckers won't sting us again!" He and every other soldier in sight were sweating profusely.

Crash!

"Three more, then change!" Drusus roared the command. A relief contubernium was charging up under the cover of shields, ready to take over the ram.

Crash!

"Put your backs into it, you sons of whores!"

Crash!

"One more, you lazy pricks!"

CRASH!

The changeover was as quick and efficient as could be, despite the exhaustion of the former group and the nervousness of the latter. But the centurion soon had a rhythm established, and the battering continued.

Marcus was exhausted but didn't dare relax as he and his comrades formed up and raised shields. An orderly march was set to start when the centurion put out a hand and stopped him.

"What did you say in there, soldier?"

"Sir?" He was so tired he didn't understand the question.

"About smoke! What did you say?"

"Yes, sir! They're like wasps, sir. They sting, but the way to kill them is to smoke them out of their nest. Sir," he added belatedly.

"Humph. Very well. Form up!" he roared. The contubernium tightened in formation and locked shields above heads, except for the last two men, who held theirs behind to protect the rear.

"March!" They left the protection of the siege tower. Drusus turned back to the new group, berating them for slackening the pace while his attention had been turned.

Smoke them out ...

* * *

"Sir." The centurion's voice was quiet, but caught Silva's attention all the same. He had dismissed various tribunes and was looking forward to reaching his tent for a bath and a meal. It had been a long day. But, then, every day for the last several weeks had been a long day. He had moved around constantly, inspecting and issuing orders regarding the construction of the ramp, the assembly of the siege tower, the deployment of the ballistae. By no means a couch-general, Lucius Flavius Silva was much admired by his men for his active involvement in the day-to-day running of his legion. No tribune would ever run rings around him.

It wore him down, though, and he felt the need to compose a letter to his wife to straighten out his thoughts. That the Sicarii were penned in, there was no doubt, but he knew that despite their numbers they held a position of immense strength by dint of geography, and he might batter his forces against those walls only to see them founder.

"What is it, Drusus?" He gestured the centurion to walk with him.

The man took a moment, then spoke in a low murmur. "The ram is wearing down the wall, sir, but it is taking a toll. We lost half a dozen men today from arrows and stones alone. I can order more up there, but it is affecting the men's morale. We will break through, but when that happens there will be a pitched battle in a narrow gap, fought by men who are tired and may be easily repulsed by the Jews who have the advantage still."

The general nodded. "Do you have some suggestion for evening up the odds, centurion?" They had reached the tent entrance and stood there a moment, looking back up towards the fortress, where torches burned like fireflies in the distance. Night had well and truly fallen, and fighting had ceased for the day.

"Perhaps." It was typical of the professional soldier to be frugal with his words. Sighing, the general gestured the officer to follow him inside.

"Gaius!" he called. "Bring wine!" He looked about the tent. The girl was nowhere to be seen. He had ordered a small annex to be added to the tent for her to bathe and sleep. He still didn't know quite what to do with her—he was loathe to send her away when it was clear the fates had placed her so firmly in his care. Best keep her close to him, where his presence could protect her from Romans and Jews alike.

He vowed silently to never let his daughter travel without a retinue of servants and bodyguards, and wondered at the idiocy of the girl's merchant father to permit her to accompany him on such a journey to foreign lands. With all the upheaval in Rome over the last few years, perhaps the man had deemed the East safer than leaving his daughter in a city where Nero's thugs or rioting crowds might have gotten at her.

Silva sat not on a couch (time for that when he was clean and ready to relax) but at his desk, indicating the centurion should also be seated. His attendant appeared quickly with a pitcher of wine and poured, watering both cups as his master indicated. Clear heads were required.

"Gaius, where is the girl?" Silva inquired.

"Sir, I believe she is reading," the young man answered. He knew for a fact she was actually bathing quickly in her annex (he'd brought the water, after all), but he didn't want to say that in front of what he considered to be two crusty old men. *Jupiter knows what thoughts they might have!* Gaius found his own thoughts on that matter vivid enough—he certainly didn't want to be responsible for heart attacks in his superior officers if they had similar opinions!

"Tell her to bathe and dress to join me for dinner," Silva instructed. "I have been busy, but I have not forgotten her. Also advise the cooks I will eat in half an hour."

Turning back to Drusus, Silva leaned back in his chair. "Well then?"

Drusus watched Gaius disappear out of the tent, then leaned forward. "Something one of my men said caught my imagination, sir. It was about wasps' nests, and using fire to smoke them out. Fire might be the leveler we need up there. It causes panic and traps people. We'll control the exit, should there be a need to retreat, but it's possible we can burn them out."

The great man nodded slowly. "How do you propose we set fire to this Jewish fortress? It's mostly stone up there. They are a disciplined lot, no matter what we might like to think, and they'll be quick to quell any flames."

Drusus continued, undeterred. "Still plenty of wood to burn. We launch burning pitch arrows as soon as we breach the gate, aiming behind the defenders. They'll have to decide which is more dangerous, the enemy at their front or the flames at their rear. They won't respond coherently at first, and that will be our moment to push in. Once we get sufficient men inside the walls, we can spread out and will be harder to pin down. We'll control the gate. It won't take long for them to fall."

Silva stared at the maps weighed out on his desk. The immediately surrounding area had been charted by scouts upon arrival in the area, but a smaller scale map showed the region of the East. Judea took a decent size bite of this land, strengthening the land corridor between Egypt and Syria and allowing better control of Nabataea—which buffered the empire from warring desert tribes. Establishing firm control over Judea was his directive from Vespasian himself. A prolonged siege in the desert opened his governance of the realm up for a reawakening of rebellion at his back. Ongoing defiance from these maniacal Jews weakened his authority, not to mention his *dignitas*.

He sat back and looked at his most reliable officer. "Where would I be without men like you in my army, Drusus? I will deliberate and decide when we should attack, but it will be soon."

Nodding at this dismissal, the centurion drained his wine and rose. "Just doing my duty, sir. Our Emperor deserves our best."

"This one does, anyway," Silva joked. Both men were Flavian supporters to the bone. Their legion had declared Vespasian Emperor, and had faith in him not only as a military leader, but a political one as well. The previous incumbents—Nero, Galba, Otho, and Vitellus—were corrupt, violent, and tyrannical; bankrupting Rome and perpetuating a reign of terror. Vespasian was fresh blood, sensible and endowed already with two grown male heirs, promising stability. He was also notorious for being tight-fisted, which bode well for a crippled imperial treasury that literally couldn't afford any more debauched or excessive Emperors.

After Drusus left, Silva attended to his own ablutions. Gaius knew his general preferred to wash off the dust of the day before dining, even when on campaign, so lukewarm water awaited him in a small hip bath inside his private chambers.

A long soak was impossible—he looked forward to returning to towns equipped with bath houses, not to mention slaves to scrape him down and massage the knots out of his shoulders. Still, Gaius was on hand to shave him and lay out a clean tunic. There was no way he was going to wear a toga when he didn't have real company—a girl didn't count. He wasn't that much of a traditionalist.

The girl was waiting quietly in the main room of the tent when he walked back in. She had improved in appearance a great deal since her precipitous arrival late that night several weeks ago, wearing filthy rags and exhausted. She was well scrubbed now, and had put on some weight, though the blue gown she wore was too big.

Silva halted and looked her over, wishing his wife was here to advise him. There hadn't been any trouble with her in the time she'd been at the camp, for which he was grateful as it reinforced his belief that keeping her here was the safest and correct thing to do. Gaius had reported that she had kept to the tent, occupying herself with scrolls. Silva himself was an avid reader and he while he didn't believe in over-educating women, a girl who read a lot was the least of his worries here. If she had been like his daughter, Flavia—whom he loved dearly, but in whom he recognized a propensity for flirtation even at such a young age—he would have been at his wits' end to keep her away from his officers. This girl seemed to be a solitary soul, and Gaius had not mentioned any difficultly in supervising her.

Gaius re-entered the tent, bearing trays of food, and Silva broached the silence. "Please sit down, Gwynia. He gestured magnanimously. "I know some people don't hold with women eating on couches, but this is an informal setting, and I am not going to hold to old-fashioned conventions in my own army. Gaius, some wine."

The young man watered hers especially, of which Silva approved. He had placed a great deal of trust in his slave, beyond the usual a general placed in the one responsible for his most personal effects. He suspected that Gaius, quite an attractive youth, might have an inclination for other men anyway, which wouldn't be unusual in the army but certainly wasn't encouraged. *This isn't Greece, after all!* Aside from that, he simply had no one else he could spare for what were effectively babysitting duties. He watched as Gwyn politely thanked Gaius for pouring, and was pleased to notice they didn't appear overly-familiar.

"Gwynia, I know this has been a difficult time for you, with the loss of your family and imprisonment by the Sicarii. I feel quite a responsibility towards your well-being since you have fallen into my care. I hope to have concluded this business in the next few weeks and we shall then proceed back to Jerusalem, whereby arrangements can be made for your return to Rome if that is what your family wish for you."

"Thank you, sir. I appreciate you keeping me safe here. It has been… most educational."

The older man raised his rather bushy eyebrows. "That is an interesting way of putting it. Most girls would find this all rather traumatic. I must say, if you were my daughter, she would have had a tantrum by now, demanding I send her home with a full military escort. Or at least throw a party for my officers so she wasn't bored. But she is rather spoiled and a little silly," he half-smiled before taking a bite of bread. He loved his silly, spoiled daughter.

"How old is she, your daughter?" She followed his lead and started on her meal.

Silva chewed and swallowed. "She is a few years younger than you, I think. You are fifteen? Sixteen?" He hadn't bothered to ask in his initial interrogation of her because it was irrelevant.

"Uh, nineteen, actually."

"Oh," he looked at her properly for once. He saw a short, thin, dark-haired girl, hair pulled back in a slightly mussed knot. Nothing really like Flavia, except for the height and hair color. His daughter was always immaculate, hair curled and pinned attractively, and she was far plumper; always bouncing around in cheery moods or pouts, depending on whether she had got her way or not. His current wife had instilled some sense of discipline and duty, but Flavia had spent too long growing up with her socialite aunts while he had mourned her mother and built his military career before he had remarried.

This girl in front of him, however, was serious and intelligent. To regard this entire experience as educational spoke of character he would not have expected in one so young. He wondered if she and his wife would get along—perhaps he would enquire into her situation back in Rome and see if something couldn't be done for her, now that she was fatherless. Her cousins might not be in a position to support her, and his success over here in Judea meant that he would be affluent enough to at least point her in the direction of an appropriate husband. It was the least he could do to repay her for the inside information on Masada.

"Sir," she was speaking again. "I know you said you couldn't spare an escort, but surely with the siege so nearly concluded you could look towards sending me north, back to Jerusalem? I feel I am a burden here."

"Oh no! I wouldn't hear of such a thing!" He was emphatic. "You are far safer staying under my immediate protection with a legion of Rome's best soldiers surrounding you. We might have subdued Judea, but brigands and other ruffians would not hesitate to carry you off or murder you. I think you have suffered enough!"

Silence was his only answer, and Silva considered the discussion closed. He moved on to ask her about what she was reading. She purported that Herodotus was imaginative, but not methodical in his historical researches.

"He shouldn't have written stuff down and call it history without at least attempting to verify it," she argued, and the older man was astonished to find himself enjoying a debate about genres, and whether it was up to the author or the reader to denote something as fiction or non-fiction. It didn't take long, though, for him to tire of the discussion and dismiss Gwyn without further thought.

When he had retired for the night, Gwyn lay on a mat in her annex. *I'm running out of time.* The spiral on the pocket watch had been shrinking faster the past few days. That frightened her more than anything. *I don't want to be stuck here until I die!* She pushed her panic down and tried to think.

The General won't let me walk out of here. Can I convince Gaius to help me? How? Steal a mule and ride with me to a random village and... what? Perform some sort of magic spell to make this damn thing work? She punched her fist gently into her left palm, tapping the embedded metal.

Maybe I can convince him to disobey the General and let me escape alone from the camp? She wondered how far she would get before another Roman scout captured her.

Gaius is too loyal to his master to even consider that, let alone deserting, she sighed. *What would I have to do to convince him? Seduce him?* She did quite like him, but while she wasn't super-romantic about losing her virginity, she didn't particularly fancy a cold, calculated first time in the tent behind the general's back. It also infuriated her that the most feasible option was the 'cunning woman entraps man through sex' scenario. *No wonder it's a damn stereotype throughout the ages that women are sneaky and manipulative. They aren't given much choice!* She sighed and rolled over. *Still, I don't want that to be me. There has to be another way.*

She lay awake for something wondering, though, if it was the best way, and what it might be like.

TWENTY

PRESENT DAY

Michelle had struck a problem. A big, big problem.

She couldn't find the chronokinetor. Not anywhere. Not anytime.

She had returned rather circuitously to twenty-first century Israel, to the historic site known as Masada. She had been cautious, flicking in and out of the day she had been captured, first determining the exact minutes she had bolted through. Then she had gone in after she knew her former self and her captors would be gone and scouted the area where she had thrown the timepiece down into the bushes.

Nothing.

She searched furtively, staying out of the way of tourists and guides who descended sporadically on the Snake Path. She flicked to different hours of the night when she needed to rest, confident in her isolation in the darkness. She didn't want to attract attention from any Israeli, military or civilian, who might spot her scrabbling over the area and believe her to be a terrorist planting a bomb, not after she had read up on the politics of the time on one of her shuttle flights. And she couldn't afford to trip over herself. While she coped far better than most with time travel, close proximity to a previous or future self nauseated her. In the highly controlled experiments run by the Agency, even people who demonstrated the ability to time travel suffered disorientation and nausea. Being in proximity to oneself very quickly brought on vomiting and unconsciousness. One of the key reasons Michelle was the best Agent was her general immunity to these effects. But this was wearing her down, and she soon ran out of the anti-nausea medication she had taken from the space-ship.

"Damn!" she muttered as she jumped forward into that night. It was cold, but she had stashed blankets and food in the lee of a large boulder. Hunkering down, she munched despondently on some travel bar rations she bought in the twenty-second century (far tastier and more nutritional than anything this time and place could come up with). It was messy and tricky doing so many little time jumps. She had been awake far longer than the day had been.

I must be close. She relived her memory. "I ran down the path, pushed that woman... girl? Doesn't matter. Pushed her out of the way and tossed the damn thing so those thugs wouldn't see. That was here, I'm sure of it!" Saying it out loud didn't make it appear though.

After snatching a few hours' sleep, Michelle used the rising sun to extend her search up and down the path, scrambling down narrow openings and peering into cracks in the rocks. Still nothing.

I'm going to have to jump to the minutes just before it all happened. Then I can see where it went. She didn't like the plan since it would risk attracting not only the attention of those tourists, including the one she'd collided with, but also her attackers. She hoped they would be too intent on chasing the other her to notice anyone else.

Some time was spent choosing a hiding spot in order to view the area she needed to see. Then she jumped and waited for the right time to approach. An hour or so passed as she dozed.

Voices came first. Michelle's eyes sprang open. Two teenagers, a boy and a girl—twins by the look of them—chattered their way past. Next came a cheerful looking couple—likely the parents. It sounded like they were debating the viability of a particular species of trees in this region. *Irrelevant.*

Another girl descended the path. Short and with the look of the man who had preceded her, she must be an older daughter. She stopped to hold up a device. Michelle peered and identified the item as an early twenty-first century portable communication device, known in this time as a mobile phone. It obviously had photographic capabilities as well.

Then the sound that made her tense. A clatter of stones, the sound of running feet. She felt the shock of seeing herself hurtle into view and shove the girl. Rather roughly, she realized now, and a twinge of guilt hit her. Or was that just her stomach heaving? Michelle saw the toss of the chronokinetor and marked it, still half-watching the retreating back of her other self.

The timepiece had fallen, not into a hole or down the cliff, but into the scraggly scrub on the side of the path. She had searched there already! Why hadn't she found it?

Frowning, Michelle growled quietly as one man thundered past and join the other in the tackle that had brought her down. Her former self and her assailants vanished in a blue haze. Her nausea subsided, and she returned her attention to the chronokinetor lying abandoned by the wayside.

But not for long. The girl was being assisted to her feet by her mother, who was trying to dust her daughter off and pat her over for injuries. Shaking the older woman off, the girl first peered intently at the spot where Michelle and the goons had last been visible in this time. Then she retraced her steps slightly and reached into the bushes to pick up her mobile phone... and the chronokinetor, which she examined very briefly, then tucked in her pocket, turning to carry on down the Snake Path in the company of her parents.

More nausea gripped Michelle—she was overlapping again. She had already been in this time, but further up the path. Fighting her roiling stomach, she slid down from her hidey-hole. But by the time she reached the bottom of the rocky track, the girl and her family were gone.

* * *

"Can I help you?" The museum attendant's English was perfect. It was obvious to him that the woman who had just wandered into the Yigal Yadin Masada Museum was not local, and so he had immediately defaulted to the most common tourist lingua franca.

"Uh, yes," Slim, dark-haired and clad in loose trousers and a conservative sleeved shirt, the woman looked pale and tired. *Probably the heat—the English often struggle in this climate.*

"Uh, I think a girl, another tourist, dropped her jacket on her way down the Snake Path. But I was a fair way above her, so she didn't hear me call out. I picked it up in case she was still here." The woman explained, proffering said jacket as evidence.

She really doesn't look well. "Please, sit down." *Never let it be said that Israeli hospitality isn't the best in the world.* "I'll fetch you some water." He guided her to a chair in the museum lobby and scooted around to the restaurant kitchen, returning with said water. She made an effort to rise, but he urged her back into the seat and watched her sip from the bottle.

"Thank you," she said. "I think I might have overdone it today." *Understatement—I've been overdoing it for several weeks now.*

"It's quite a hike in this heat, even downhill. Have you drunk enough water today? Are you with a group?" His solicitousness was kind yet professional.

"Yes, but the other members of my group wanted to take their time at the ruins and then catch the cable car down. I thought I'd hike and spend some time at the museum. But I saw this girl drop her jacket on the path—have you seen her? Looked like she was with a family group. She obviously wasn't wearing it because it was so hot, but she might want it later. I know I hate to lose something while I'm traveling."

The attendant had to confess that he believed that family had already left. "They didn't come into the museum; I saw a van pick them up. They had a private driver. You can leave it at lost and found if you like? They might come back."

"Oh," the woman deflated. "I wonder where they might be headed. Possibly the same place as my tour group?"

"En Gedi, perhaps? For swimming in the Dead Sea and lunch?" More tourists entered the lobby, and he returned to the ticketing desk. When he looked up next, she was gone. Shrugging, he went back to work and thought no more of it.

* * *

A friendly tour bus operator felt sorry for the foreign lady who had, by all accounts, been left behind by her own tour group as Masada.

"I'm so terribly sorry, I really don't want to inconvenience anybody—I simply can't imagine how they must have forgotten me! Ridiculous, really. Spend five minutes too long taking photographs, turn around and—whoosh! Off drives your bus with the rest of the group!

Absolutely ridiculous!"

After assuring her that, yes, his bus also was headed to En Gedi. Knowing the public transport in the area was infrequent to none, he offered her the lift partly out of pity, and partly to shut her up. That seemed to work, though she spent the next twenty minutes muttering quietly out the window. He caught "utterly ridiculous" several times and tuned out.

"Thank you, thank you very much!" she was off like a shot as soon as they arrived at the oasis. Rolling his eyes, he returned his attention to his own tour group who flocked around him like little lambs (some milling near him expectantly, others already drifting off erratically). They were excited to be visiting the lowest place on Earth and ready to bathe in the Dead Sea.

* * *

Michelle strode down from the oasis car park to the public beach, looking about her intently, hoping to see the girl who had picked up her chronokinetor. Tourists in bathing suits were either covered in black mud or floating in the shallow water. She spotted the twins. They were cackling and throwing mud at each other while their father admonished them. The mother was chatting with another group of tourists.

But where was the girl? She didn't appear to be swimming, nor mud-bathing. Was it possible she wasn't part of this family after all?

Michelle kept moving, not wanting to attract attention. She was feeling better now she was away from Masada. There was only one of her in this time and place.

Not in the water, not on the beach. Maybe getting changed? She whirled and aimed for the women's change rooms. They were extensive (only two rooms) and no one was in the first. She supposed it was lunchtime, so anyone not bathing might be up in the restaurant near here.

Then a sound—so minute as to have been imagined—came from the back room. A blurry, distant roar, like the sound a big ocean wave made as it hissed across a sandy beach, but from far, far away.

It was the sound of time travel.

Most people couldn't hear it. Michelle could. It was what had given her warning that she was about to be attacked.

Even rarer was Michelle's ability to detect the difference between incoming and outgoing time jumps. She didn't know of anyone else who had it, but then there weren't enough Agents to be able to say that it wasn't there in others. She'd tried to explain it to the scientists at the Agency, it was like the difference between the wave coming in and then going out. Most of them had never been out of Vivaldis Central, let alone to an isolated ocean retreat. Waves and beaches were something that happened in holocasts and stories.

The sound of this wave was the retreating kind—someone was leaving this time zone.

Abandoning all attempts at quiet, she hurtled around the corner into the back change room—only to see a fading blue haze with the figure of a startled girl outlined in it.

"Shit!"

How the hell did she manage to activate it? It should be tuned to me! And when the hell has she gone!? Argh! Spitting with fury that she had been so close to her goal, only to have it snatched from her, Michelle thumped the wall.

"Ow!" She cradled her fist, even more angry that she'd lost her temper.

Right. Focus. When could she have gone?

A strange sense of foreboding crept over her. She thought about her primary mission.

Go to the Siege of Masada. Make sure the Romans prevail quickly. If the Romans spent too long subduing the last pocket of resistance, then other rebels would take heart from Masada's defiance and regroup to cause havoc. Being forced to continue to quell insurgents would undermine Vespasian's rule and leave Rome unable to solidify their foothold on the eastern edge of the Mediterranean. Thus, the future of the Empire and future Western Civilization would be jeopardized. As biased as that sounded, it was Western twentieth century technology that launched humanity off the planet and into space. If that did not take place at that critical juncture, they would not have been advanced enough to be welcomed into the Allied Planets. And if that didn't happen...

She had been sworn to top-level secrecy, and understood the

importance of this mission, which is why she needed this particular chronokinetor to undertake it. Small time jumps were inefficient, too much could go wrong with an agent.

Somehow, incredibly, this dumb girl had activated the pre-programmed destination and gone back in time to Masada at the time of the siege.

Michelle blew out a deep breath, cricked her neck and composed herself. She connected to her own timepiece and started jumping.

Flick!

* * *

1911 AD

At her fastest, Michelle could manage a two-year time jump every five seconds. That was time to jump, check and reset the time piece. Jump again.

Almost two thousand years to jump. No one, not even she, the Time Space Agency's best Agent to date, could manage that. One hundred years straight was the most she could manage on this homemade chronokinetor without needing a break.

"Piece of shite," she muttered as she halted. She always picked the early hours of the morning to stop if she was uncertain about the terrain, so to speak. Fewer people to see her.

She spent twenty or so minutes stretching and breathing meditatively, overcoming her irritation. Then she focused and began another fifty jumps.

By the fourteenth century, she had to stop. Although, relatively speaking, not a whole lot of time had passed for her personally, it was exhausting. One's body was trying to adjust to all sorts of environmental factors, slight atmospheric changes, magnetic shifts in the Earth's field—it was like old-fashioned jet lag, but far worse.

Fortunately, one of the other handy items she'd picked up on her way back from Vivaldis was a cute little device that projected an electronic field in a three meter radius. Not quite a force field, not in the sense that spaceships with their massive power sources had them to deflect space debris, but sufficient to obscure anything inside the field and cause a sharp shock to anything outside that touched it. It could be breached, but at least it provided some protection and would alert her out of even the deepest sleep. She walked herself some distance away from the oasis, trusting to the natural isolation of the area, and rolled herself up in a twenty-second century space blanket, and went to sleep.

TWENTY-ONE

74 AD

"Gaius."

"Yes?" he smiled as he looked up at her, mending yet another article of the General's gear. Tunics, boots, armor—Silva was not a vain man but took pride in being well-presented, so the lad always had something to clean or repair.

It was mid-morning; Silva was out inspecting the goings on of the siege, which seemed to be progressing quickly. As un-dramatic as it was, Gwyn had specifically chosen this time as opposed to the cover of darkness. She wasn't going to invite speculation and misinterpretation. This morning was like any other—she read in the tent while Gaius attended to his various chores.

Except this morning she had an agenda. But it didn't help when he smiled like that at her. She couldn't afford to get romantically entangled with someone who had died two millennia before she had even been born, but...

"Gaius, I need your help. I don't have anyone else I can trust. Only you." *Laying it on too thick? Maybe.* She had to appeal to his friendship if she was to have any hope of succeeding in this escape plan.

The young Roman looked at her quizzically. "What's wrong?"

She exhaled through her nose. "I need to leave the camp—yes, I know I'm not allowed to! But I think it might be my only hope of getting home. Please, just listen for a moment."

He continued to frown, but subsided and listened.

"I'm not from here. Don't laugh, I know, neither are you. But... I'm not from here or now. I don't belong here. Let me explain.

"Imagine, for a moment, that you'd discovered some magic that took you back to the Age of Heroes. Hercules, Perseus, Jason and the Argonauts. They are all alive and battling monsters and winning names for themselves.

"There they are, fighting with swords of bronze and shields of hide and thinking that Greece is the whole world. How do you, a modern Roman, explain things like steel and aqueducts? Or tell them that places like Gaul and Britannia are real and conquerable? Back when all you had to do to be a king was to own an island like Odysseus?"

A small smile twisted his lips as he nodded. "They'd think I was mad. Or a seer." He shrugged. "Or a mad seer."

"Exactly," Gwyn pressed on. "Rome was just a cluster of seven hills back then. How could you make them believe that one day it would build an empire that stretched from Africa to Germania? You couldn't!"

"No, you couldn't," he agreed.

She sighed, feeling mournful. "So you can understand how hard it is for me to tell you that I'm not from this time... That the world is so much bigger than you can possibly imagine. That you'll be dead and buried... or burned, almost two thousand years before I am even born... The Jews in Masada will commit mass suicide before surrendering to Rome. Emperor Vespasian will be succeeded briefly by Titus, then Domitian, who will prove to be a paranoid and vicious ruler just like Nero. His wife will murder him. There'll be other Emperors after him who will expand the Empire incredibly. Rome will have several centuries before its ultimate decline and fall, Europe will descend into the Dark Ages, Christianity will rise and dominate society in a thousand years' time. The world will undergo such incredible changes so as to be unrecognizable in the time I am from ... But I have to get back to that time. I don't belong here."

He stared, open-mouthed. His forehead crinkled. "Have you been drinking?" he asked at last.

If I didn't dislike the taste so much, I think I would! She had expected such a reaction. "No, I have not been drinking. You've been with me since breakfast. How could I have been? I know it sounds crazy. I thought I was going mad when I first got here. But remember—try to explain to

Jason that his voyage for the Golden Fleece only took place in a tiny part of the Aegean and the Black Sea? That the Mediterranean is so much bigger than that! You wouldn't be able to prove it to him, he'd just have to trust you."

Please believe me.

He huffed in confusion, looking hard at her before standing up and pacing the tent. He spun around to look at her.

"Maybe you have a fever. Or maybe you've eaten something bad?"

She nodded solemnly. "Check me, if you like. I haven't eaten anything you haven't. I'm not warm."

His eyes narrowed, then he crossed to rest a hand on her cheek and forehead. Her skin thrummed with his touch, but she knew she wasn't overly warm. She gazed at him seriously while his eyes flicked over her face, indecisive.

"Gwynia," he said softly, eyes kind.

Gwyn gave him a small smile, hiding her desperation. "I'm not crazy, Gaius." *Really doesn't help having him so close. Can't concentrate!*

He looked her in the eye. "Even if you're absolutely telling the truth, there is no way I'm going to help you leave the camp. General Silva put you under my protection and you need to be kept safe! There is nowhere safer than a general's tent surrounding by the best Roman legion in the world!"

Gwyn slumped. "Yes, okay, I know. But if I don't try to get back to where I'm from, I think I'll be stuck here forever. The only way I can think of to get back is to return to the place I first came through, at En Gedi."

"What's En Gedi?" He looked crestfallen to have upset her.

"It's a village north of here, on the shore of the Dead Sea. I was there with my family in my time when this device somehow sent me back in time." She waved her left palm towards him, cradling her face with her right hand, rubbing her eyes.

He peered at the pocket watch, embedded into her hand.

"What is that? It looks like a pattern but ..."" He reached out gently and touched the device, feeling the demarcation between metal and skin. "How did this metal get into your skin?""

"I don't know," she answered. "It happened when it sent me back in time. Kinda burned into my skin, but it doesn't hurt. But this spiral pattern used to be much bigger. It's like it's winding down. I think I'm running out of time."

He sat down next to her, holding her hand. Her pulse quickened, and she fought the distraction. The moments stretched out in silence.

"I don't know, it seems pretty far-fetched," he said, shaking his head.

"Tell me about it. If it were the other way around, I'd think me crazy too." She sighed.

They sat for a while. Holding hands with him felt good. Finally, Gaius spoke. "Titus really doesn't last? His brother is a weasel. Everyone says so."

"Unfortunately, yes."

"How long will he rule for?"

"I don't know exactly. Quite a few years, I think. I haven't studied much Roman history."

He contemplated this. "You've studied Rome's history? But wait— you said the Empire would decline and fall—why?"

"Lots of reasons. Overstretched resources. External attacks, internal dissent. But many, many years from now. It'll be long after you're dead."

A longer silence.

"Christianity? Seriously? I've seen a few of those whack jobs since I've come to Judea. They think there is only one god and have some other really weird ideas."

She snorted. "Yeah ... They think a lot of other stuff that is pretty crazy. It gets better ... Eventually." *I suppose. Gets a lot worse first.*

He sighed. "Even if it's true, I'd be flogged at the very least for disobeying the General. He can legally crucify me, you know."

You can't ask this of him, Gwyn sighed. "I understand." *It was worth a shot.* She squeezed his hand, and it sent a jolt between them.

He had obviously felt it too. Raising his eyebrows in slight question. "May I ...?"

Oh well, might as well. "Alright," she whispered, a smile ghosted across her face, her heart beginning to race, "Just once."

Her lips tingled where his met hers. The kiss only lasted a few seconds, but when he pulled back, she leaned in to kiss him again, quashing the logical part of her brain. Once became twice, then more, as she moved her hand to the back of his neck, enjoying the feel of his hair in her fingers. He reached for her waist, and the thrill of being touched made her shiver.

If she was being honest with herself, Gwyn had idly daydreamed about Gaius since that first day he had offered to bathe her. And while he had surprised her with that kiss, the time she had spent thinking about it in the meantime meant that she didn't freeze up and panic. *Plus, he did ask this time, and I said yes.* She smiled inwardly. Warmth rose between her legs and she guessed by the hardness pressing against her thigh that a similar effect was happening to him.

This wasn't part of your plan! Her inner voice snapped. *What happened to not pandering to stereotypes!*

Yeah, yeah, I know, but… He's already said he can't help me! I'm not trying to change his mind, I just want to find out what this feels like! She couldn't help but wonder at her real motives.

He was kissing her neck now—one hand had dropped to her waist and circled gently over her thighs.

"Gaius," she breathed. *Oh wow, his hand is getting closer to my, to my…* Tell him to stop? But she really did want to know what it would feel like.

"Mmm?"

"I can't." She pulled back with a gasp and grabbed his hand. "I'm sorry. You have no idea how much I want to, but I just can't."

He stared at her, confusion apparent. He took a deep breath and sat back, disentangling his fingers from hers.

Gwyn tried to smile to take the sting out of the situation, but failed. *He is as disappointed as me, I bet.* "Gaius, I really, really like you," she whispered, "but I can't stay here. I don't belong here. And as much as I want to, well, you know… I don't want you to think it was to try and manipulate you into helping me get away from here."

He looked at her incredulously. "You really believe it, don't you? That you're from the future?"

"It's the truth," she replied simply.

TWENTY-TWO

74 AD

Gaius didn't bring up their conversation in the following days, and neither did Gwyn. She wondered if he was thinking about it as much as her. She would give him no cause for suspicion, but she knew she would have to go it alone. The spiral had almost run out.

And there was no better time than tonight. The Roman forces had come so close to breaching the wall today, and Silva had decided that at dawn, they would make the final push.

With them so distracted, Gwyn hoped her whereabouts would be the last thing on their minds. She had taken precautions the whole time she had been in the Roman camp, secreting bits of food and swiping a water skin—hiding them under the cushions in the annex where she slept. She estimated she had been at least two to three weeks living in Masada, and a further three to four amongst the Romans. She still didn't know if the shrinking spiral on the pocket watch was battery life or countdown, but she was going to find out very, very soon.

Come nightfall, she ate her supper quietly in her annex while Silva spent his evening in intense final discussions with his officers. She tipped her well-watered wine into the skin and wrapped cheese, bread, dates and olives in a cloth. She pretended to be asleep when Gaius came to clear her meal, staying still and feigning deep breathing even as she felt him stand and watch her for some time. *If this was a stupid romance novel, the guy would declare his feelings for the heroine and they'd make out passionately. But no. I'm tossing and turning and wondering what I've missed out on!*

The more ruthless part of her considered cracking him over the head with a metal wine goblet and stealing his uniform, but she knew she had no skill at incapacitating people, and she would either end up killing him if she hit too hard, or simply alert him that she was making a break for it. No, she would have to find some way over the palisade and across the ditch herself.

Finally, the camp fell quiet, or as quiet as could be expected. The sound of animals shifting in their pickets drifted on the breeze. Occasionally, a legionary shuffled from his tent to use the latrine, murmur to the sentries and return to snoring. It was the sentries that concerned her the most, but she didn't want to run into a soldier taking a leak either, so she was silent and cautious as she wrapped her cloak around herself and crept from the tent.

Memory was her ally as she recalled the day Gaius had taken her to see the siege ramp. It ran up the western face of Masada, so she knew which way was north. She had seen defensive ditches and outward-facing wooden spikes around the perimeter—getting through those would be harder than climbing over a wall.

It had been a gibbous moon the night she'd scrambled down the Snake Path, and she had needed every photon to avoid plunging to her death over a cliff. Tonight was a crescent moon. She would need the light later and it wasn't really sufficient, but at least for now it wasn't shining brightly as she crept through the shadows of the camp.

Picking her way through tent ropes, Gwyn aimed for the north-western corner of the square encampment. Sentries stood guard at each end of the Via which ran north to south, others at the east to west. Her heart leaped several times as a soldier stumbled past in the dark, but no one spotted her and she snuck towards the ten foot high wall.

The wide gap between the last row of tents and the wall offered no cover, so she crouched in the darkness considering her next move. It was a lot higher than she could jump—she would need something to step on. And those sharpened points offered no forgiveness if she slipped.

Intent on what to do, she didn't notice the hand coming round to cover her mouth until the last second.

"Mmmph!" Gwyn thrashed backwards, elbowing her attacker.

A grunt, then "Gwynia!" in a half-choked whisper. "It's me!"

She relaxed the fingers she had been about to gouge into eyeballs. The hand on her mouth released, and she turned.

"Gaius? What the hell are you doing here?" she demanded.

"What in Hades are *you* doing here? Were you about to try climb that wall? Are you crazy?"

"Enough with the crazy!" she snarled, peering over his shoulder. Had anyone heard? Leaning in close, she breathed "I *told* you, I have to get back to En Gedi. By tomorrow, almost all the Jews in Masada will be dead and Silva will be finished here. I have to go tonight."

He looked at her, gaze unreadable in the darkness.

She sighed. "Please, I don't want to get you in trouble. Just help me get over that wall and I'll be out of your hair. I can walk to En Gedi by dawn, I expect it's about thirteen Roman miles." She remembered the drive with her family not taking much time at all, maybe twenty minutes, so she guessed it to be about twenty kilometers. Average walking speed of five kilometers an hour, slow it down because of the dark, add in rests... she estimated dawn to be an achievable target. Determination would lend her stamina, she hoped.

"Gaius?" she prompted when he didn't say anything. "Trade you a boost over the wall for a kiss?" She tried to inject some humor the because the truth was she was desperate and he was about to march her to right back to Silva.

Finally, he gave a half-hearted chuckle. "I must be the crazy one. You have some nerve. You escaped an impregnable fortress, climbing down that death trap of a path in the dark. Now you want to jump over a sharpened, ten-foot high wall, crawl through a ditch full of spikes and walk thirteen miles—in the dark!—to a village on the edge of a salty lake in the hope that your magical amulet will take you back into the future!"

"Sshh," she shushed him anxiously as his voice rose, but her heart leapt with hope. "Does this mean you'll boost me over the wall?"

He smiled—she could see his teeth shining in the moonlight—and leaned in slowly, carefully, raising her chin with a callused hand. Hope danced with excitement in her heart as he kissed her gently, then he straightened up and grinned again.

"I must be the crazy one. I'll do better than that," he said. "I'll get you there."

* * *

This isn't exactly what I had in mind as a disguise. She hid her grimace and tweaked her dress to show more cleavage. Her cloak hung impractically over her shoulders and she had teased her hair out, flipping it over her shoulders in what she hoped was a suggestive manner.

Gaius grinned like an idiot beside her as they waltzed up to the north gate. Hanging off his arm, she attempted to simper. *Ugh, this is pathetic. Give me spikes and ditches over this any day...*

"Going somewhere?" the sentry smirked as he toyed with his spear.

All sorts of innuendo ran through her mind, and Gwyn tried not to roll her eyes.

Gaius puffed his chest out. "Got to escort this lovely lady back to her sisters before they miss her! She's had a busy night, entertaining the high-ups!"

The other sentry guffawed.

"She going to make a man out of you before she finishes for the night? We are going into battle tomorrow, after all!" Winks and nods had Gaius grinning all the wider.

Giggling as though she was slightly drunk, Gwyn tugged gently and stood on tiptoes to whisper in his ear as she smiled, "If you don't hurry up with this charade I will find somewhere very creative to put that spear he's holding!" Sinking back, she giggled again and batted her eyelashes.

Gaius' expression froze for a second, then he broke into laughter and moved forward, slapping the sentries on the shoulder and saying, "Got to go lads, she's promised me special treatment, and I've got to get back to my tribune's tent within the hour!"

"It won't take you an hour, lad!" one called after him.

"It might not even take you a minute!" the other joined in. "If we weren't on duty, we'd come and show you how it's done!"

Their leers and whistles subsided into the darkness with a final reminder not to forget the camp password. Gaius and Gwyn veered quickly off the path and took a sharp right once out of sight.

"Sorry," he said after a while, as if he could sense her simmering rage.

"It was the only reason I could think of that I might be sneaking out of camp with a girl at night."

"I know. I'm not angry at you." Gwyn heaved her cloak back around her. "I just get pissed off at the world, men treating women like objects, abusing them, not respecting them. People like that are scum."

"I know," he answered quietly. "But it's the way the world is."

She shot a glance at him. "But it's not how the world has to be. You will never change the world if you don't think it can be done."

He was quiet for a while as they trudged eastwards. Then he said, "So things are different in your time? The way men and women treat each other?"

Gwyn sighed. "Sometimes," she replied. "It's pretty good where I live. There are still plenty of things that could be a lot better. In most places, it is a lot worse. At least in Rome in this time, women are allowed to own property and to divorce. But there is a lot more to it than that. Don't you ever wonder about what's fair?"

"I do." He reached out and grabbed her hand gently, raising his eyebrows in that questioning way of his to indicate that handholding was by no means obligatory if she didn't want it. She didn't pull away. "You see, my sister was a prostitute," he remarked, staring ahead. "She sold herself to keep us from starving when we ran away from our uncle. She knew what he was like. She knew I'd try to stop him once I found out what he was doing to her. But I was only eleven—he would have killed me. So we ran away to Rome instead, and she kept us alive and made sure I wouldn't have to follow in her footsteps. That's why we got into debt; she borrowed money to send me to school, to give me a start, a chance of making something more of myself."

Gwyn found herself unable to say anything for several minutes, squeezing his hand tightly instead. She was overwhelmed by the love she heard in his voice for his sister, and the undeniable respect he had for her for making such hard decisions.

"She sounds like an incredibly strong woman," she said at last, after they picked their way over a rocky section and found a narrow track that offered some easier progress.

She could see his smile in the moonlight. "She is," he replied. "But so are you. Being around you is an adventure." He chuckled.

Gwyn was subdued in contrast. *I used to dream of having adventures. I'd read and dream. But my dreams usually involved a lot less walking.* A glance up at the dark bulk of Masada panged her with guilt. Somewhere inside there, Adi was perhaps sleeping, or maybe lying awake in sick fear. *In my dreams, I'd charge up there heroically, drag her to safety. Instead, I'm a coward trying to save my own skin.*

They marched in silence for quite some time, until she called a break, figuring them a few miles from the Roman camp.

Gwyn sat, taking a deep breath. "Gaius, you really should head back now. I'm well on my way. I know I have to head east till I hit the Dead Sea, then turn north and follow the shore. I don't want you to be missed."

He considered. "You know, I don't think I can. I'd be forever wondering what had happened to you, whether you'd gotten lost, or fallen and broken an ankle in the dark, or been attacked by bandits. I don't know how you will make this amulet thing of yours work, but I have to see it to believe it."

"But…" she was both stupidly grateful and annoyed he didn't want to abandon her. *Is it the pocket watch making him think like this? Or his own feelings? He is risking everything.*

Maybe it was the quiet recklessness he was displaying, but something infected her mood and made her want to be as daring. Side by side, they leaned companionably against the large boulder behind them. Gwyn turned and kneeled before him, resting her hands on his thighs.

She thought his face registered surprise, but it was hard to tell in the dark. She leaned in and kissed him clumsily on the corner of his mouth. His hands only took seconds took reach up and take her face in them, guiding her more firmly as he kissed her back.

No agenda now, her brain whispered.

Moving her hands to his shoulders to balance, she shifted until she was astride him. The heat and excitement built as he ran his hands all over her neck, shoulders, back and hips, both of them making little murmuring noises as they explored each other.

His hands stroked her thighs, rubbing firm circles inwards until he reached the same spot where she had stopped him last time. Gaius paused, leaning back to stare into her eyes. Gwyn swallowed and placed her own hand over his, encouraging it onwards. Her eyes closed and breath quickened as his fingers brushed sensitive skin through the fabric of her dress.

Oh my God, please don't stop! She hoped like hell he was getting the message because she was too embarrassed to say it out loud. He seemed to be, because he didn't stop as she bit her lip and fought not to make a sound at that wonderful feeling building and rising in her core. The heat, pooling and expanding, dampness against the cloth.

"You're beautiful," he breathed in her ear.

She jerked hard three times, making a little whimper and subsiding against him, eyes closed and breathing hard.

Gaius' arms pulled her into a tight embrace, his arousal pressed hard against her stomach. Kissing her neck, grazing his teeth against the soft skin, Gwyn moaned and rocked against him. He dragged up her dress, baring pale legs, fumbling under his own tunic and grasping himself to guide her onto him. Her eyes flew open again, heart racing. *This is it, Gwyn. You can still stop if you want to.* But she didn't want to. She let him push against her, feeling it slip slightly, then return to that point of resistance. *Um, I'm not sure it's going to go in…*

"Ow!" She froze as sharp pain ripped between her legs. Tears sprang to her eyes as she gasped.

"I'm sorry, I'm sorry!" Gaius gripped her shoulders and kissed her. "Are you alright? I didn't want to hurt you!" They were suspended awkwardly, her still straddling his lap, him half in her, and she wasn't sure whether pulling away or staying still would hurt more.

"It's okay!" *You idiot, you knew it would hurt the first time.* Mortification set in—everything had been going so well! "Um, I just didn't expect it…" *To hurt so much.*

"Here." Gaius raised her gently by her hips and off him, settling her on his lap. "I'm sorry." He kissed her gently, hands rubbing her shoulders. She tried to relax. "You don't have to," he whispered. "I don't want to hurt you."

She could feel his hardness and took a slightly shuddery breath. "No, I want to," she whispered. *I do, I just don't want it to hurt. Need to get past that!* She kissed him back, trying to recapture the feeling she had before, the one where her brain wanted to explode. *Maybe if he…* She guided his hand back to that spot it had reached before, only this time it was on her bare skin, not through the dress, and he followed her lead, rubbing gently, and then harder as a small moan escaped her lips. Kneeling up again, she tried to position herself so he could guide himself in.

Ow! It still hurt like hell, a sharp, stabbing pain, but she pushed down onto him, trying to concentrate on his fingers rubbing her instead. The pain subsided a little, but it still was stronger than the nice feelings she of before, which were fading fast. She grabbed his wrist, looking down into his eyes.

"I'm sorry," she whispered. "I just don't think I can. It hurts too much." She lifted herself off him and sat to the side, pushing her dress back down. Tears of embarrassment, disappointment, and pain welled up in her eyes and she bit her lip hard to stop them from pouring out. *What a mess. Your first attempt at sex and you can't even go through with it.* She stared at the ground, too humiliated to look at Gaius.

"Hey," he leaned over and turned her chin towards him. "It's not the end of the world! I'm so sorry I hurt you—I never want to be that man." He hugged around her shoulders and rocked her gently. "Are you alright?"

She sniffed slightly, wiping her nose on her cloak. "Surely that's not what all the fuss is about?"

"Erm... well, I've only been with a few women and they seemed to enjoy it. My first time was with another slave—she took a fancy to me."

Gwyn swallowed and frowned. "How old were you?"

"Fourteen—I was a man, not a child, though I expect I seemed like one. Didn't really know what to do, but she was kind and didn't make fun of me." He shrugged. "I never really wanted to visit prostitutes."

His prosaic tone calmed her, though embarrassment still ran deep. The awkward silence broke when Gaius cleared his throat.

"So, yes, I think could have been a lot better. I didn't realize that you hadn't... I would have been more careful." His tone was so dejected that she half laughed, then sniffed again.

"I knew it was supposed to hurt, the first time, but everything I've ever read makes it seem like you can get past that quickly and then it's amazing. Guess books lie."

He digested that. "You read books about it?" He sounded shocked.

"Not many!" she retorted. "It doesn't matter. Anyway, we should keep moving."

She half smiled at him and then pulled herself gently out of his embrace and stood, fussing with her skirt to smooth it down. "I'm just going to go, uh, find a rock or tree or something."

He was standing, waiting when she returned. The moon was overhead now. Half the night had passed. She gave a lopsided smile and offered him the water skin. He took a sip, and they started to walk.

"You still can go back, you know," she said.

"I know," he replied.

They marched on into the night.

* * *

551 AD

Dzzzt!

"Baaaa!"

Michelle sat bolt upright and tensed for the fight. Then she snorted quietly with laughter as she watched the startled sheep scamper back towards its shepherd. She saw the boy peer confusedly towards her—the electronic field obscured everything under its dome, including her, but in the pre-dawn light she knew he would be able to see a strange shape, so she quickly disappeared in a blue haze.

She was almost there. It was the sixth century AD—she had stopped to eat and had even managed to sleep for quite a few hours. Refreshed, she managed the next fifty jumps and then had to jump once more to avoid a band of startled bandits creeping towards the oasis in the dark hours before dawn.

She continued to jump until the need for food and another sleep pressed upon her. This kind of time travel was extremely draining, and she wanted to have her wits about her when she got to the right time. Problem was, she wasn't sure the exact day, week or month she was aiming for. That information had been stored in the other chronokinetor. She didn't want to overlap herself again either, so she figured she would start at the end of the year and use the translator on this timepiece to ask if anyone had seen a strange girl appear in the village, then she'd aim for closer to that time. Which meant she would have to start appearing in the day time. *Oh well, I could use some sun after centuries of night.*

When she got to the village of En Gedi at the end of 74 AD, however, she was stunned by what she saw.

TWENTY-THREE

74 AD

Ashes. En Gedi had been burned to ashes. The buildings that still stood were burnt-out ruins hosting the ghosts of those who had lived, and died, at the oasis village.

The dawn breeze blew gently off the Dead Sea as the ground began to heat up, rustling the palm fronds that hung desiccated from the blackened trunks. Gwyn and Gaius stood staring at the desolation.

"What happened here?" the young man asked at last. "We never came this way." He referred to the Tenth Legion.

"It was the Sicarii," Gwyn answered slowly. "This is where they took me. It was a raid. I didn't realize they'd destroyed everything and…" she trailed off as she spotted the charred bones of a crumpled skeleton lying where a hut had once stood.

"They killed everyone. Why didn't they kill you?" he asked.

Sheer dumb luck? "I'm not entirely sure," she waved the pocket watch hand vaguely. "I think this may have had something to do with it. It seems to affect the minds of those around it somehow—maybe making them less likely to kill me. It's how I can speak Latin. And Hebrew. Or Aramaic. The Jews in Masada had no trouble understanding me. It may even be why you are helping me, despite the trouble you are going to get in when you return."

There. She'd said it. It had plagued her through the night—every time they'd stopped to rest, she'd badgered him to return to camp before he was missed. It didn't follow that the pocket watch would assist in persuading him to help her escape, but then ignore her persuasions

135

for him to return. Maybe once set on a course, a person's mind wouldn't be deterred? All she knew is that he was going to be in a hell of a lot of trouble over this. Sinking to the ground, she sat and took the weight off her blistered feet. Used to marching, Gaius was unaffected by their nocturnal tramping.

He sat next to her nonetheless and replied, "You think so? Maybe I couldn't resist my own adventure with a woman like you?" His light gallantry made her laugh briefly, but then worry. By now, the General would have missed him. When he reappeared, he would be severely punished for deserting, particularly on the eve of battle, even if he wasn't a soldier. She shivered.

"Now what?" Gaius asked. "How does this amulet of yours work?"

She looked at it. "I honestly don't know. I don't know exactly where in the village I was—they hit me over the head and I didn't see anywhere outside that hut. I guess I should just try something."

She took a deep breath and pressed the spiral.

Nothing.

Tracing patterns, trying to twist it between her palms, clapping it, poking it. She tried speaking to it, whispering at it, swearing at it—Gaius was astonished at her range of vocabulary—nothing worked.

Finally, she slumped to the ground, muttering in frustration. The sun had risen high by now; oppressive heat bore down on them. Gaius had located the village well, but it was fouled by the corpse of a sheep. Gwyn had gagged at the smell, and even the Roman lad pulled a face.

"Terrific," she declared bitterly. "We are going to die of thirst in this blasted hell-hole, you'll be called a runaway or a deserter and punished, and my family will never know why I disappeared without a trace." Tears trickled down her cheeks. She dashed them away.

Gaius looked as though he had been starting to have similar thoughts, despite all his previous positivity. "What are we going to do?" he asked, dejection creeping into his tone.

"For a start, young man, you are going to not make sudden moves. And you, young lady, are going to stop trying to break the most advanced and expensive bit of time-space technology ever created to date!"

The voice came from behind them. Gaius disobeyed immediately, leaping up and moving defensively in front of Gwyn, while she complied effortlessly, since she could only stare in astonishment.

"What the …?" she managed.

"Calm down, lad, I'm not here to fight," the woman replied.

By the looks of her, she could probably handle herself, Gwyn thought, recognizing her as the woman from the Snake Path at Masada. *She knocked me flying and dropped the pocket watch before disappearing.*

Gwyn scrambled to her feet and pushed gently past Gaius, then stopped. There were so many things she wanted to say, to ask. She had been at the end of her hope, and suddenly this beacon had appeared. She settled for, "Please tell me you know how to work this thing and send me home?" her voice cracked and she reached out with her left hand, showing the pocket watch with her palm facing up.

Something akin to pity crossed the woman's stern features. She relaxed and advanced slowly, watching Gaius carefully in case he decided she was dangerous. He returned the assessment.

"Who are you?" he demanded, once again trying to move protectively in front of Gwyn. She neatly nudged him to the side again.

The woman shot him a look, then looked at Gwyn. "How long have you been in this time, girl, that you've already acquired a boyfriend?"

Gwyn blushed fiercely, and the woman choked back a laugh. She arranged her features in a more serious expression, stepping forward.

"No, really," she asked as she took Gwyn's hand gently and examined the timepiece, "how long have you been here?"

"Uh, seven weeks, I think. Maybe more, or less. I lost track."

"Seven weeks." The woman stared searchingly at Gwyn's face. "How in the stars did you survive alone for seven weeks in this time and place? And how did you manage to activate the chronokinetor?" she asked.

"The what?" Gwyn asked.

"Time-mover." The two women turned with surprise to the Roman. "What?" he said. "You have to speak Greek at this end of the Empire."

Gwyn sighed resignedly. "I have no idea. I'm so sorry I ever picked it up. It is yours, isn't it? You dropped it on the Snake Path."

"Yes." The woman's face was contemplative, then businesslike. "Look, the spiral has almost run down. We have to charge this thing."

She pressed the back of Gwyn's left hand and frowned in

concentration. Then there was a weird popping noise, and Gwyn gasped at the creepy sensation of metal leaving her skin. Suddenly the pocket watch, or chrono-whatever thingy was free. The chain left her wrist, and it sat innocuously on her palm, just like that.

"How did you do that!?" she demanded.

"It's a knack," the older woman replied. "Come on, there isn't much time."

Gaius uttered something unintelligible to Gwyn and she turned to stare at him in puzzlement.

"What did you … say?" She stopped as he stared back at her. Her brain turned over the words in her head. *You're speaking English. He's speaking Latin. You can't understand each other without the pocket watch!*

"Ah. Hang on a minute and I'll fix that." The woman repeated herself to Gaius in Latin, then starting walking away.

"Eh?" he replied, as he trailed after them. They marched down from the oasis towards the Dead Sea. It was at a much higher level now that it was in modern times.

The woman stopped on the shore edge and plunged the chronokinetor into the water. "It was almost out of power. If you let it run out completely, it's stuffed, so you and I are very lucky it's got a bit left. Water is its main power source. Salt water is best—this should work a treat. Lots of ions."

"You are kidding me, right?" Gwyn asked. "Do you know how careful I was not to let that thing get wet in case I broke it?" Her voice cracked. "Argh! And you say it was almost out? I would have been trapped here forever! Unless … how did you get here then? Who are you? You didn't answer before."

The woman chuckled and pulled the timepiece out of the water to examine it. "Right, that should do it. Here, hold out your hand." Gwyn saw another pocket watch sitting in the woman's own left palm, which she popped out in that same strange way and placed it in Gwyn's.

"Just a tick," she pulled out a tweezer-like object, tinkered with the edges and then pushed it into Gwyn's skin. It buzzed warm and melded in there, feeling weird but not painful like last time.

"What is going on?" Gaius' voice broke in. He had been watching the exchange, baffled.

"I understand you!" Gwyn was delighted. "So it does somehow translate."

"Yes," the woman advised, "but I've blocked any fourth dimension functionality, so you shouldn't be able to activate it. Don't attempt it."

"I don't even know how I did that last time."

"Hmm…" The woman's gaze was thoughtful. "Well, let's sit down in the shade and we can work that out. You two look like you could use something to eat and drink."

"The well is fouled," Gaius pointed out.

"That's alright, I have supplies. Come on." They made their way further down the shore to a cluster of palm trees. The breeze blew straight across from what would one day be Jordan, so the smell of death and decay from the village did not reach them.

Gwyn felt as if she would burst with all the questions, but she waited until they were settled cross-legged on the ground, gladly drinking the water offered. It occurred to her that she had to keep this woman on side to get back to her own time, and maybe even get Gaius back to the Roman camp before the battle so that Silva never realized he'd been gone. *You need to find out if she can even do that first,* she whispered to herself. *Then make sure she will do it. You don't know what her agenda is yet. At least she doesn't seem pissed off that I took her device.*

For the first time in weeks, hope truly bloomed in her heart.

* * *

The woman introduced herself as Michelle, an agent from a future organization that dealt with Space and Time.

"So this is common?" Gaius wanted to know. "This traveling between times?" He shot a puzzled looked at Gwyn.

"No," Michelle replied. "I am from several hundred years in her future. The technology has not been developed in her time. It is relatively recent in mine. And few people cope with it—there are side effects. Fewer of us cope well. How did you feel when you arrived in this time?" she asked Gwyn. "Were you vomiting, nauseous? Did you pass out?"

"I was confused, but I don't remember feeling sick," Gwyn said.

"Then I was cracked over the head and knocked out." The tale that followed was more or less what she'd told Silva and Gaius, with the addition of her impersonation of a prophetess. Anxiety built as she recounted it, hesitating in spots until Michelle prompted her and pressed for more detail. Gaius sat riveted, hearing it in full context. She relayed the previous night's escape and journey here (a few private details omitted, though she blushed to glance at Gaius, and he gently laid an encouraging hand on her knee).

Michelle was most particular is ascertaining the time they left and the layout of the camp. But all through this her heart was sinking as a thought grew louder and louder in her head: *What if I've done some terrible damage and history is all skewed because of this? What if this Michelle woman tries to take me back to my time and it's not the same?*

Gwyn fell silent. Michelle sat back and looked thoughtful. She nibbled on a ration bar she had shared out of her backpack earlier—they were delicious and most rejuvenating—and leaned back against a palm tree. Legs crossed in front of her, gazing out over the Dead Sea, the quiet surreal after the tale of war and siege.

"You've got quite a talent there," she said simply.

Gwyn looked puzzled. Gaius beamed proudly.

"She is one of the bravest women I've ever met," he asserted.

Gwyn's eyes fell on the chronokinetor, resting innocently in Michelle's own palm now. "I think that had a lot to do with it," she said slowly. "It affects people somehow, doesn't it? Makes them more susceptible to suggestion. How does that work? Some way of influencing the brains of people in the vicinity? Is that an inbuilt feature of all chrono-thingys?"

"Chronokinetor," came the gentle correction. Michelle stood and stretched, then looked down at the pair. "I've been wondering all this time how you managed to operate it in the first place, nothing in your story has really explained that, but I have a suspicion you have a great deal of inbuilt talent relating to time travel. I'd like to test that."

The girl barely heard that last comment. "But can you take me home?" she blurted. "Back to my time? My family will be wondering where I am. They'll be frantic. And Gaius here doesn't deserve to be flogged for deserting. Can you get him back in time for the battle? Will there be a battle? Have I wrecked history?" *Not logical, you duffer … if she can get him back in time for battle, surely she can get you back to Mom and Dad before you are missed. Unless you really have screwed up history…*

Michelle's smile was kind. "Relax," she said. "We have plenty of time."

She swung her backpack onto her shoulders and reached her right hand towards Gwyn, pulling the girl to her feet. Gaius scrambled up as well.

"Where are you going?" he asked.

"*When* are we going," she corrected. "I'll take you back to your camp," indicating him, "then I want to check out Masada itself, then we'll see about getting you," a nod at Gwyn, "back to your family. You might want to say goodbye now, it could get hectic later."

Gwyn and Gaius stared at each other.

"Um," said Gwyn, looking at the young Roman. "Thank you for all your help. I couldn't have got out here without you. And thank you for looking after me in camp. It really helped having a friend there."

"You're welcome," he replied miserably.

Her heart wrenched. She really liked him. Maybe if they had existed in the same time, something could have come of it, but it wasn't like they had fallen madly in love. She wasn't about to stay with him, and he wasn't about to come with her—stuff like that only happened in books and movies.

But with a sudden impulse born out of her sense of narrative, she moved forward and reached up to take his shoulders in her hands and kissed him. It was a better kiss than their others, and despite the raised eyebrows of their amused observer, it was unembarrassed and sincere.

Gwyn broke off gently and sank back, blushing. She patted Gaius gently on the shoulder.

"You take care of yourself," she said. He nodded and clasped his hand over hers.

"You too," he whispered, brushing her cheek gently with the back of his other hand.

The moment was broken when Michelle moved forward and announced, "Holding hands already? Good. Everyone hang on to each other, and me. Especially me." She placed her right hand over their already-joined ones, reaching awkwardly and trying not to look too amused. She raised her left hand with the chronokinetor ready in her palm. A blue haze started at the edge of her vision, and the whooshing noise opened up in her ears.

Flick!

TWENTY-FOUR

74 AD

The crash woke Adi from her sleep. She started, then listened as the ram struck the western wall again. It was fully dark, and that in itself was unusual—normally the Romans began their attack around dawn. They were in the northern palace, but the fortress wasn't so large that the sound couldn't be heard from anywhere in Masada.

She hastened to dress and ran to check on Sarah. The crone was already awake, looking more aged than ever.

"This is it," she foretold portentously. "Our last dawn."

"Don't say that," Adi begged, but was distracted by Elizabeth entering the room.

Eleazar's wife ordered imperiously, "Everyone is to go to the throne room. My husband's orders. Come now." She turned and left without bothering to seek acknowledgement.

Sarah straightened from the chair where she had been sleeping, "Help me now, Adi, these bones have never felt older. Let us go and see what my nephew wants." Adi had never seen her look more shrunk in stature or presence.

They found the rest of the household hustling out of doors, disturbed and anxious, frightened by the ominous booming from the wall and from the predawn awakening. Adi's own nephew, Joel, was in front of her, crying because his adoptive mother had been separated from him in the rush.

Frowning with exasperation, Adi scooped him up and jiggled him, making soothing shushing noises. The two-year-old stared at her, then wailed all the louder, and she was highly tempted to put him straight back down to fend for himself. Instead, she grudgingly carried the squalling brat down the hallways until they squeezed into the back of the great hall which was now brimming with Masada's entire population.

The eight-year-old girl who was Joel's adoptive sister saw the toddler crying and Adi looking disgusted, so she pushed back through the crowd, her four-year-old brother trailing after her. She appropriated Joel, who quietened upon seeing a familiar face. Adi turned her attention to trying to find a seat for Sarah, but the hall was jammed so they squished into a small alcove near the door.

Sarah cast a pitying gaze upon the children. "They don't deserve this," she muttered to Adi. "Stupid decisions by cruel men and the children suffer." Her voice held some of her old fire. In the dim light of the throne room, her eyes narrowed and her jaw tightened. Someone had thought to light a few torches, but the shadows still made it hard to see. Eleazar's voice, however, rang out clearly.

"The hour is upon us, my brave brothers and sisters! God has seen fit to test us, time and time again, and we have proved ourselves worthy! We have thrown back the Romans, we have resisted their efforts to breach our walls, we have been defiant in the face of their unholy invasion and enslavement of our race!"

A ragged cheer broke out and echoed through the shifting shadows. Adi noticed Sarah stiffen.

"What's wrong, Sarah?" she whispered.

The old woman merely shushed her with a wave of the hand and concentrated on her nephew. He waited until the cheers died down, let the silence reign for a moment, then the echo of the Roman ram boomed again in the distance.

"But that is the sound of Death knocking at our door!" he continued. Waited again.

Boom!

"And the Devil marches with him!" Silence.

Boom!

"Now, we could wait for the Devil to come into our homes, butcher our men, rape our women, and enslave our children … But I say no!"

This last was delivered at a shout.

A defiant "No!" resounded in the chamber, drowning out the distant *boom* of the ram.

"We can cheat the Devil of his prize, cheat those murdering, heathen scum of their slaves! We can march ahead into Death before the Devil has the chance to reach us! We are not afraid! *We are not afraid!*" His voice rose hysterically and cheers joined him, but decidedly fewer than before.

Fierce mutterings broke out amidst the dozens of families clustered near Adi, and by the flaring of Sarah's nostrils she guessed the old woman had foreseen this.

What was it that Eleazar was actually proposing? March into Death? In a flash, it was on her.

He wants us all to die before the Romans break through. If no one is left alive that cheats the Romans of any slaves, cheats them of parading us through their God-forsaken cesspit of a city. They had all had heard about the Triumphs whereby victorious Roman generals displayed booty and captives taken from defeated nations. She knew she would be raped and made a slave, or raped and then simply executed in front of a jeering Roman crowd if she was taken. Adi shivered. Surely death was preferable to that?

Others in the crowd were also following this line of thought. Shouts started to break out and argue, and it was several minutes before order was regained and Eleazar could speak uninterrupted.

"I know there are some who question this! I understand! But that is your fear talking!"

More mutterings, none of the men liked to be accused of cowardice—they were brave men who had fought the Romans fiercely for years, risking lives and family in the process. Anxious mothers gathered their children close. Adi saw Joel's foster mother casting about, spotting her children over in the alcove. She started to struggle towards them, but there were too many people between them.

"But think on this, my brothers. We men may fight fiercely and die a brave death on the Roman sword, but what about your wives? What about your children? Would you consign your dearly beloved to the Roman yoke? They will possess your wives and daughters—yea! Even those so young! Sullied and soiled, would you risk a heathen bastard to be got on your precious women?"

Murmurs of anger rippled through the hall, and many women recoiled in fear, shaking their heads, Adi amongst them.

"And your sons! Those not slaughtered as men, cut down protecting their sisters and mothers—they will be enslaved! Would you suffer your proud sons to pass under the Roman yoke, to be sold off like cattle and sent far from their homes? And as slaves, subject to the worst cruelties and degradations the filthy Roman mind can think of? If you think what might be done to your pure innocent daughters is terrible, think far worse on what the Romans might do to your sons ..." His voice ended low pitched and quiet, trembling with disgust. The crowd rose first in indignation and then in fury as minds worked out what Eleazar meant.

He let the furor die down and gestured for silence, his audience captive. "This is what will happen, my brothers and sisters, if we wait until the Romans come through that wall ... *Will you let that happen!?*"

His shout triggered a massive roar of "*No!*"

And the spirit of defiance rippled through the air.

* * *

Adi found her hand gripped hard by Sarah, and the old woman pulled her ear low.

"We have to leave now, my girl, here is our chance."

For a second Adi didn't understand, then she saw a man struggling through the doors from outside, shoving his way through the crowd towards their leader.

Adi stared between the exultant Eleazar and then back to his aunt, who suddenly did not look so beaten and weary. Aged, yes, but determined—with flint in her eyes.

To die or risk a life of slavery and degradation ...

Adi's mind whirled for several seconds before she made her decision.

* * *

The man struggled through the doors of the throne room. He shoved his way through the crowd and managed to reach Eleazar, who bent to hear the man's message. He straightened and gestured for quiet again.

It took some time, but finally he bellowed, "The fortress is breached! Our wall across the palace will hold them for a time, but we need to act now. Listen to me carefully!"

He began to issue instruction on how this wholesale death was to take place. Each man was to take a sword, and turn it on first his children, then his wife. They would then draw lots to assign ten men to kill all the other men. Another lot would decide which of the ten would dispatch his nine comrades, then set fire to the palace and finally turn the sword on himself. It was an ironic reversal of the Roman military punishment of decimation, not that any there realized that.

Eleazar ordered the final man to make sure the food stores weren't fired.

"We will show this Roman filth that we did not succumb to hunger nor thirst, our deaths will show not desperation, but defiance!"

While this organization was going on, families began to say their farewells. Tears flowed as people embraced. The youngest children didn't understand what was going on, but copied the examples of their siblings who cried in fear. Adolescents were tight-lipped, trying to be brave, but the sight of their father's beards glistening with tears broke many. A cacophony of wails sounded through the chamber.

In all this, Joshua stood straight and stern by his revered leader's side. His eyes cast about the hall, searching. He had a responsibility towards one person in particular...

His sharp gaze spotted her, right at the back of the chamber, slipping out the door.

* * *

Adi made her decision. Whether this was madness or extreme sanity, she didn't know, but she knew in her heart that she wasn't ready to die quite yet. She would risk life.

She nodded determinedly at Sarah and raised the old woman to her feet. Glancing up, she caught the eye of Joel's foster mother, who was still struggling to reach her children through the crowd. Seeing Adi move, the woman stopped struggling and looked beseechingly first at Adi, then and the three children squished into the alcove.

Silently, her eyes begged a question. *Don't let them die, please. Let my children live. Give them a chance.*

Adi felt tears spring to her own eyes, and she nodded once more, scooping Joel up gently this time and smiling at him.

"Come on, nephew, time to go. Maria, take your brother's hand. We must be quick, but quiet."

The eight-year-old looked back at her mother. With a maturity that belied her years, she gripped her brother's hand firmly and followed Sarah and Adi as they gently pushed their way out to the main door. They were deft, and Sarah's agility astonished Adi, the old woman slipping between distracted people with the younger ones following quietly behind. So much confusion was in the hall that no one noticed them gone.

Almost.

Adi turned back one last time and saw her betrothed leaving Eleazar's side, pushing through the crowd towards them. Eyes wide, she shoved through the door into the emptiness of the corridor.

"Quickly!" she urged. "Joshua saw us. He will try to stop us. We must hurry!" Joel whimpered and little Maria hastened her steps. Even Sarah hobbled faster.

They raced through rooms and corridors, panic snapping at their heels. Away from the hall, they could hear a crackling roar coming from outside the palace. Adi could smell smoke.

"Fire!" she whispered in fear.

"We cannot run, we have to hide," Sarah wheezed.

"He will find us!" Adi's voice rose. "Even if he does not, we will still burn in the fire!"

Fire … In case of fire …

The words echoed through her head. Who had said that?

If the Romans break through … In case of fire …

"Gwyna!" she exclaimed.

"What?"

"Sarah, the water cisterns! We could hide there!"

"Quickly then!" The old woman lost no time is changing direction, away from the Romans and the fire. They hurried across courtyards and down steps, the stone walls getting cooler as they descended.

They stopped quickly to decide which turn to take next.

"It is right, I believe. Come now," Sarah gestured, then froze as she heard the same sound that chilled Adi. Footsteps scraping on the stairs. Someone was following them.

The young Jewish girl turned and without hesitation passed her whimpering nephew to his foster sister, who stood wide eyed, with her other brother clutching at her skirts. She reached out and squeezed Sarah's upper arm.

"Go," Adi whispered. "I'll lead him the other way."

Tears welled in the old woman's eyes as her mouth twisted in grief. "I've failed you, my girl."

"No, you haven't. But don't fail them," she indicated the children. "Go!"

The once proud matriarch and the three children scuttled to where the cooler air hinted at the awaiting water cisterns. Turning, Adi placed her back to the wall and held her breath.

TWENTY-FIVE

74 AD

As the blue faded, Gwyn heard retching. Gaius was doubled over, hands on his knees and sounding as though he was about to be sick. Michelle had turned away and was examining their surrounds, so it was left to Gwyn to help her friend as he heaved and gasped for air.

"Urgh," he straightened and clasped Gwyn's arm for balance. "That was awful."

"What's wrong with him?" she demanded of Michelle, who motioned her to shush. They were outside of the General's tent, next to her annex. It was fully dark, the stars were twinkling overhead and the camp was mostly quiet.

"Side effect of time travel," the woman whispered. "Fairly standard for most people, I've seen a lot worse. Sit him down, he'll be alright in a few minutes."

Gwyn pushed the tent flap and guided Gaius inside, plonking him down on what had been her pallet.

"Take it easy," she said quietly, brushing his hair out of his eyes. His eyes flew to hers.

"Come on, Gwyn," Michelle crouched guardedly beside the tent. "Let's get out of here before anyone spots us. Good luck, young man. We might see you in the morning, but chances are you won't see us."

"Wait!" Gwyn turned back to her Roman friend. "Gaius, after the siege, there may be several survivors. Everyone else will be dead already—they will have killed themselves. But some women and children might still be alive."

She wasn't sure how to put it. Might it be Adi who survived? Would she remember what Gwyn had said about hiding in the cisterns? Or was it someone else, someone Gwyn didn't know?

They deserve better than slavery, whoever they are, her brain reminded her.

"Gwyn..." Michelle's voice held a tinge of annoyance.

"Please," she gripped Gaius hands. His eyes focused on her. "Try to help these women, and the children. Don't let them suffer at the hands of the soldiers. One of them ... she was my friend up there. She knew me as Gwyna." *Please let it be Adi who survives.*

Gaius stared for a second, then nodded. He still looked dazed. She had to hope he understood and would try to help. She kissed him on the forehead and whispered, "Good bye. Thank you."

She backed out of the tent, trying not to cry.

"Time to go." Michelle gripped her wrist and

Flick!

* * *

Joshua came down the steps slowly, holding a torch that threw dancing shadows against the walls. His tread was determined. His dark eyes lit on Adi, backed against the wall at the base of the stairs.

"Where did you think you would go?" he asked softly, voice full of menace.

Not answering, Adi sidled along the wall opposite to where Sarah and the children had gone.

He advanced. "You cannot escape from here! Or did you think to whore yourself off to the Roman scum like that little bitch friend of yours? Is that it? Your own people aren't good enough for you?" His voice dripped with hatred and barely suppressed fury.

She increased her pace, still half facing him. The corridor darkened. It was practically a tunnel down here, cut into the rock of Masada itself. She hoped it would lead out to one of the lower terraces that protruded out from the northern point of the plateau. Perhaps there she could entice him close to the edge, and even grapple with him so that they both fell. If death truly was unavoidable, she wanted to at least prevent him from causing it to others.

No such luck. In the gloom, she bumped into a solid wooden door. She fumbled for a handle, found one, but it refused to turn. Desperately she pushed, but to no avail.

Joshua's figure loomed. He carefully placed the torch into a bracket, then stepped towards her. She tried to dart past him, but he was too quick, catching her wrists and shoving her hard against the door.

"You are *my* betrothed, and you shall do as *I* say," he hissed. "How dare you abandon your people for those heathens? You are only a woman, so I expect you would be afraid of death, but you should obey regardless!"

She struggled uselessly—his hands were like clamps on her thin arms. Kicking at his shins was ineffectual—he was too strong a brute to be bothered by her desperate flailing. She knew trying to talk to him would be pointless; in the months that she had been betrothed to him she had seen a man who, once fixed on an idea, would not deter for any reason. His hatred of the Romans she understood—she had once admired it in him—but she now saw that hatred encompassed anything and anyone who did not fit in with his view of the world. He would not tolerate a future wife who had her own ideas, nor one who did not obey him completely, and his anger at her insubordination was incandescent. Panicky defiance seized her.

"I do *not* have to obey you!" she hissed from between her teeth, voice cracking. "You are not my husband, you never will be!" He was going to kill her, she knew, but she knew finally that she didn't have to go meekly.

Furious, he shook her and pinned both her wrists above her head with one hand. With the other hand, he ripped at her dress, tearing the material down to expose her breasts. She screamed in fear and indignation as he squeezed them roughly, then hiked up her skirt. Thrashing in panic only made him angrier, and he struck, the blow snapping her head sideways. Dazed, a rushing noise sounded in her ears.

He fumbled with his own robe. "You will learn obedience like a proper wife!" he snarled. "You will do your duty as a woman, then you will die as I see fit!"

The shadows spun wildly, and she heard an almighty *crack!* The pressure on her wrists released. Slumping to the floor, Adi sobbed in pain and terror. It was completely dark, the torch must have gone out. She heard a bewildered grunt, a scuffling sound then a sickening *snap*. Suddenly, the tunnel was quiet except for her own ragged breathing and...

"Adi!" a shape morphed out of the darkness. Hands patted her gently, trying to find her head. "Adi, are you alright? My God, what did he do to you?"

"Gwyna?" Adi couldn't believe it, but it was her voice, distinctly. "What are you doing here? What happened to ...?" She peered into the shadows.

"He won't be hurting anyone anymore." Another woman's voice spoke as a small glow emitted from her hand. She stood over the fallen body of Joshua, neck lolling sideways at a strange angle as he lay on the ground.

Confusion gripped Adi. "Who is she? What happened? Have you been down here the whole time?" She shook, taking in her friend, the strange woman, and Joshua's fallen form.

He was dead, it appeared, but there was no blood, no wound that she could see. It looked as if his neck had been broken, but how could that woman have been strong enough to do that? And had Gwyna not left Masada after all—had she been hiding down here all this time?

Adi heard the other girl sigh.

"It's hard to explain. Are you able to get up? I'm so sorry we didn't get here sooner. That bastard." Her voice shook with anger, but her hands were gentle as they tried to straighten Adi's dress, draping the shawl to cover her front and tugging skirts back down. "You poor thing," she muttered.

"Come on, Gwyn," the other woman gestured. "I'm afraid she's going to have to hide down here. I believe the Romans will break through shortly. It's not going to be pretty."

"Sarah!" the Jewish girl burst out. "She took the children to hide in the water cisterns. Just like you said!"

"Where is she?" her friend hoisted her to her feet.

"Back that way," she pointed. "But Joshua came after us, so I tried to lead him away. He... He wanted to kill me. Eleazar is making everyone kill each other, so no one will be left alive when the Romans come. But

Sarah and I escaped with some of the children. They went down that passage while I came down here."

The other woman half-smiled. "You are a brave girl, Adi, is it? I'm Michelle. Let's get you back to your Sarah and the others… they are children, you said? Now isn't that interesting…" The last was half to herself.

Stepping over the deceased Joshua, Adi closed her eyes and let Gwyna guide her. She didn't look back, so she never saw the blood pooled at the back of his head or the cast-aside torch that had been used to crack him in the skull. They made their way back along the tunnel by the light of that mysterious glow from Michelle's hand. Passing the stairs, they continued down the corridor sloped down into the rock of the plateau.

After whispering, and then calling, they discovered Sarah and the children wedged up on a ledge beside one of the water cisterns. It was a natural collection point in the rock, one of the lowest on the plateau that began at the southern end and continued in a series until this final one that serviced the bath house in the palace. The rocky pool was brimming, and they were lucky to have not slipped in and drowned. None of them knew how to swim.

"Adi!" Sarah was relieved, then astonished. "Gwyna? Where have you been, girl? We have been worried sick about you? And who is this?" she pointed at Michelle, looking outlandish in her garb of loose, lightweight trousers and a strange shirt.

"I can't explain," her friend apologized, "but you have to hide here until everything is over. The Romans have fired the wall. They are coming."

"But what will happen to you?" Adi wanted to know, looking distraught. *I've only just found you, now you're leaving?* Adi found herself engulfed in a tight embrace.

"I'm going home," her friend said. "Thank you for taking care of me, you and Sarah. I'm sorry I had to leave you before, and have to leave again, but if I don't go now…" She stepped back. "If you can find a young Roman man called Gaius, make him understand that you know me, that you are my friends. He serves the General. But only after everything is all over. Until then, stay in here."

"I don't understand," Adi pleaded.

Her friend looked sorrowfully at her. "I'm sorry, Adi. If you find Gaius, he can explain. I've asked him to look for you."

Gwyna nodded at Sarah. The three solemn faces of the children stared out uncomprehendingly.

"Be strong," she told Adi as she gripped Michelle's wrist. "I hope it'll be alright."

And then a blue mist rose up around her and Michelle, and they were gone.

TWENTY-SIX

74 AD

Dawn was a hellish affair. With almost zero sleep in the last thirty-six hours, Gaius was reliving some of those hours again, exhausted and nauseated. Silva was distinctly unimpressed.

"Hurry up, Gaius! This will be the defining battle of my career here in Judea, and if you don't find my greaves right away, I'll be forever known as the general who couldn't get dressed in time to conquer the Jews!"

Bleary-eyed and horribly disoriented, Gaius located the errant pieces of armor and got Silva ready to march out, almost crying with relief when he was finally dismissed with a snarl. He stumbled into what had been Gwynia's annex and collapsed on her pallet, falling straight asleep.

Not five seconds had passed when he was rudely awakened by Silva's shout, "Gaius, I expect you ready for running messages at the gate by the time I walk through it or I will have you flogged! What is the matter with you?"

Gaius struggled up and lurched to the gate in a daze. He blinked, rubbing his eyes as he observed a scene of minimal torches and silent men assembled in various positions up Silva's great ramp. The vanguard formed the arrow point of his attack, artillery arranged to target the wall either side of the where the ram worked. Everything was in place and ready for the final attack.

"The men are ready, General," Drusus murmured.

"Sound the attack," came the order, and at a signal from Drusus, a horn blew.

No roar of charge, no sudden onslaught uphill. Instead, the crunch of boots and the groan of huge wooden levers brought the legion to life. More torches lit and in the shadows cast, Gaius watched the Roman military machine grind into action.

* * *

CRASH!

The ram smashed through the weakened wall shortly after dawn. Marcus charged through screaming, short Roman sword ready to slash, hack, and skewer. Flaming arrows sizzled past his ear from behind to strike...

No one. Several arrows thunked solidly into the palace buildings, but Marcus' sword failed to maim, kill, or even menace a single Jew. Not one Sicarii awaited the Roman assault.

The momentum of assault petered out and the murmur of confusion crept awkwardly into its place.

Drusus stomped through the shattered remains of the wall and glared at his men milling about, sword points drooping.

"Form up!" he roared. They scrambled to obey. "You think that just because there isn't a sword in your face means you can drop yours? The enemy is cunning! Advance cautiously and find out where in Hades they are!"

Marcus and other soldiers spread out in units, spears and swords at the ready, but there wasn't a single defender in sight. It didn't take long for them to discover the wall which enclosed them in the palatial buildings that stood over the Western Wall. A spear from a lone Jewish defender killed one careless legionary before they retreated back to Drusus.

Their report had him brood briefly, then sent a messenger sprinting back down the ramp to General Silva.

* * *

By now the sun had risen, though its rays had yet to reach this side of the plateau. Where Gaius stood as part of the general's personal guard lay yet in shadow. He was more awake now, having passed beyond the bounds of extreme fatigue into an odd alertness, running on adrenaline buffered with the bread he had managed to snatch and scoff on his run to back to camp, delivering a message.

Silva watched the attack, messengers sprinting back and forth between his artillery, infantry and scouts that ranged around the plateau. Other divisions held positions to ensure that not one single Jew would escape this time, even if they reached as far as the circumvallation wall.

For the first time Gaius saw it much like Gwynia must have—a giant crushing a bug for daring to buzz in its face. He knew logically that it had to be done, the pride and honor of the Empire was at stake, but her voice echoed sarcastically in his head and he wondered where the honor was in fighting women and children and a few crazy, desperate men.

He was about to find out. Squinting up, it looked like the wall had been breached as legionaries vanished into the rubble.

Long minutes passed, then a runner hurtled down the ramp towards them. Someone nearby grunted dismay as the runner tripped, arms wheeling. He couldn't stop his momentum and crashed with an impact that made several wince. The runner slid down the remainder of the slope in a cloud of dust.

Gaius hurried forward with the others.

"Damn fool," Silva barked. "Is he alright?"

The messenger clutched his leg, scraped raw by the gravel. A medic knelt beside, examining the injury. "Broken leg, General. Needs cleaning and splinting."

"Report, first," Silva ordered.

Face white, the runner obeyed. Blood leaked between his fingers as he pressed them to his wound. "We breached the wall, General, and have entered the Western Palace."

"And?"

"There are no Jews there to fight there, sir!" the runner gasped.

"What? They have killed them all already?" Silva's voice was perplexed, but unflustered.

"No, sir," the runner sucked in air, pain in his voice. He had a reputation for making clear reports even after running, which was why the centurion had sent him, and no amount of pain or injury was going to prevent him from trying to fulfill his duty. "No Jews met us to fight, but we are encircled by an additional wall that prevents us from advancing any further. The wall is barely defended; it is going to be difficult to assault because we are forced into a choke point before we can attack it."

"Of what is the wall made?" There had been no reports of an internal wall from the Roman garrison who had held Masada before the Sicarii had overtaken it.

"Wood and earth, sir."

"Are you certain?"

"Yes, sir."

Silva nodded, then dismissed the broken man. The medic signaled two soldiers to load the patient onto a wooden stretcher and followed them back to camp.

The General considered very briefly, then turned to his young attendant. "Gaius. My orders to Drusus are: continue with assault, using fire to burn this wall. Kill the defenders, then search every corner of that fortress until all the Jews are found. All women and children are to be captured. Kill all men over the age of fourteen. I don't want any future slaves who might foment rebellion. Go now, as fast as you can, but for Mars' sake, don't break your damn ankle!"

The young man nodded and obeyed, running carefully up the steep ramp. Silva's words drummed through his head as his arms pumped for momentum.

All women and children are to be captured. Kill all the men.

But then another voice sprang into his mind.

There may be several survivors. Everyone else will be dead already.

His legs ached, but he kept running.

I have to find those survivors.

TWENTY-SEVEN

74 AD

Drusus nodded before Gaius even finished, as if he had been expecting the order. "Fire the wall," he bellowed.

Soldiers with torches and buckets of pitch moved into position. Their comrades held shields in interlocking formation to provide cover in front and above and as one they tramped towards the wall, setting fires in three different locations as arrows hailed around them.

Slow at first, the wood caught, licking upwards until it crackled, finding more and more fuel. The Jews didn't even try to put it out, merely throwing what must have been their last spears before abandoning their posts.

Then the fire turned, catching on the wood in the surrounding buildings. It threatened to ravage the men who had laid and lit it, and, while not panicking, the Drusus experienced the gripping fear that he had doomed himself and his men to a horrible death.

But Mars' breath blew for them at the last moment, and the wind changed direction to force the fire back onto the wall, consuming it. Now smoke drifted across the plateau, belying the carnage that lay below it. The Western Palace was gutted, and not a few Roman soldiers were suffering a nasty cough caused by smoke inhalation.

Several hours passed before sections had died down enough for safe passage across, and in his direction of operations Drusus had no time to notice where the General's young messenger had gone. Back to Silva, he assumed, not realizing Gaius had braved the still-hot earth and ashes to clamber over and venture into the rest of the fortress.

The lad had stopped feeling nauseated at last, and took the chance to find out if what Gwynia had said would be true. He hoped beyond hopes that he might see her again, remembering Michelle's words.

Might see you in the morning…

Was that what she had said? It was all rather hazy in his mind, more like a dream than reality. He had to find out. And if there were indeed survivors, he wanted to find them before anyone else did. *Maybe they'll have some answers.*

* * *

The two women stood in silence, watching the young Roman man venture into the northern palace, following the stench of death. He never looked up, never spotted them in the tower, Michelle feeling solemn, Gwyn looking ill.

"It's done," the older woman said quietly. "The momentum will carry it forward. At this point in history, the Roman Empire will continue to grow and prosper, which will shape the future of Europe for quite some time."

She knew she had fulfilled her mission, but it wasn't easy to overcome what they had seen in that hall. All the Jews who had committed suicide rather than become subjects to that empire.

"All those people… families, children." Gwyn whispered. "They're all dead. It's so… brutal. They just wanted to live in their own country according to their own customs. They didn't ask for any of this."

Michelle patted her shoulder awkwardly. *Poor thing. I guess she's never seen anything like that before. Even for me, it's horrific.* She sighed. "I find throughout history, people never ask to be butchered and oppressed. Other people just do it."

"Does it ever change?" came the question. "Are people still doing this in the future? Endlessly being cruel and greedy and full of hate?" Her voice cracked, and Michelle realized she needed to move Gwyn on before the girl completely broke down. The ghastly array of corpses in their hundreds shook even Michelle, not to mention the smell of death.

"It does change, eventually, in a lot of ways," she said. "Look, your boyfriend has found the survivors." She pointed down to where Gaius emerged with a slow-moving Sarah, a dazed Adi, and the three children. Soldiers appeared. Gaius held his ground against one man and prevented him from advancing any further towards the group. Gesticulating pointedly, it became apparent to all onlookers that he was insisting on taking them to the General, and would brook no interference with his 'prisoners'. His determination seemed to baffle the legionaries, who stood, deflated, after their near brush with a fiery death and no enemy left to fight.

"They will tell the story of Masada," Michelle observed. "Or as much as that twat Josephus gives them a voice. More of a sycophant than a historian, but you work with what you've got."

"Mm." Gwyn wasn't listening, gazing instead at her friends, one Jewish, one Roman, standing within a stone's throw.

Michelle interrupted before the girl could do anything stupid. "It was a good hit with the torch, by the way. When you rescued that girl. I wouldn't have guessed you had such a swing."

"Huh?" Gwyn answered distractedly. "Oh, yeah…" She looked even sicker than before. She swayed unsteadily on her feet.

"Time to get out of here," Michelle said abruptly. "Hold on to me."

"You're taking me home?" It was almost a plea, and she added plaintively, "but… I didn't really say goodbye."

Flick!

Up in a tower Gaius thought he saw a flickering of a blue haze. He stopped and his eyes snapped upwards.

Adi to follow his gaze and ask in Greek, "What's wrong?"

She remained suspicious of him, for which he couldn't blame her, but she seemed relieved when he had stopped those soldiers from coming too close. He knew that convincing her that he was Gwynia's friend might take some time, but she was the only other person to whom he might be able to speak about the girl from another time.

Sadness welled in him as he continued to stare briefly upwards, then slowly replied, "Nothing." *And no answers either.* "Just thought I saw something…"

TWENTY-EIGHT

2572 AD

It seemed like a long time that the rushing, whooshing azure haze enveloped them. Then the lurching stopped and Gwyn found her vision clearing yet again.

Where... No, when the hell am I? She wondered as she looked about. They were in a room with shining white walls, interspersed with screens or... *Holograms,* she realized, seeing them project from the wall. The pictures shifted and changed, showing bright colors, happy people and grand vistas. *It looks almost like... advertising?*

"What's going on?" she turned to Michelle, who quickly strode to the doorway and peered out suspiciously. "This isn't En Gedi. I thought you were taking me back to my time? When is this?"

Satisfied that no one was out there, the other woman moved to a wall and waved her hands in front of it, activating a stream of water that flowed into a backwards-sloping bench. *It's a sink.* Gwyn realized. *This room is some sort of bathroom.*

"What's going on?" she demanded. "Where are we? *When* are we?"

"We are in En Gedi, actually," Michelle splashed her face and neck, washing up her arms as well. "Just not in your time. Sorry." She straightened and a warm jet of air blew gently onto her face and outstretched hands.

"Sorry?" Exhaustion and fear bloomed. Gwyn had contributed to the murder of Joshua and then had to witness the harrowing aftermath of the mass suicide by the Sicarii—now this time traveling agent hadn't even taken her to the right time?

"Yes, I'm sorry," Michelle turned to face Gwyn. "I will get you back to your own time, I promise, but I have to clear up a few things first and I need your help. You've proved your ability to deal with time travel exceptionally well. I need someone who can do that so that I don't end up in the same place as I did before."

"You want *me* to help *you*?" Gwyn rubbed her eyes. She had been *this* close to going home, and now this future woman was kidnapping her. "Just take me home! Please! How could I possibly help you?" Her voice rose plaintively. *What use could I possibly be to this, this time-space-whatever agent who zips about casually watching the world come crashing down around people's ears? She's crazy!*

"Gwyn." Michelle rested her hands gently on Gwyn's shoulders. "I promise I will take you home, but please let me explain why I need your help first. Here, wash your face, it'll make you feel better."

Like an obedient child, Gwyn washed her face in warm water and allowed it to dry. It did make her feel better, but she glared sulkily up at her new captor all the same.

"Let's go sit outside," Michelle suggested. "I don't enjoy being stuck in a room with only one exit."

They walked out and Gwyn gazed about in astonishment. She recognized the scene to a certain degree. The beach lay before them, sun rising over the horizon. It was early morning, and the place was deserted. Hotels encircled the area. They were ecologically blended into their surroundings, faux rock and much greenery incorporated into their design, so they weren't eyesores, but clearly hotels all the same.

"It's still a resort," Michelle answered Gwyn's unspoken question. "They managed to avoid draining the Dead Sea entirely, and rehabilitated it to a certain extent, though some of the sinkholes were irreparable. Very popular tourist destination for Earth dwellers and off-worlders alike. Come on, there's a nice spot to watch the sunrise."

Déjà vu struck Gwyn as it seemed that it was almost the same spot they had sat more than two thousand years before. Of course, the tree couldn't possibly be the same, but another like it grew in its place. She stared at it, feeling as though she was right back where she had started.

* * *

Michelle told her extraordinary tale, starting with her encounter with Gwyn on the Snake Path at Masada.

"I was attacked and captured," she explained. "They were after this." She held up the palm with the chronokinetor. "It's the most advanced, valuable timepiece ever to yet exist. I dumped it to keep it from them when I realized I wasn't going to escape. Believe me, I tried. But they just kept appearing! I never expected anyone to find it, let alone be able to use it! It's more than a physical thing, you see—it requires a mental connection. I have no idea how you formed that connection without training. I would like to find out, but first I have to get this back to the Commissioner of the Space-Time Agency before anyone else can get a hold of it.

"That's where you come in. I'll be the decoy, the one they are looking for. You can waltz on in without any symptoms of time-travel sickness. I'll work out a way for you to get to the Commissioner, she can rescue me and bust these crooks at the same time. Then I'll take you home."

The words rolled through and over Gwyn's head. *So many questions!* But eventually she understood, or at least she thought she did. This was the only way to get back home. She didn't know how to operate the timepiece blended into her hand, and even if she did, Michelle had mentioned she had 'blocked any fourth dimension functionality' so she figured that meant that independent time travel was out.

"Alright," she said, finally. "What do I have to do?"

The other woman smiled. "You are a serious hard-shell," she said. "I appreciate your help. But first things first, both you and I need some rest, food, and cleanup time. I think the hotel reception over there should be open by now. Let's check in and gather ourselves, then we'll go from there. Just let me do the talking."

* * *

Gwyn woke from the deepest sleep she'd had in weeks. The bed had seemed too soft at first. It was like drowning in marshmallow, but that hadn't mattered after the first two seconds. Sleep had washed over her and she sank into oblivion like a stone to the bottom of a deep pool.

Waking slowly, she luxuriated in the squishy pillows and comforting duvet. The smell of fresh linen was a delight, and she realized in amusement that she had had the strangest dream—a dream about time travel, ancient battles, strange people from past and future. She was home, of course. It must be the weekend for Mom and Dad to have let her sleep in so long.

That's strange, her brain was groggy but insistent in its logic. *I thought they were away. Aren't they working overseas, in Israel?*

Israel. En Gedi! Masada...

She dragged her reluctant eyes open to take in the strange hotel room in which she resided. Gaze falling on the faux rock walls and decorative flora, combined with discreet but extremely modern facilities. Screens; soft-toned lights; the short, wheeled robot rolling in with a tray of food.

Reality hit her and she spoke aloud. "It wasn't a dream." Dejection hung over her. She was still a long way from getting home.

"No, it wasn't," Michelle strode out from behind an opaque panel and assisted the robot in unloading the tray. "Thank you," she told it, and it whirred briefly before executing a neat three-point turn and rolled from the room. "Something to eat? You must be hungry. You slept for so long."

Gwyn was starving. Clambering out of the soft, beautiful bed she could smell something tasty—it looked like bread rolls with mini pastries stuffed with egg and spinach, bordered by colorful fruit and topped off by a glass of some sort of juice. She glanced down at her attire even as she seated herself at the small table where Michelle now sat helping herself to breakfast.

"Where did this come from?" she asked. She was in soft white shorts and a singlet. *Pajamas.*

"Standard hotel-issue sleep attire. I sent the dress you were wearing to be incinerated, I'm afraid. It was in pretty bad shape. I've ordered some clothes—hope they fit." She indicated a small pile next to the bed. "You were pretty zonked by the time we checked in. I don't know if you remember, so I shoved you in the shower and then put you to bed. Hope you don't mind—I figured you'd rather be clean."

And clean she was, unbelievably so compared to the standards she had been forced to endure during her time in the past. She vaguely recalled showering and collapsing. *Huh,* she snorted. *All that time dreaming of a hot shower and clean bed and you were too tired to enjoy it. Figures.*

They finished the meal in record time, both women eating voraciously. Michelle showed Gwyn how to operate the bathroom facilities by herself, and she enjoyed properly her second hot—and very fantastic—shower, not to mention teeth cleaning and brushing her hideously tangled hair.

The clothes did fit; the simple, lightweight trousers and sleeved shirt much better than anything she had worn while at Masada. She emerged after a lengthy period to find Michelle stretching elegantly on the semi-enclosed balcony that overlooked the beach and the Dead Sea.

"Ok, so what now?" Having steeled herself to helping this woman in her mission in exchange for passage home, Gwyn was determined to get it over and done with as soon as possible.

"Now?" Michelle straightened and twisted her back with a satisfying crack of her spine. "Now, we need to get back to my own time. I'll instruct you on what you are to do when we reach Vivaldis Prime and how you are to get to Commissioner Hera. She is the director of the Space-Time Agency and the only one who can get to the bottom of this mess. I want to know who attacked me and tried to steal the chronokinetor, and I want them caught and tried."

"How on earth am I going to find this Commissioner without help?" Gwyn wanted to know. "I couldn't even operate the toilet in there without you telling me how. I'm out of my depth in this time! And where is Vilval … Vivalda … where are we going?"

Michelle smiled. "Vivaldis Prime. It's the capital world of the human reach of the Allied Planets. Most of Earth is akin to a nature reserve now, the parts that aren't simply a wasteland or radioactive. Heritage listed, you might call it. And you managed alright out of time before. This time, you will have help. I'll send a message to a friend of mine. He'll meet you and escort you to the Agency Headquarters, and get you in too. The code words you have to remember are 'time to find missing person'."

Gwyn stared at her. "Another planet. You're kidding, right?"

"'Time to find missing person'—remember that!" Michelle

admonished gently. "It'll be fine. We're going to skip forward to a time where space travel is frequent and direct, then make the last time jump on Vivaldis. I suspect they'll attempt to capture me again if I go anywhere near the Agency, but they won't look twice at you. You've demonstrated no signs of time-travel sickness in all our jumps, no disorientation. You'll blend in, and my friend Owen will take it from there. All you have to remember are the code words—that'll get you access to the Commissioner, then you explain everything to her."

Gwyn's mind raced. "But you said they were after that," she pointed to the chronokinetor, lodged in Michelle's palm still. "Won't they just take it off you when they nab you?"

The other woman smiled. "But it won't be on me. It's going to be with you."

TWENTY-NINE

2572 AD

To the best of her knowledge, Gwyn figured she was the first person from her era to have ever traveled so far from the Earth. And so easily too! No intense training to be an astronaut, no years undergoing selection for missions, no attempts at the moon. She was light years from home. To have traveled this far by the fastest means of space travel in her time would have been impossible. So far that even if speed of light travel had been achieved in her time, it would take hundreds of years, and by the time she reached her destination everyone she knew would be dead.

They were dead, she realized, and it saddened her. Hundreds of years dead, in this time. She wondered if she had descendants living now, and where they were, and who they were.

Michelle interrupted her melancholy train (or spaceship) of thought.

"We'll be docking soon. Do you remember what you have to do?"

Gwyn turned from the view available to passengers: the planet that filled the panoramic screen in front of them. It was incredible, but surreal. None of the familiar landforms she had learned from movies to expect from space. The oceans were smaller, the continents strange. This was not Earth.

She recited to Michelle, "After we land, you and I will jump forward to your time, approximately several hours after you escaped from the Detention Center. We'll split up immediately and I'll make my way to the Arrivals Gate in the Spaceport. Your friend Owen will be waiting there to meet me. You will attempt to reach the Agency, but in the event that you are arrested or similar, Owen will assist me in getting to the Agency, whereby I will ask to speak to Commissioner Hera, and advise that it is 'time to find missing person.' This should gain me access to her and then gain her confidence that I have been sent by you. Tell her you have been captured in an effort to steal the chron … chronokinetor," she still stumbled over the awkward words.

"And then?" Michelle prompted.

"Then tell her that Owen can locate the one that you have, that you used to come back and find me. They locate it, find you, bust the baddies and you take me home." *Seems easy, it's just all happening so fast, after weeks and weeks of lying low and hiding.*

"Hmm," the other woman exhaled softly through her nose. "Let's hope it's all that simple. I have a strange feeling there is something else I don't know, something critical, but I can't work out what. Still, it's the best plan I have. The Commissioner holds the ear of some of the most powerful people on the planet. If anyone can get to the bottom of this, it's her. She's ex-military, tough as tough can be, fought the Clarish on behalf of the Allied Planets when humans first were permitted to join."

"She sounds impressive," Gwyn observed unenthusiastically.

"She is," Michelle frowned at the younger woman's reaction. "She sponsored my entry into the Agency, even though I was the youngest by a decade. I didn't have any parents to help me, I had to study and work hard and bust my ass to get ahead. The Commissioner noticed me, and argued for my joining. Most of the other senior members of the Agency said I was way too young. But no one else had my aptitude for time travel. In actual fact, I've never seen anyone cope with it as well as me— until I met you. Those goons who ran me down back in your time must have been doped up to the eyeballs on anti-nausea drugs to have kept up with me. I could hear them slur even before they tackled me."

Gwyn filed this information away in her mind, leaving it to ponder upon later. *She isn't exactly arrogant, just matter of fact. Still a little annoying that she's so confident about herself. I suppose I should find it reassuring.* She wondered why she had this natural ability, same as Michelle. Perhaps they were related somewhere along the line? *Distant descendant, perhaps?*

She didn't have time to finish that line of thought. The ship was docking as they spoke. They shuffled off onto the main Space Station orbiting Vivaldis, the same one Michelle had utilized to make her escape, albeit in a different year to this one. Descent to the planet's surface was straightforward, if tedious (gray walls of the space elevator made for boring viewing). Space Port officials found that the sight of the rapid transition between the ground and the station affected most people badly, so while plain walls were unexciting, they did not induce vertigo or visually accentuate the change in the atmospheric pressure that passengers experienced during the trip up or down.

Having gained the ground, Michelle ducked into a hygiene facility to swap chronokinetors with Gwyn. The basic one she'd acquired from Owen had remained lodged in Gwyn's palm all this time, except when Michelle decided it needed charging.

"Safest place for it," she explained. "You can't drop it, lose it or have it stolen. It's literally part of you."

"Yes, but you haven't taught me how to get it in or out." She still couldn't fathom the simple way Michelle managed to concentrate, then pop the timepiece out with minimal pressure.

"We'll get to that later, I promise," Michelle said blithely.

Gwyn hid her frown. The Time-Space Agent promised easily, but as yet had not delivered on anything. *Can you really trust her …?*

Still, somehow the original chronokinetor, the one that had taken Gwyn back in time, felt far more comfortable than its basic cousin. It was weird; maybe weeks of wearing it had engendered a familiarity. *Michelle did say there was a mental connection. I wonder how that works.*

Michelle seemed to notice the quickness with which the timepiece melded back into Gwyn's skin, but while her lips tightened, she didn't say anything.

Gwyn noticed, and wondered what it signified. A genetic predisposition? Michelle had mentioned tests… An inner part of her baulked at that, but she took a deep breath and nodded that she was ready.

Flick.

They jumped into Michelle's time.

* * *

2623 AD

The blue haze had barely faded when Michelle pushed her way past Gwyn and disappeared out the door. An astonished-looking man stared at them in the mirror, speechless at the appearance of two women out of nowhere.

"Um," Gwyn hesitated, then said with some incredulity, "Did you see that hologram? Malfunctioning if I ever saw one." *Wonder if he'll buy that. Aaand obviously, these toilets are unisex. Would have been nice if she'd mentioned that!* After the separation of the sexes in Masada and the all-male environment of Silva's camp, she wasn't used to men and women sharing the same space so casually.

"Huh?" the man turned to stare after the departed Michelle. Gwyn made hasty her own exit from the opposite door. She found herself in a windowless corridor, a replica of the one she'd disembarked into from the space elevator. It was busier, with newer furnishings that didn't quite disguise the worn floor surface and wall colors. It *was* several decades on, she supposed. *You think they'd have at least changed the color scheme.*

She tried not to look tentative as she made her way with the general flow of people along the corridor and down a moving ramp to a lower level. The real test came when she saw her first alien. It was all she could do not to stare. More or less humanoid but blue: bipedal with two arms, much shorter than her and furry with a tail that twitched back and forth, it paced by, putting her in mind of a cat in a hurry. Michelle had warned her, in an offhand fashion, that while Vivaldis was predominantly a human planet, various other members of the Allied Planets had embassies, businesses, schools, and exchange programs here.

"The Shanista are the most important, if most elusive," Michelle had instructed her while on their space flight from Earth. "Highly scientific but with strict ethical and moral codes, they were key to the development of the Agency and have a facility adjoining our headquarters. They tend towards tall and dark, bipedal like us, but with two pairs of wings for extra limbs.

"Don't get into an argument with a Mayash—they get agitated easily and have a tendency to smack things with their tail. Rilans and Nolii are less common. Rilans are amphibious, and can ooze if left out in the air too long—you'll know one when you meet one. They are a lot bigger than humans and slide about on their tails. The Nolii don't travel much—they grow a really heavy shell upon reaching maturity, makes them clumsy. The younger ones like to come to our schools, though. Great sense of humor."

Head buzzing with information, Gwyn tried to memorize the details and gave up. She favored a bored look when inside her mind was screaming,

It's an alien! Oh my God! We are not alone in the universe! I can't believe it— I'm on another planet and casually sauntering past real live aliens! Just act cool, just act cool.

"Gwyn?"

She'd reached the arrivals gate without realizing, following the crowd until it dumped her into a general morass of people that pooled and eddied as friends sought friends, families reunited, and business people marched purposefully through the flow. More hologram advertising flashed around her, distracting her.

"Gwyn?" The speaker was a tall young man, a few years older than her. He shifted nervously, glancing often over his shoulder.

"Ah, yes. Owen?" *Who else would be expecting you?* He fit the description Michelle had given her. *Tall, pale skin, and dark hair. Needs a new shirt.* It was rather shabby, and seemed to be inside out. She wondered if he realized.

"Yeah," he gestured for her to follow, and they edged their way through the crowd, following another corridor to a busy platform. It seemed to be a bus or train stop. Music chimed as an announcement warned all Citizens to stand back as the transport approached. No wheels or track were apparent; the carriage glided to a halt with a swish of warm air. Owen handed her a crystal, indicating that she should copy him and wave it over a sensor as they boarded the carriage. Behind them, more passengers boarded, and the doors closed. She didn't know want to call the vehicle—she had seen no form of locomotive-like engine—departed smoothly, accelerating through into a dark tunnel, then into bright golden sunlight.

They traveled ten stops, Owen clearly too edgy to say anything, and Gwyn both too hesitant to initiate conversation and too enraptured by the scenes around them to want to try. They flashed past buildings and open spaces, leaving her little opportunity to study anything in detail, but each stop saw a general shifting of passengers on and off that left her engrossed. At first it was the aliens, but the variety of humans and their apparel left her feeling quite drab by comparison. She forced herself not to stare as a massive dark-skinned bearded man strolled past in a hot pink miniskirt and bowed a greeting to an Asiatic-looking woman in a grey patchwork overall. The woman bowed back, and they began chatting avidly. Nobody else batted an eyelid. *Maybe clothing choices aren't a big deal here and now. That's kinda cool, actually.*

Owen tapped her elbow. He finally seemed satisfied that no one was following them or eavesdropping, and he leaned close to ask in a breathy whisper, "Is Michelle alright? She's in some sort of trouble, but she wouldn't say what. Just that I had to help you get to the Commissioner of the Time Space Agency."

"Um," Gwyn muttered back, still absorbed in people-watching. "Yeah, she is, I guess. That's why she wants me to get help. How much further is it?" She glanced at him.

He pursed his lips, fidgeting again. He was good looking, not in the earthy, capable way that Gaius had been, but in a tall, dark and moody sense. Looked like he needed a few good meals and some sunshine to bring him out of himself. Then she felt a pang of guilt for even looking at another guy, so soon after leaving the kind young Roman man in the past.

"Next stop," Owen advised, and swiped his crystal pass off as they disembarked the transport. Gwyn trailed him across the platform and up another moving ramp, emerging from a bustling archway, where the warmth of the sun hit them.

Gwyn got out of the way of commuters and halted, gazing in awe. They stood in a large square, paved with grey and blue and adorned by beautiful buildings around the outside. An elaborate fountain shot sparkly, colorful liquid in the center of the square, and people (humans and aliens) milled about. Walking, talking, sitting, eating—some even seemed to be tourists, taking photos of the surroundings. At least, that's what she assumed they were doing, judging by the cheesy smiles, since she couldn't see anything that resembled what she would recognize to be a camera. They were threw pink crystals up in the air, got into position and posed as the crystal floated down in a rotating fashion. *Could be a weird game? You have no idea what people do for fun in this time. I'm definitely getting a tourist vibe, though.* More holograms leapt up out of the ground, spruiking accommodation and restaurants, tours and credit facilities. Everything was clean, too—she watched impressed as a child, not more than five she guessed, waved her empty drink cup in the air and a robot trundled over and opened a receptacle for the girl to place the cup into. *Even the kids know to not litter.*

"This way," Owen muttered and tugged her jacket sleeve gently. They crossed the square, Gwyn still staring, and scooted down an alleyway to a plain walled building. An ugly solid doorway graced the wall—no windows, no columns or intricate carvings dancing up the walls. *Oh. I guess I thought the Time Space Agency building might be one of those fancy ones out in the square. Obviously not.* The only thing that indicated any difference between this doorway and the few others that lurked in this alley was a small spiral symbol etched to the top left of the portal. Gwyn stared at it for a second, then quickly glanced at the timepiece embedded in her palm. The same spiral resided there.

"It's the mark of the Agency." Owen noticed her staring at the symbol on the wall. "Kind of a corporate logo, I suppose. It only appeared in the last few years. But I make a point of keeping up to date with Agency developments."

"Why?" she wanted to know. "You don't work for them just yet, Michelle said. What's the interest?"

He started, and quickly shot glances behind to see if anyone was nearby. The alley was deserted.

"What do you mean, just yet? What did she tell you? She can't travel beyond her own future, no one can! So how can she know about my future?" He demanded to know, leaning in close, wide eyed with frustration and fear.

She jerked forward, forcing him to lean back.

"*I* don't know!" she growled. "And I've had enough of dudes getting up in my grill and being all agro, so back off! I just want to go home, and apparently the only way to do this is talk to this Commissioner lady, so let's go get it over with!" *Wow, okay, calm down Gwyn. Guess I'm a bit touchy about personal space after all everything that's gone on recently.*

He stared at her, agape.

"Uh, okay …" He was silent a moment. "Who are you anyway, and how do you know her? She basically told me she was protecting a timepiece, that you knew about it, and people were trying to abduct her and steal the piece. And that the Commissioner needed to be told or there could be serious ramifications for the entire Allied Planets." He paused and seem to weigh his next words. "She also said her life was in danger. That's the real reason I'm here—I have serious reservations about this. The Agency is no friend to me."

Gwyn sighed. "It's a long, confusing, convoluted story. I got mixed up in it by accident." She didn't mention that she had the protected timepiece. She kept her sleeve pulled down over her hand. The fewer people who knew, the better, just in case Michelle was wrong about whom to trust.

Owen blew out a long breath, then nodded. "Okay. Well, the sooner we find her, the sooner I can wring the truth out of her. I'm really not happy about this." He turned to the door and tapped on a covered panel. It slid back, and he tapped in a code on a screen. The door slid open. He stood back, indicating that she should enter.

The room was small, a reception of some sort. A squishy orange couch occupied the wall to their left, with a high fronted desk opposite it on their right. In front of them, a plain door with no handle.

A breath of air made her turn and realize the door had closed behind her, and for a second she thought Owen had abandoned her and run away, but then she saw he had merely crossed to the couch and had seated himself in a broody fashion.

"Can I help you?"

An androgynous human with short green hair was seated behind the reception desk, uniformed in a black skin-tight coverall with the Agency spiral emblazoned on the sleeve. Gwyn couldn't tell the person's gender, so opted to address the person as 'citizen', as was considered the polite form of address for all species of the Allied Planets, according to Michelle, in lieu of a rank or occupational honorific. It eliminate the risk of incorrect or offensive titles, and Gwyn wondered at the society in which she now stood. Was anyone not a citizen? What did that entail?

She pulled her attention back to her immediate surroundings, clearing her throat as her chest tightened, "Citizen, I need to speak with Commission Hera as a matter of extreme importance and urgency. It is time to find missing person." The words tumbled out just as she'd rehearsed them.

Despite the polite and correct address, the receptionist looked blank. "I beg your pardon? Do you have an appointment with the Commissioner? She is an extremely busy person and I'm afraid if you don't have an appointment, she can't see you."

"Yes, I have an appointment. Please check with her secretary." *Buy time*, Michelle had instructed. *You'll have to get past the gatekeeper, but 'time to find' should trigger a response from higher up. There will be an audio sensor in the reception.*

Citizen Receptionist smiled in polite puzzlement and spoke quietly to the computer, tapping the screen occasionally with long, elegant fingers.

"I'm afraid there are no appointments scheduled for the Commissioner this afternoon," they informed Gwyn. "I can submit an application for one for you if you like. What is your name, citizen?"

Gwyn's stomach churned. "My name is Gwyn, Gwyn Turner." It felt slightly strange to be using her full name again after so many weeks of variations. "Perhaps the appointment isn't showing. I really just need a message passed on immediately: time to find missing person." Her voice threatened to tremble. *Come on*, her brain urged silently. *It was a simple plan. Please let it work! Pass on the message.*

Citizen Receptionist looked doubtful. "I'm afraid I can only forward your message to the Commissioner's secretary. If you don't have an appointment, I can take your contact details and ask Secretary Romero to get in touch, but you'll have to submit an application, as I said. The Commissioner doesn't see just anyone, you see."

Gwyn could sense Owen getting agitated behind her. She was afraid he would walk out, and she knew that without him, they wouldn't be able to locate Michelle. Why he was so afraid of the Agency she wasn't sure. Michelle had only briefly alluded to the fact that he had had a run in with them during their university days, and he preferred to keep under their scanner, so to speak. His demeanor had discouraged any questions she might have tried.

"Please," she tried again. "It really is a matter of extreme urgency and importance. I really need the Commissioner to get that message. Someone's life could be in danger."

Citizen Receptionist shook their head. "Then you really ought to alert the police. This isn't a matter for the Time Space Agency. I'm going to have to ask you to leave, please."

"Time to find missing person," she blurted out again. "I'm sorry, I can't leave. I have to get that message to the Commissioner." This was not working out how it was supposed to. Michelle had said those words would trigger the Commissioner to respond, but the receptionist was blocking her all too effectively.

"Come on, Gwyn," Owen was at her elbow, muttering. "This isn't working. We have to go." He shifted uneasily from foot to foot, clearly keen to leave.

Frustrated, Gwyn glared at him and turned back to the receptionist, struggling to arrange her features into a more conciliatory appearance.

"Please," she said quietly. "I'm aware this is highly unusual and you don't think we should be here. But I really do promise you there is no one else who can help us in this situation, and if the Commissioner doesn't get that message, terrible things could happen."

Citizen Receptionist's beautifully arched eyebrows snapped together, annoyance at Gwyn's persistence giving way to extreme displeasure. "Please leave now," they ordered abruptly. "If you think to threaten an employee of the Agency, you are mistaken. Get out."

"I'm not threatening!" Gwyn insisted, shrugging off Owen's hand and ignoring his whining voice that was pleading to leave. "I need your help. I need the Commissioner's help! Please pass on the message!"

Where was all the persuasiveness she had been able to muster at Masada? Religious zealots and war-hungry soldiers she had been able to sway, but a green-haired receptionist? Had she lost the ability?

Citizen Receptionist muttered into a com on their collar. Owen's hand pulled harder and Gwyn couldn't keep the desperation out of her voice as she begged, "Please!"

Suddenly another door opened, admitting two black-uniformed figures, also bearing the spiral symbol of the Agency. One was human, burly and female; the other an alien she recognized as a Mayash, blue, short and furry, just like the one she had seen in the space port. Its tail twitched back and forth, as if it were sensing the mood in the reception area.

Citizen Receptionist looked relieved. Obviously, this was security of some sort, here to eject them from the premises. Owen was already edging conspicuously towards the outer door, but Gwyn held her ground, facing the newcomers. *I might be getting kicked out of here, but damned if I'm going to skulk out with my tail between my legs. Figuratively speaking.*

"Gwyn Turner?" it was the Mayash who spoke. His voice purred deeply, like a tiger seducing its meal.

Gwyn's stomach turned to jelly. "Yes?" she returned, squaring her shoulders and praying the creature wouldn't strike her down. She couldn't believe the words that were spoken next.

"The Commissioner will see you now." The female security guard stepped back and indicated the door through which she had just come. Her voice was flat, eyes expressionless, and Gwyn was not sure if that was an improvement on the predatory timbre of the Mayash.

"What?" Citizen Receptionist sounded outraged.

"What?" Owen had stopped, back to the outer door, and was staring suspiciously at the guards.

Gwyn managed to nod her head. "Very good," she said, sounding like a po-faced butler from the nineteenth century. "Thank you." *At last, we're getting somewhere!*

"Is he with you?" the Mayash pointed his tail at Owen, grinning with all its teeth.

"Yes," Gwyn replied before Owen could get the chance to say anything. "Yes, we are both here to see the Commissioner."

THIRTY

2623 AD

Michelle had been sedated heavily this time, and her mind wandered back and forth in a haze as she struggled to fight the drug-induced haze. Someone had quite expertly relieved her of the chronokinetor from her left hand. He had been one of the guys who had chased and captured her the first time; she was pretty sure, or as sure as she could be of anything in this state. Swearing and threats from him confirmed that her captors realized this was not the timepiece they were after.

After leaving Gwyn at the Spaceport, she had made her way swiftly to the center of the city by air taxi, registering her name in order to pay for it by credit. *That should get the attention of anyone scanning the system.* The computer-driven taxi took off and patiently merged into the streams of air traffic that crisscrossed Vivaldis on routes carefully marked by colorful hovering beacons.

As she approached the Time Space Agency's entrance she made no efforts to hide herself or conceal her trajectory as she crossed the Central Square, passing the fountain and skirting the crowds of tourists. She was not even halfway into the alley when an electroshock from behind sent her plummeting to her knees.

What a cheap shot! Her mind exclaimed as a wave of pain swept over her.

Two guys dressed in the black uniform of Agency security guards appeared out of nowhere and bundled her into a hover-car clearly stamped with the spiral logo.

More than anything, that spiral worried her. She had been surprised they had taken her so blatantly, impersonating Agency staff right in front of the building itself, and just off the public square. Like the first time she'd been captured, that stank of corruption high up and someone powerful abusing their position. *Surely someone witnessed it and reported it?* There were hundreds of people in that square. But if they thought it legitimate, why would they question it?

Because citizens of the Allied Planets aren't used to arbitrary arrests, she mused. Vivaldis and the other human inhabited planets were democratic and generally safe places to be, barring certain areas. To snatch someone straight off the street would need a cover-up story for the media. Arresting a terrorist about to stage an attack on a public building, perhaps?

It still niggled at her. Her head lolled as she slumped against the corner of the room, trying to think through the fuzziness. Angry Man had left—was it the same aggressive asshole from the Detention Center? He would wait until she was coherent before coming back to question her. She could see surveillance scanners in the ceiling, but it definitely wasn't an official holding cell like the one she'd been in last time. The scanners were rigged up in a temporary fashion, and the smell in the room was one she associated with space cargo—stale and mechanical— making her wonder if they were near the spaceport. There was nothing else in the room, however, to give her a clue, and as her wrists and ankles were electro-cuffed to the bench, she couldn't even attempt to explore. They weren't taking any chances this time.

Despite the wooziness, she wasn't unhappy about the sedative. They might think it was preventing her escape, but in actual fact it was buying her time. She would play up the effects for as long as she could. She only hoped that once Gwyn and Owen had reached the Commissioner, they would work fast to locate her. She didn't fancy undergoing questioning by Angry Man, he had already demonstrated he was trigger happy with the shock baton.

Come on, Gwyn, she urged as her thoughts became clearer. *I know it's ironic, but I really am running out of time.*

* * *

Gwyn's first impression of Commissioner Hera was a stern, figure; lean and muscled despite her greying hair and weathered brown skin. The office was large, but her presence filled it and left Gwyn in no doubt who was in charge here. Dim holograms flickered on the walls. The far wall appeared to be one large window, looking out over rooftops. Gwyn could see the corner of the square they had crossed before.

The window dimmed, and Hera turned to face the visitors, nodding dismissal to the security guards. Gwyn noticed the Commissioner's face twitch, nostrils flaring ever so slightly as she faced the Mayash guard who lingered just a moment too long before exiting the room.

Woah, she really doesn't like that guard, it would seem? Gwyn wondered. *Insubordinate, perhaps, or a personal beef?*

She wasn't given a chance to wonder further as stern eyes swept briefly over Gwyn before resting on her companion with intense scrutiny.

"Owen Chang," Commissioner Hera stated deliberately.

Owen swallowed and nodded nervously in response, more agitated than before.

He really doesn't want to be here, she realized. *All those nerves, the edginess as we were traveling here—this is what he was afraid of: being in this room facing this woman. Why?*

The stern old woman smiled. It was an interesting effect. It was no grandmotherly smile, kind and indulgent. Rather, it was a satisfied smile, like the proverbial cat that ate the canary.

It made Gwyn uneasy and seemed to have the same effect on Owen.

"Owen, it's been a long time since that misunderstanding over your university exploits," Commissioner Hera gestured magnanimously for them to sit down.

They sidled into two swivel chairs facing the big desk that took pride of place in the office. The mention of university made Gwyn feel like a naughty student called to the Dean's office. *Why is the Commissioner so interested in him? I was the one kicking up a ruckus in the reception.* She tried not to feel disgruntled.

"Ah, yes, misunderstanding," Owen nodded hopefully. "Does that mean I'm not in trouble anymore?"

That's why he's so nervous about being here, Gwyn figured. *He's had some sort of run in with the Commissioner in the past and doesn't want to be hit with repercussions.*

"In trouble? Of course you're not in trouble," Hera chuckled darkly. "If I'd been in the Commissioner's chair at the time, there never would have been this... malarkey. Skills like yours are much too useful to be restricted by university policy."

Owen looked relieved, though Gwyn didn't find it completely convincing. She found herself the focus of that steely gaze and any feelings of being overshadowed vanished.

"Now," Hera seated herself in the high-backed chair behind the desk. "Who do we have here? Your name is Gwyn Turner, I understand? You were rather earnest in trying to get a message to me."

"Uh, yes," Gwyn tried to regain the confidence she had felt in the reception. "Time to find missing agent, uh, I mean, person." *Get it right, you muppet!*

Hera leaned closer, her dark eyes focusing directly on Gwyn. "There is only one missing Agent, of whom I am aware, and I am aware of everything that happens in this Agency. We have been frantically trying to locate her, but lack the resources and staff to mount a search party. Not to mention it is our policy is that Agents are completely self-sufficient. But a strange message surfaced at the City Detention Centre several days ago, which would imply that she was active but in some sort of trouble. Can you tell me why she hasn't reported in?"

Those eyes bored into Gwyn, intent on finding answers. She swallowed, glad that she had some.

"She's been detained," she explained. "She was attacked and captured, but managed to escape her captors. She knew they'd try again, so she sent me to inform you so you could locate her. She knew you were the only person who could make something happen quickly enough to both retrieve her and find out who these people are."

"She doesn't know?"

The question surprised Gwyn. Surely Michelle would have said if she had known who had kidnapped her? *Maybe. But then she seems to keep her cards pretty close to her chest. I get the sinking feeling I'm some sort of dupe but I'm not yet sure why...*

"Not that she told me." Gwyn shifted in her seat. "But I think she's in trouble. She was meant to get here first, but since she's not here, I'm guessing they recaptured her. She thought that might happen if she tried to reach you, which is why she sent me. Us." She glanced at Owen. "You see, she thinks the reason she was attacked in the first place was to steal the device she had. But she hid it. She has another, but it's nowhere near as good. Owen can use it to locate her."

"Indeed!" Hera exclaimed. "She hid it! But can she find it again? That device is a prototype—worth millions of credits! We're under a lot of scrutiny and to lose it…" Hera clenched her fits.

Gwyn could sympathize. To discover your best Agent—she was assuming, since who else would they trust with an expensive prototype? —had been captured by an unknown group in order to steal said expensive prototype on your watch would be extremely embarrassing and stressful. But, all the same, she clenched her left fist kept it out of sight in her lap, shielded by the desk. Some instinct that had been awakened during her fourth dimensional travails made her decide it would be best if she kept something to herself rather than lay it all out there. After all, her bargain to get home was with Michelle—if she gave it up to the Commissioner, Hera might confiscate it and then where would she be? Also…

Why is she being so open about how important this thing is? She doesn't know me from a bar of soap. I'd be a lot more circumspect if some random showed up in my office making allegations like this.

Still, she answered Hera truthfully. "Yes, she can find it. But we need to find her." She hoped she was doing the right thing. She didn't entirely trust Michelle, but the woman had rescued her from siege, fire, and either death or a lifetime in ancient Rome… *Which might not have been terrible…* She pictured Gaius in her mind, *but certainly not to be preferred over to family, home, and clean sanitation.*

"If you can allow me access to some of the Agency computers," Owen piped up. "I can locate the device she has on her. Even if these kidnappers have taken it from her, it should at least narrow down our search options."

The Commissioner pursed her lips, and then nodded. "Very well," she rose, and they copied automatically. "Come with me. We'll use the programming room to search for her."

* * *

"What's taking so long?" Gwyn whispered as Owen tapped furiously at the computer screen before reaching out to rotate a hologram.

She was trying not to stand too close to anything in this room—it all looked technical and expensive. Screens and holograms and columns of little lights on the metal walls made it look more futuristic than anything else she had seen so far in this time, save an actual spaceship itself. Even those had been confusing—the one she had arrived on had been egg shaped with several spindly protrusions, putting her in mind of a half-bald sea urchin. Nothing like the streamlined, forward-facing craft she'd envisioned, with large engines at the back.

Why would they need to be streamlined if they never enter an atmosphere? her brain chimed in. She had forgotten to ask Michelle what propelled them. *Actually, you forgot to ask her a lot of things, which is weird. You had plenty of time to ask questions.*

"It's not that simple," Owen replied, sounding short. "Every agency chronokinetor emits an automatic signal every twelve hours, and with the right equipment, you can pinpoint where it is. Together with the tracker implanted in the agent—which emits a different signal every time the agent makes a jump—you can use a very complicated algorithm I designed to roughly locate the agent in time and space. But you have to know when to look before you try for where. For this timepiece, I know that the when is now."

"Why not combine the two?" Gwyn wanted to know. "Why have two separate tracking devices?"

"It's to do with interference, and the way each timepiece is tuned to the bearer," he answered, tapping strange symbols into the computer. "I'd have to spend some time looking at their systems to know for sure. But it looks like the implanted tracker is also designed to act as a backup in case the agent is separated from their timepiece. A rescue team could be sent to the correct time, and then search manually from there."

That would explain why Michelle's attackers couldn't find the chrono-thingy on its own, I guess. They might have known where it was, but not when. She realized Owen was still talking.

"This, however," he went on, "is not an agency timepiece, but one of my own, so I'm modifying the algorithm because I used a different kind of signal. I didn't want them to be able to find it. So it's taking longer." He lowered his voice. "And I'm taking the time to embed an erasing program so they can't find it again without me. A little insurance so they don't throw me out again," he added cryptically.

"Oh." She fell silent, not wanting to ask further questions in case she gave too much of her ignorance away. She had been warned by Michelle to keep quiet about coming from a different time. Owen knew she was from Earth, but not from the past.

"They might not want you to go back," Michelle had reluctantly disclosed. "The Agency has an agenda to keep certain timelines on track, and they wouldn't want to risk you going back and destabilizing any of them, even if it meant keeping you against your will."

Oh, there was so much she didn't know about this world and time. If she had felt overwhelmed back in ancient Judea, this was ten times worse! Fortunately, the chronokinetor in her palm seemed to be doing its own trick again of allaying the suspicions of those around her. Despite his reservations, Owen had helped her. The Commissioner hadn't questioned her on where she had come from, or how she knew Michelle. Strange that it hadn't worked on the receptionist. Maybe some people's minds were more resilient? *Should really have gotten Michelle to clarify that.*

"Hmpf!" Owen exclaimed quietly, then shot a dark look at Gwyn, who was hovering awkwardly at his elbow. Flicking his eyes back to the screen, he muttered out of the corner of his mouth, "No wonder I'm having trouble finding the signal from the timepiece I gave her, you're interfering. Why didn't you say you had it?"

"Had what?" she muttered back, trying not to look back at where the Commissioner stood a little way away, speaking quietly into some sort of communication device. No one else was present in the room. "She gave it to me to keep safe. I don't know how to use it."

Owen was still frowning, but didn't say anything to Hera. Despite the Commissioner's assurances, he obviously retained a sense of caution.

"What happened that got you in so much trouble?" Gwyn murmured.

Owen glared. "None of your business!"

Gwyn bit her tongue and watched him return to his work with an unnecessary intensity. After a few more minutes, she whispered, "Sorry. I didn't mean to be nosy. I just feel like I don't know what's going on here—things Michelle didn't tell me."

He snorted. "Just like her." Then reflectively, he added, "She learned the hard way when I got arrested. She didn't sell me out, though. I owe her that."

Gwyn nodded, even though his words hadn't made anything clearer to her.

Owen shrugged. "She's always been persuasive, but she said it wasn't just life or death for her. She said it would affect all of us. Something big is going down, and I want to know what."

"Oh." *Affect all of us? Surely he means just in this time. I just need to find her and make her take me home.*

She wondered if Owen was a little paranoid, and Michelle had leaned into that to convince him to help. His aversion to authority, being out in public—he struck her as someone who was very intelligent, but possibly a little unhinged.

"Anyway," he muttered. "I'm reconfiguring the search algorithm to account for..." his eyes flicked to Gwyn's hand.

She nodded, not bothering to ask how. Chances were she wouldn't have been able to understand his explanation, anyway. Probably the scientific principles were taught in primary schools now and she would be more ignorant than a child.

"Ah ha!" he straightened, pleased with himself.

"Yes?" Hera appeared at their side, startling them both. "You have managed to locate her?"

"I've located the chronokinetor she was using," he corrected. "Chances are she's still near it, but in any case it gives us a place to start looking. We ought to hurry before it moves."

"Where do we need to look?" Hera asked.

The door to the programming room slid silently open and Hera gestured to the same human and Mayash security guards who had been standing to attention outside. Again Gwyn noticed the semi-concealed distaste for the non-human guard.

Owen frowned. "Looks like the industrial area near the spaceport. Here." He used finger and thumb to drag the image on the screen, enlarging a map.

The Commissioner dispatched the human guard to assemble a small squad and instructed them to proceed immediately to the location Owen had found. The Mayash she ordered to form part of the backup perimeter with the other squad. Speaking into her communicator, she requested that her vehicle be made ready for immediate departure

"You two, come with me," she ordered Owen and Gwyn.

They trailed her along a corridor and up an elevator to the roof, whereupon they boarded a small hover-car. It did not resemble any automobile from Gwyn's time, having a comfortable but functional interior and short, stubby wings that had little to do with lift in the traditional sense. Anti-gravity engines allowed the car to take off and accelerate well above the legal speed limits, but the emblazoned Agency logo meant the Commissioner could pilot through low air traffic without being held up.

Gwyn gazed out the window, watching as they zoomed by buildings and ground vehicles well below, interspersed with tiny pedestrians. The city stretched on, threaded with large nature reserves and parks. Some of the parks were huge, with strange tall trees that tended towards blue rather than the green. Lagoons interspersed the foliage, connected by streams and canals. Despite all the parks, or gardens, or whatever they were, the buildings continued on to the horizon without any sign of city limits.

The scene underneath began to change as they drew closer to the industrial area about which Owen had spoken; a solid slab of grey and brown structures with nothing to brighten it except for garish hologram signage. They descended on what appeared to be a warehouse, judging by the words flashing on the roof: *Sensitive Space Freight*. The manager on duty scrambled out onto the rooftop space as they landed, but the Commissioner brusquely brushed him aside.

"The Agency needs to search the building immediately," she declared. "Assemble all your staff so they can be accounted for."

Gwyn looked around curiously as the first squad landed in a car just after them. Rooftops were by and large flat and rectangular, even if the building below had curves to its walls. Lights marked out landing areas for hover-cars and pedestrian walkways, making it clear this wasn't wasted space. There were no cranes to lift freight, but as they descended into the building, they passed through a massive warehouse space and she could see floating platforms trundling slowly about, guided by human staff carrying what she guessed to be remote controls. Much yelling and confusion ensued as the warehouse manager announced over an intercom that all staff were to halt activities and present to the main dock. Hera ordered the humans from the first squad car to spread out and search everywhere, but the original female guard stayed with them and they marched downstairs into the warehouse.

She seems to know where she is going ... Gwyn was uneasy as she and Owen trailed after Hera. They took a lift down two basements levels and followed a corridor, Hera tapping open doors which clamped shut automatically behind them. It was poorly lit, down here, and had the dank, stale air of being disused space. Gwyn sniffed nervously but the presence of the guard behind her discouraged her from pausing, and she was forced to keep up. They reached a locked room, and the Commissioner nodded to the guard with them, who spoke into her communicator.

A man opened the door, and they proceeded inside.

"Michelle!" Gwyn and Owen exclaimed at the same time, spotting the woman on the far side of the room, hand- and foot-cuffed to the bench she was sitting on.

"What the...?" Owen was flabbergasted, but Gwyn reacted quicker. She whirled and ducked under the outstretched arms of female security guard who had accompanied them, but made it only as far as the doorway when an electric current hit her legs and she went down hard. Groaning, she felt herself being unceremoniously dragged back inside the room and propped next to Michelle. The man who had opened the room for them had already cuffed Owen and was affixing him to Michelle's bench.

"Well, then," Commissioner Hera spoke. "Seems like we have our missing Agent and some rather inept companions. Now, Michelle, they told me you know where the chronokinetor is, so give it up now before anyone else gets hurt."

THIRTY-ONE

2623 AD

Michelle's heart had leapt when she had seen the Commissioner walk into the room. She had just undergone half an hour of questioning by Rickas. The angry guard had enabled the shock baton enabled. She had barely managed to keep the dopey-headed, glazed eye appearance in the face of the electric currents. She reacted, but slowed everything down and gibbered as if her brain couldn't comprehend the source of the pain. It was hard.

Relief had come in the form of a communication and Rickas had stopped his torture, contenting himself glaring in frustration. She continued to let her head loll, even drooling out of the corner of her mouth.

When Hera strode through that door preceded by Owen and Gwyn, she thought all her troubles were over. *They found me!* But immediately she realized it was all wrong, that her captor had willingly let them in, that the Commissioner wasn't arresting or tasing him. In fact, the confidence with which she had walked through the door made it seem almost like she had known where Michelle was all along…

That's because she did, her mind whispered disconsolately. *You wanted to know who the high up, powerful person was pulling strings in this affair—you've found her.*

"It's no good, Commissioner," the man gestured violently. "She's doped up from the sedative, nothing but shit and dribble coming out of her mouth."

"Is that so?" Hera cocked her head.

Michelle she knew there was no point in pretending. This woman had overseen her training, after all, she knew her best agent was playing dumb.

"Why?" she asked the Commissioner, speaking quietly but clearly.

Rickas gaped in shock, then fury, to realize he had been duped. The other guard stood stolidly by the door, expressionless.

Owen and Gwyn sat silent, eyes darting between Michelle and their captors, trying to work out what was going on. Michelle shot a despairing glance at Gwyn—this was not part of the plan. Gwyn seemed to understand, dismay written across her face. They had not come as a rescue team after all.

"Why?" Hera smiled in amusement. "Do you really expect me to spend time providing exposition while you attempt to overcome me and escape? I trained you, Michelle, I know how you operate. You came up through the university, a child of the state, brilliant and hardworking, with a natural aptitude for time travel. I got you into the Agency, advanced your career. Why do you think you always got the cutting edge missions? The best assignments?"

Again, Michelle's voice was steady and quiet. "Because I'm the best. The best Agent, the best at time travel. My missions are always successful."

Hera stopped to consider her. She answered quietly, too. "Yes, you were the best. But I don't need the best. Not with this new chronokinetor. You've proved it works, but I can put it to far better use than tipping history in small and insignificant ways. So you are going to tell me where it is."

"What better use?" Michelle wasn't just stalling for time. She genuinely wanted to know. Upset and disappointed beyond belief that the Commissioner she had looked up to and trusted was behaving in an illegal and unethical fashion, she wanted to know why. The calm, calculating part of her also realized that Hera obviously didn't know Gwyn had the timepiece.

Hera sighed, barely concealing her impatience. "It is for the good of our species and our future. Humans have been subordinate in the Allied Planets when they should be running the place. Our rights have been suppressed in favor of aliens. I'm sorry you had to get caught up in it— you'd have been recruited to our organization if you hadn't showed disturbing tendencies towards xenophobia that rendered you ineligible. And if you hadn't run from my agents, this would have been a lot simpler. You would have been relieved of the device and escorted back to our time."

"What?" Michelle screwed up her face, baffled. "You gave me the damn device! You gave me a mission. No one was supposed to interfere with that. When I heard those dopes trying to sneak up on me, of course, I ran. I wasn't hanging around to chat. Especially not to some Purity Politics nut-jobs."

Hera turned to the man who'd been holding Michelle prisoner. "Rickas, you told me she'd never know you were coming. She has just made it clear that she did." She spoke flatly, but it was clear she was nearing the end of her patience and wanted someone to blame.

"I don't know how she managed that!" Rickas protested. "But it doesn't matter now—she just needs to tell us where the damn timepiece is!" He fingered the trigger of the shock-baton.

Hera turned back to Michelle, face stern. "You heard him. Where is the chronokinetor?"

"Don't know, must have dropped it," Michelle spoke sarcastically.

"You're lying. The algorithms showed it moved, then disappeared. Where did you hide it?"

"Up your ass."

Hera sighed, tapping her fingertips together. "When you sent your little message from the Detention Center, I knew you would attempt to retrieve it. That's why I let you escape. Clever reaching out to Mr. Chang, here—because of you we located him too and he *will* become a useful part of our programming team."

Owen shot Michelle a look of alarm. He was paler than usual and she felt a pang of guilt, but she shook her head. "I can't believe you're a xenophobe. Like humans weren't the last to join the Allied Planets. They let us in!"

Hera growled. "These two," she indicated Gwyn and Owen, "came to my Agency and told me you knew where it was. If you don't cooperate…"

"Or what?" Michelle snarled back. "Trigger-happy here will shock me some more? You trained me, you said so yourself. How much time will you waste trying to break me while that timepiece is getting further and further away from you?"

* * *

Gwyn saw the flash in Hera's eyes at this—triumph, then uncertainty. *She doesn't know if Michelle is baiting her or if that was a real slip,* she thought.

"No," Hera replied. "But there are other people in this room who don't have your Agency training…" She left the threat hanging.

Gwyn knew what she meant. Owen started hyperventilating quietly. Gwyn's eyes widened. She was still aching from the zap she had received, and the memory was worse than being shocked by an electric fence as a child. If these guys had already tortured Michelle, what was going to stop them from torturing her and Owen as well? No one knew they were here, no one was going to rescue them—they were the rescue party, for heaven's sake! *And look how that turned out!* Her brain said sarcastically.

I've got to get us out of here, she began to think desperately. *Michelle's plan has failed. Owen is next to useless. But they don't know I've got the chronokinetor.*

So what? she demanded of herself. *You don't know how to use it. You've never been able to, Michelle never taught you to. And it's only by sheer luck that no one has yet noticed it in your hand because you've been bloody careful to keep it hidden! But they'll find it pretty soon when they start zapping you! And then the show's over!*

Rickas grabbed Owen by the arm, dragging him onto his knees.

"Hey!" Michelle struggled in her cuffs and tried to kick at the man, but couldn't reach. He administered a light zap to Owen's nose, resulting in a scream of shocked pain.

"I don't know anything!" he bleated. "Michelle didn't tell me!" His stream of protests continued, that *he didn't know, he didn't know, he just got dragged into this, he knew nothing!*

Gwyn stared at Michelle in horror. It wouldn't be long before Owen fessed up. She didn't know what to do. She couldn't get close enough to Michelle to give her the thing undetected. Besides, Michelle's hands weren't free to get it off her. *I have to make this thing work somehow!* But how could she? It hadn't ever worked when she'd tried back in Masada.

This is the part in the books or movies where the hero reaches their most desperate moment, and suddenly the thing works! She agonized. *But it never worked for me, no matter how desperate or frightened or hopeful I was...*

She looked at Michelle, frantic, but the woman had tilted her head back and closed her eyes, breathing calmly. *How can she be so calm!? What is she thinking?*

Thinking. Gwyn's heart skipped a beat. *Michelle said this thing forms a mental link. A mental link involves thinking. Not desperate emotions. I have to be calm and think.*

She closed her eyes and tried to remember what she was thinking when she had activated the chronokinetor for the first time, back at En Gedi. She had been curious, wondering what it was, what it did.

It was no good—Owen's scream cut through the air as the Commissioner looked on impatiently.

Gwyn felt tears well in her eyes.

Think of something that will make you calm! her brain commanded.

It was hard. She tried to shed emotion in order to clear her mind, but the feelings kept crowding in. She ran through her mind frantically for thoughts and notions to distract her from her current situation.

Thinking of her family only made her feel anxious. She would never see them again! They would never know what happened to her. She would never see home again, she was trapped, just like she had been at Masada, just like she had been at the Roman camp.

Gaius' sunny face rose in her mind. The cheerful, polite young Roman, who had been interesting and courteous, brave and kind...

She focused on that feeling. The friendship they had formed. Their growing attraction. The fact he had listened and did his best to help her, even when it seemed so crazy to him.

She almost smiled. Outside sounds dulled, then faded, her breathing slowed, her mind relaxed and then—*there!* On the edge of her mind, she could feel the timepiece.

It was incredible how she hadn't noticed it before. Her brain had been so full of confusion and fear and the fight to survive in a time that wasn't her own, but there, shining like a beacon, was this *thing,* like a bionic limb—part of her, yet so much more.

She concentrated on reaching out mentally to it. It was elusive at first, like reeling in a fish that danced on the line. She probed it gently—there was so much to it. She knew it could move her, sink her through the soft spots of time and space to emerge in a new place, an old place, a different place. It was all there, like opening a book that had once been in another language, only to find that one simply had to turn the book upside-down to make sense of it after all. She just had to find the right page.

"I'll tell you! Please, stop—I'll tell you!" Owen's scream sounded loudly in her ears. Her eyes snapped open, and she almost lost the link. But having found it, she knew logically it was still there. The fear and panic could only rabble around the edges—she acknowledged them, but didn't let them control her. She focused on what she had to do.

"Her! Her!" Owen pointed frantically. "She's got it!"

All heads in the room swung to stare at Gwyn.

Flick!

THIRTY-TWO

THIRTY MINUTES EARLIER

"You two, come with me."

The blue haze faded, and Gwyn experienced real déjà vu. It was Commissioner Hera's voice she heard echoing in the corridor, and she experienced a lurch of sickness and she watched herself walk out of the room, and then she was alone.

She stared about her at the flickering computer screens and dimly lit holograms. She was back in the programming room at the Agency.

Well done, her brain whispered. *You traveled through time at will. Now what?*

It was a good question. She needed to get help. But who could she trust? And why would they believe her?

Just then, the door slid open and the Mayash guard who had been deployed to organize a backup perimeter re-entered, then stopped in astonishment.

"What in the Two-Tails...? You just left! I saw you leave!" His tail twitched in bewilderment and blue fur hackled.

She hates aliens, she remembered. The interrogation by the Commissioner showed a pro-human agenda, and her almost-rudeness towards the Mayash guard earlier had been obvious to Gwyn. *The enemy of my enemy...*

"I did," she blurted. "I've come back in time from half an hour from now. It's a trap. I need your help. The Commissioner is—" *How to tell this person that their superior officer is a politically demented criminal who tortures people?*

"The Commissioner is...?" The guard's eyes narrowed and his tail whipped violently.

She took a deep breath. "The Commissioner is corrupt. She is torturing a Time Space Agent and a civilian in order to find... well, this." She brandished her palm at the guard, displaying the chronokinetor embedded in her palm. It felt so comfortable there, it was incredible.

The Mayash leapt towards her in one bound. Tail gently snaked to encircle her wrist while clawed fingers held her hand delicately. He examined the timepiece.

Dark, dark blue eyes raised to meet hers, unfathomable and, literally, alien. She wondered if she had made a terrible mistake.

Then the guard smiled, sharp teeth displaying, and the tail patted her gently on the shoulder.

"Help you shall have, young Citizen. Come with me."

* * *

Brrrys, as it turned out his name was, was probably the best possible person she could have found to help her.

He explained he was part of a group that had suspected the Commissioner of corruption for quite some time now, but her position and cunning had thwarted them from finding solid evidence. They were made up of five Mayash, several humans and a scaly young Nolii, all of whom had been recruited by the Shanista scientists in the Agency to watch the Commissioner's activities and uncover unethical or illegal behavior.

Gwyn's appearance out of thin air had been just what they needed. Lacking hard evidence, and frustrated in their efforts, they had watched as certain humans had been promoted where there had either been a more qualified Citizen of another species, or a human whose tolerant politics had been unpalatable to Hera and her growing group of cronies. At first it had been subtle, but in the last year the restructuring of staff had accelerated, and non-humans or tolerant humans found themselves increasingly sidelined in less important projects. Michelle had been the last tolerant Agent left on important missions, due to her brilliance and skill for time travel. Her support crew and programmers had gradually been shuffled, but she spent so much time in the past she hadn't seemed to notice, and Brrrys hadn't wanted to jeopardize the investigation, given Hera's patronage of Michelle.

He explained this as their hover-car, not as flash and sleek as the Commissioner's, rose and sped towards the industrial area. Standard police vehicles flanked them. He had questioned Gwyn intently, undeterred by the chronokinetor's usual function of dispelling curiosity about the wearer. She commented on it, hoping to get answers, and he smiled that sharp toothed grin again.

"My brain doesn't respond to it. They tested it. Some people simply have a natural resistance to the waves it emits. Very rare for a human to have it, and no one of the Rilans or Nolii have ever demonstrated it. But a few of us Mayash, and of course all of the Shanista. They built the thing, after all."

She was very curious to meet one of these Shanista. None had been in evidence anywhere she had seen in the Agency Headquarters, and certainly none made up the team she was traveling with now. But they seemed to have great influence upon the Agency.

"Commissioner hates it," Brrrys observed when she voiced that opinion tentatively. "She keeps trying to get humans into their labs, but they won't have it. So polite they are, always gentle. Not much good in a fight, but clever as anything. And impeccable ethics. They are the true leaders of our Allied Planets." His tone was very respectful and proud.

He had been astonished to learn that she had time traveled from several hundred years in the past. She knew she was taking a risk, but once she realized he wouldn't be deterred from questioning her she didn't want to appear deceptive. He took it in his short, furry stride, tail a-twitching as they had boarded the hover-car.

Now as they descended upon the warehouse, she wound up the extremely summarized version of her accidentally going back into Michelle's mission. Michelle's getting captured, escaping, rescuing her— *well, the jury is still out on that one*—and bringing her to this time in the hopes of blowing this plot wide open.

"It's going to happen now," he smiled once more, fiercely this time, and turned to issue orders to the other members of the team.

"Stay close to me," he instructed Gwyn as they leapt out of the craft.

"Hey! You're meant to stay on the back-up perimeter!" a human Agency guard yelled as they marched in without hesitation. The guard stood at the rooftop entrance to the warehouse, and seemed to take a moment to realize that there were far more vehicles and personnel approaching than warranted for a backup that hadn't been called in.

Even if the guard hadn't delayed, he never would have reached his com in time. One of Brrrys' colleagues moved like a whirlwind and—tail lashing out—administered a crack to the skull that incapacitated him immediately. Collapsing, he was dragged away unconscious by the regular police officers that had landed on the warehouse, swarming from their vehicles and moving swiftly to secure the premises. Working with Brrrys' team of Agency guards, they arrested the personnel Hera had planted, reassuring the warehouse manager that everything was in hand, but they would need to take statements from each and every staff member and anyone else on the premises. They wanted to find out why this warehouse was being used, and who had authorized it.

"Hurry," Gwyn muttered as she urged Brrrys onwards, remembering the route she'd taken not thirty minutes before... Or only a few minutes before, depending how you looked at it. It was hard to realize that for everyone else, less than ten minutes had passed since the Commissioner had passed through. No wonder the warehouse manager was confused.

"Stop," Brrrys hissed, holding up a clawed, blue-furred hand. Gwyn did so, swaying slightly as she felt increasingly sick. Michelle had mentioned something about feeling sick if you were in the same place at the same time as yourself. *Of course, I'm still there, in the room. I haven't gone yet.*

The Mayash peered in her face. "Are you alright, Gwyn Turner?" His eyes flashed in alarm.

"Yeah," she muttered, leaning a hand on the hallway wall. "I'm still there. I can feel it."

"Ah, yes. Proximity sickness." He considered momentarily, then whispered.

"There is a guard up ahead. The one who was with me when I came to collect you from the Reception. I can smell her. The second you stop feeling sick, I'm going to take her out, then enter the room. We will have the element of surprise, because you will have just disappeared, and they'll be distracted by that. Grrrel will cover me." He indicated the lightning-fast female Mayash who had taken out the first guard, standing silently behind them. Gwyn nodded her understanding and paid close attention to the queasiness wracking her. Grrrel and Brrrys crouched, readying themselves.

The sudden relief from the sick feeling was so wonderful she almost forgot to signal. The nausea lifted, and she chopped her hand down in the ancient gesture to charge. Like missiles, the two Mayash shot around the bend in the corridor and she heard another *crack!*

Following as fast as she could, she stepped over the unconscious human guard and into the room.

"Gwyn!" Michelle's cry of astonishment was tinged with delight. Hera and Rickas had spun as the Mayash had burst into the room. Rickas managed to raise his shock baton in defense, but he was no match for Grrrel. He was quickly overwhelmed by another of those whip-cracking tail shots.

Hera stepped forward and Michelle lashed out with both feet, striking the Hera hard in the shins. The older woman stumbled and Brrrys rendered her unconscious with another tail strike.

"Michelle!" Gwyn raced to the other woman's side. "How do I get you out of these things?" Grrrel leapt to her side and showed Gwyn the release code for the cuffs.

"Agency issued," the female purred. "Nice bit of evidence, thank you very much!" She slipped them into a foil evidence bag and pulled Michelle to her feet.

Michelle gripped Gwyn's shoulder and smiled. "You did it." Her tone was proud. "When did you go? Can't have been long ago."

"Not even an hour," Gwyn glanced around at Owen, sobbing silently as Brrrys helped him up.

"I'm so sorry, I'm sorry," he was distraught. "I didn't mean to tell. I'm so, so sorry."

"S'all right, Owen," Michelle patted him on the shoulder. "Brrrys, boy, am I glad to see you. Can we get a medic down here? They roughed him up pretty badly."

"Of course," Brrrys glanced at Michelle, disheveled and with several burn marks from the shock baton. "Looks like they had a go at you, too. We'll need to take holos for evidence."

"Evidence? Against the Commissioner? Of course. I couldn't believe it when I realized…" The shock seemed to sink in she glanced down. "She was my mentor," she murmured. Gwyn and Brrrys were too polite to say anything.

Michelle cleared her throat. "How did you get here so quickly?" she wanted to know. "What did Gwyn tell you?"

He laughed. "She told us enough about Hera to warrant an immediate response. We've been set to watch her for quite a few months now. The Shanista in the Agency suspected her of corruption, but weren't sure how far it went, and needed solid evidence before moving against her."

For the second time in five minutes, Michelle was astonished. "The Shanista sent you? No wonder you acted so fast. What about the other guards up there in the warehouse? She had quite a number acting in her interests—all human, of course—but whether they were part of it or following orders, I couldn't tell."

Brrrys grinned his toothy smile. "All taken care of. We'll find out soon enough who was in and who was following orders." He listened quickly to his com. "Someone's called the media. There are hover scanners all over this place. I'll find out if there is a more discreet way out of here."

He listened to his com again, and replied in the affirmative.

"Now," he directed his attention at Gwyn. "There are some very important Shanista who are quite keen to meet *you*."

THIRTY-THREE

2623 AD

If Michelle was distraught at Hera's betrayal, she hid it well. Little seemed to faze this woman. Gwyn wondered how someone could be so unflappable after being kidnapped and tortured, not to mention have their world turned upside-down with the betrayal of the leader she had trusted.

Owen had been taken away by a medic in the hangar to be treated. Though she hadn't particularly liked him Gwyn hoped he would be okay.

Brrrys' team had managed to bring a vehicle inside the warehouse so he, Michelle and Gwyn could board without being seen by the media scanners that flocked in the building's airspace. They flew out a low exit and wend their way through city streets before rising up to accelerate. They were going, he had said, to see the Shanista scientists who apparently held such sway.

Gwyn stared through the windows, opaque to outsiders, and listened to Michelle and Brrrys, who were deep in conversation about the implications for the Time-Space Agency.

"There'll be an investigation," she heard Brrrys say.

"The Government will question the Agency's operational powers," Michelle replied. "There might be some big changes. They've always been afraid of what we can do. It's not going to look good for us."

Listening, Gwyn mused that it was not simply technology that made living in another time challenging and confusing. She didn't have enough knowledge about the last few hundred years to grasp the nuances of the politics, let alone the social attitudes. The rough outline Michelle had given before they had come to this time had only been her point of view, too, and listening to Brrrys speak made her wonder at the variety of opinions and beliefs that must be held in this truly multi-cultural universe. She tried to line up her thoughts to ask some questions, but didn't know where to start, so her minded drifted until they landed in an enclosed underground hanger.

Curved walls and rounded edges made the rooms in this building different from any other she had been in so far. It reminded her of the egg-shaped spaceship, and the way corridors wound their way with a variety of alcoves put her in mind of a bee hive. Colors were varied, with hexagonal patterns featured—whether decorative or purposeful, she couldn't tell.

Several hard-shelled Nolii and one very squishy-looking Rilan had met them in the hanger and politely escorted them to the top level via a spherical elevator. Under a large dome encompassing the entire roof, a pleasant garden filled the space. The garden consisted of *very* tall flowers rising up on single stems, with smaller bushes that sprouted an array of blue-green fern-like tendrils instead of leaves. Looking up at the covering dome, she realized it was the first rooftop she had seen that didn't have a flat surface to be utilized for hovercraft. She also noticed that she and Michelle were the only humans present.

From amongst the foliage, three Shanista approached.

Over two meters tall, impossibly thin and with sepia-colored skin, the Shanista put Gwyn in the mind of Masai tribespeople crossed with dragonflies. They had faceted eyes and two sets of gossamer wings each, fluttering in a non-existent breeze. They were beautiful but eerie, clicking gently to each other before addressing the group made up of Brrrys, Michelle, and Gwyn.

"Welcome, Citizens, thank you for coming to our facility." The one who spoke had a pink and orange shimmer to the wings, and wore a white flowing robe streaked with hues of the same.

"Citizen Colsa, you know Agent Michelle," Brrrys gestured. "Our companion is Gwyn Turner, about whom I reported while undertaking to apprehend ex-Commissioner Hera." He explained to Gwyn, "I had a live feed on once I realized what you were. Colsa is the head scientist here. It and its colleagues are aware of your situation."

Gwyn felt the attention focus on her. It was not threatening, not like it had been when she'd been interrogated by the Rabbi and Joshua, not patronizing, like when Silva had questioned her. It was just… intense. She could feel their interest, and she realized oddly that the clicking that took place quietly between them must be their way of speaking, but for once the chronokinetor wasn't doing its translation trick. Yet she could understand and speak the language used between the Shanista and Brrrys. It was not the modern English she spoke, and but timepiece had no trouble translating that straight into her brain. *Why not the clicking?*

Colsa nodded at Gwyn. "Forgive our scrutiny, young Citizen, you are an anomaly we did not predict. Yet we owe you our thanks for your critical actions in apprehending the misguided Hera, whose political agenda would have threatened our society."

"Um, you're welcome," Gwyn replied after several seconds of silence, as a response seemed warranted. *Wow, they are really formal. But they seem to be in charge so here is your chance.* "Um, may I ask a question?"

"Of course," Colsa fluttered its wings, sending ripples of air into the surrounding plant life. The exotic flowers and strange shrubbery waved gently in the breeze created, and a gentle perfume rose in the air. Its effect was relaxing, and Gwyn felt more confident as she went on.

"I'm glad I could help, really, I am. It's just that," she glanced at Michelle, "I really would like to go home, or at least get back to my family. I don't belong here; I had an agreement with Michelle here, that I would help her, and she would help me get back to my time. And while I can use this thing," she waved her palm and the timepiece, "it isn't mine, and I need help to get back to Earth so I can get to the right place *and* time."

Quiet clicking ensued amongst the Shanista, but not for long. Colsa spoke again for all of them.

"If that is your wish, then of course we will help you return to your own time and place. But, as you correctly point out, the chronokinetor in your possession is not yours, however it seems to have bonded to you quite intensely. May I?"

Gwyn stood quietly while the cool, almost metallic hands of the scientist touched several points of the timepiece in her palm. She expected it to pop out like it had when Michelle had removed it from her back by the Dead Sea. It failed to do so.

"The lateral functionality of the chronokinetor has been damaged somehow," it observed. "The fourth dimensional capability remains intact, as does its other features."

"So jumps in time, but not space." Michelle asked. "Can you fix it?"

Colsa probed further, then turned to Michelle, changing the subject. "You made this young Citizen assist you in a dangerous situation when you had in your power the means to return her to family? This was not an ethical bargain, Agent Michelle."

Michelle had the grace to look embarrassed. "I know," she apologized to Gwyn and to the Shanista. "I am sorry, but I made the decision to use the resources at hand, and she was one of them. Plus, I knew you would have to examine her—she formed a link with a chronokinetor with no training or knowledge whatsoever. That thing was supposed to be tuned to me. I thought perhaps by testing her we could determine why some people have a natural aptitude for time travel and seek them out. There aren't enough Agents. Cracks are beginning to show in some timelines. It's getting too dangerous."

"We know," Colsa's voice continued gently, but uncompromising. "The Shift is coming. However, we will not keep young Gwyn here against her will. And it appears also that this timepiece has fixed itself to her."

"Huh?" Gwyn exclaimed.

"What?" Michelle demanded. Brrrys' tail twitched in agitation.

Gwyn felt like panicking for a second, then resigned herself. "Does that mean this thing is stuck in me?" *Seriously? It just doesn't stop, does it? Every time I think I'm closer to getting home, something else comes up to prevent it! Now they'll want to run tests and get this thing out of me. Or is it all just a ruse to keep me here? Michelle did warn me that people here might not want me to go back. Guess she forgot to mention she is one of those people!*

She didn't realize Colsa had spoken to her. "Sorry?" She blushed.

Clicking and a fluttering of wings seem to signal gentle amusement amongst the Shanista.

"I said, that does not pose a problem if you will undertake to return to us at some point in our near future." The other Shanista nodded as

Colsa went on. "It would be cruel and unnecessary to keep you here when you so clearly wish to return to your family. If it is acceptable to you, after several weeks we can dispatch Michelle to collect you and have you visit a facility on Earth. Of course we would require you to guarantee not to use the chronokinetor, as that could seriously affect timelines that have critical turning points."

"But what about the timepiece?" burst out Michelle. "It's one of a kind!"

"We will build another. The technology is not lost. But there will be an investigation into the Agency and ex-Commissioner Hera's corruption, which will include a thorough examination of all Agency technology. It would be best, perhaps, if this chronokinetor stays in a safe place until that furor dies down, or it will merely draw attention from more... unsavory parties. We cannot afford to lose momentum before the Shift happens."

The what? Before she had a chance to ask, all but one of the Shanista clicked and whirred their wings, bowing a farewell to Gwyn, Michelle and Brrrys. *Guess that interview is over.* She tried to feel frustrated at the lack of answers, but somehow she couldn't be bothered. What was wrong with her?

One Shanista remained. It introduced itself as Arenns, a doctor who would give them a brief medical examination to ensure they suffered no serious harm from their travails. They were taken to another level; Michelle was treated for minor burns from the shock-baton torture. A painless blood test revealed that Gwyn had a couple of nasty—and ancient—parasites she had no doubt picked up from her time in Ancient Judea. They hadn't manifested themselves as anything serious yet, but did go some way towards explaining her exhaustion as her immune system sought to fight the drain on her body. A light radiation bath and a carefully administered dose of what she understood to be futuristic antibiotics, followed up with a balancing dose of probiotics, reset her immune system. Gel patches covered up scrapes and bruises—the doctor advised her that by the time they boarded the spaceship back to Earth they would dissolve and her skin would be healed completely.

No STIs, at least. The thought of Gaius made her feel sad. *It was never going to work, I know, but it would have been nice to have a bit longer with him.*

207

What are the odds that I'd meet someone so ahead of his time two thousand years in the past? She fought her dejection. *Come on, Gwyn, you are going home.*

Finally…

* * *

The doctor had taken some blood. Gwyn wondered idly what tests they might run on it, and what it would tell them. *They didn't really invite questions, but I'm annoyed I didn't find out more. I guess they don't want me to know too much about the future.* They didn't seem to want her to stick around either, bundling her and Michelle straight into a private transport to the Spaceport, bypassing normal security and protocols to put them on the first ship back to Earth.

And she was almost back! She stared out the viewing deck of the spaceship at Saturn's rings and they cruised past at what would have been an impossible speed in her time. It was incredible. Both the view and what she had been through. In the past two months she had traveled into the past, the future *and* across the galaxy, meeting ancient humans and aliens from other planets. And now she was set to return to only a few minutes after she had left. It was a lot to take in.

Will it all seem like a dream, I wonder? She looked down at her palm, and the outline of the timepiece that once again looked like no more than a shiny henna tattoo traced onto her skin.

"It's a big deal, isn't it?" she turned to ask Michelle, who stood silent on the viewing deck beside her. "Them trusting me to keep it? How do they know I won't use it?"

The older woman considered this. "I've been thinking about that myself. I don't know if they have a whole lot of choice." She crossed her arms and stared at Titan receding in the viewport. "They weren't kidding about the investigation—there are a lot of people who are against time travel. Say it's meddling. But I know that what we do is important. If history doesn't happen the way it's supposed to, there are serious ramifications for all the species of the Allied Planets."

"Like what?" Gwyn started to ask.

An announcement to prepare for docking by securing all personal items and returning to one's allocated pod came over the ship's system.

It was remarkably similar in principle to the instructions she had received on the flight to Israel. She didn't get a chance to talk privately to Michelle again as passengers swirled around them. Shortly afterwards they entered Earth's largest space station, then followed the crowds to connect to the planet's surface.

The shuttle ride down also distracted her from questioning Michelle further. No space elevator here. Familiar land masses took shape underneath the gently rotating clouds. She was almost there.

Private transport was arranged and the penultimate leg of her journey was quick—a hover-jet returning them to the popular tourist resort of En Gedi. It was busy and crowded, and Michelle's demeanor discouraged any chit chat. *You know I actually think her timepiece might be doing that thing on me... Preventing too much curiosity... I feel like that should annoy me but I can't be bothered, which logically suggests that I'm right. Oh well.* The knowledge didn't help her overcome the apathy, and she entertained herself again by people watching.

They ate a quiet evening meal in the hotel restaurant, and waited for night to fall before wandering down onto the beach, away from tourists and partygoers.

"Well," Michelle said as they contemplated the stars. They were dim compared to those Gwyn remembered from Masada. Light pollution had been nil, the darkness of the desert all-encompassing, and the brilliance of starlight on Gaius' face... She stopped that thought.

Clearing her throat, she asked, "So... How are we doing this?" She rubbed the timepiece with her thumb. "I mean, I think I can probably manage the jump, I can feel how it works and all."

"Oh no! Wow—no—I wouldn't make you do that!" Michelle looked astonished and then distraught. "Anything could happen to you—that would be very irresponsible of me!"

"Oh." Gwyn subsided. *And here I thought I was supposed to be a responsible adult now, surviving in a hostile time and place for months and saving her in the future. Guess I'm not.* She stopped reaching out mentally for the timepiece's connection, and looked to Michelle for direction.

"No, no," Michelle assured her. "I'm going to take you. Or rather, you are going to take me, since yours is the superior device." She showed Gwyn the homemade chronokinetor Owen had created in his apartment. Rickas had confiscated it but obviously never made a record as her imprisonment was illegal. She had retrieved but not reported it, so the Agency didn't know it existed.

Colsa had deemed it best that things remained that way—just as they had left Vivaldis a freeze had been put on all Agency staff, missions, and materials. Michelle had escaped that by being off planet, escorting Gwyn home, but she would be facing questioning—as would everyone involved—when she returned.

"So," she began. "You are going to take my hand, then connect and concentrate on the time you want to go. I suggest aiming for a few minutes after you left, reduces the risk of crossover—you should be able to feel when that is. Talk it through with me. When you are sure and ready, squeeze my hand and we'll make the jump. Once we are there, I'll check to make sure we are in the right time and place, but then I won't stick around. I have a lot of jumps to make to get back to now, and I don't want to waste time." She grinned at the pun. "Keep it safe, disguise it if you can, and remember to charge it every week. Keep an eye on the spiral. Plain water is fine. Salt water is better, since it charges slower when still attached to someone. But you won't be using it, so it shouldn't run down in a hurry. And I'll get in touch with you in your near future. I don't know what will happen exactly to the Agency, but I might be hamstrung for a while. But that won't affect the relative time for you."

"Give me a couple of weeks, at least," Gwyn mumbled. *This is it. This is it!* Her brain shouted. *Going home! Well, kind of.*

Michelle flashed a smile. "Of course. Otherwise you will age too fast relative to your time. But I will be coming back for you."

Gwyn wasn't quite sure if that was a promise or a threat. Either way, that was a future... a past future... that was a problem she would deal with when it happened.

"Okay, let's do it," she said, reaching out for Michelle's hand.

She made the mental connection—it was like to plugging her phone into a power-point. The surge of energy made her brain buzz with excitement and possibility. She took a deep breath, then started to sort through the impulses and concentrated on where—on when—she had to go. It took a while, but she found what seemed to be the right time in her mind. Her brain forced it to shift forward by a few minutes. She squeezed Michelle's hand.

Flick!

THIRTY-FOUR

74 AD

Waves washed gently against the sea wall of the port, and for a moment there was a sense of peace amidst the overhead screaming of seagulls and the distant clatter of ships unloading at the dock. The lack of answers Gaius had found over the last few months had contributed to his overwhelming desire to be gone from Judea, and back home to Rome.

Fortunately, Silva was also inclined to send him back, pleased with the overall success of his campaign to finish quashing the rebellion, but disappointed in his servant for losing the mysterious Gwynia Antonia—she had vanished during the breach of Masada and no trace of her remained. Still, he was far too important a personage to waste time chasing teenage girls in the desert. No doubt she'd managed to get herself involved with a soldier and it had ended badly, despite his best efforts to protect her. He conveniently forgot that nothing in the girl's personality had showed her inclined to make those sorts of decisions and sighed that not every woman could be as sensible as his wife.

The Jewish survivors were another matter. Titus' sycophant Josephus arrived in camp shortly after the siege had ended, and Silva permitted him to question the two women briefly about the events inside the fortress leading up to the breach. He didn't glean much, except that it had been decided that suicide was preferable to surrender, and Silva had to admit he admired their collective courage. He had sent the two women and three children to Jaffa with Gaius under orders to take the first ship to Rome. The girl and the children were young and could be absorbed into the slaves of his household, and the old woman had to go with them to avoid any kind of focus for future Jewish rebels. Besides, keeping them alive did his *dignitas* no harm. He could afford to be magnanimous now—he was headed for a Consulship, after all!

"There are lots of Jews in Rome," Gaius had tried to reassure Adi. She had begun learning Latin and was teaching it to the children, realizing that the ability to communicate would serve them well in their new home.

"Yes, but we are slaves now," she replied flatly. Still, they were alive and relatively unharmed, and after so many brushes with death, she was learning to take each day as it came. She had been skeptical of the tale Gaius told of Gwyna, that she was from another time and had used magic to go back there, but neither of them could come up with a better explanation. Sarah had commented that the Roman was pining for their mysterious friend, and it was on this strange absence that a kind of comradeship was formed between the Roman boy and the Jewish girl.

Maybe one day I'll see her again. Gaius turned from contemplating the sea and strode down the docks to board the ship. After all, who knew what the future held?

**Read on for a sneak peek at Gwyn's
next time-travel adventure:**

Transylvanian Knight.

JODIE LANE

ONE

Sticky pools of blood oozed against her rough sandals. Nausea welled up in Gwyn, but she was paralysed with shock, unable to turn, flee, or even shut her eyes against the scene in front of her. She retched as the smell hit her nostrils, and breathing through her mouth only tainted her tongue with a thick, coppery taste.

It was the faces that affected her the most. Bodies were everywhere, limbs askew, smeared with gore. She might have been able to pretend they weren't real, if it weren't for the faces. Despite the blood stains and bruises, she could recognise the foremost ones in the pile of corpses.

Sarah. Adi. Silva. Gaius.

Gaius… Please, no!

Empty-eyed, ashen skin and slack jawed. There was no doubt they were dead, even if she couldn't see the swords, arrows, and spears that pierced their flesh. Flies buzzed into open mouths, maggots crawled in congealing wounds. The bodies of other men and women from Masada slumped further back, children too, as well as soldiers from the Tenth Frentensis. Some she recognised—Eleazar, Elizabeth, Gad, the old Rabbi—but plenty she didn't. Their numbers staggered her, filling the throne room, crammed against the walls.

This is a dream, just a dream. But she'd thought it was a dream once before, when she'd gone back in time, and it had all been real…

Someone was missing. One sinister, ominous face lacked a presence in the hall of death. Gwyn had to run or he would find her, only, to her horror, the blood that had merely crept along the floor had risen to her knees and was as thick as mud. Arms pin wheeling, she fought to maintain her balance. Eyes sought the entrance to the throne room—it was clear! Wading fiercely, the room seemed to tilt against her and each step made a nasty sucking sound. *Almost there…*

She strained a little too hard and lost her balance. Gwyn shrieked in panic and threw out her hands as she fell. Pushing back up to her knees, she saw her arms were dripping to the elbows. Choking with terror and disgust and with tears pouring down her face, she reached the doorway. As she touched the stone frame, the blood vanished. A shadow fell on her.

"You can't escape your fate," Joshua rasped.

The man who'd frightened her so much at Masada loomed over her. There was something *wrong* with his head.

She gulped back vomit—half his skull was smashed in, leaving a lopsided horror that glared. His hands gripped her face and squeezed. She twisted and clawed frantically at his filthy skin, but as the pressure mounted, she began to black out. The last things she heard were her own screams and his hateful voice.

"You can't escape me…"

* * *

PRESENT DAY

"Gwyn. Gwyn. *Gwyn!*"

She gasped awake and lurched up in her bed, almost braining her sister Naomi. Cold sweat clung to the back of her neck and shoulders, the clamminess driving her to pull at her t-shirt. Naomi grasped her by the upper arm.

"You had a nightmare, sis. You were yelling in your sleep."

Wide-eyed, Gwyn stared uncomprehendingly, then she let out a massive, tense breath. She looked hopelessly at her sister and their brother Justin, who was sitting up in the top bunk across the hostel room. She couldn't read his face in the dim light, but she'd wager the thirteen-year-old was alarmed.

"S-sorry guys." *It was a nightmare. A dream. Not real. Calm down.* "Thanks for waking me." She reached for her phone. It was five a.m. Dim light crept into the sky outside the window, but they didn't have to get up for breakfast for another two hours. She lay back on the bed then sat up, turned her sweat-soaked pillow over, and tried again.

"Must have been a bad one," Naomi said, still standing at her bedside. "What was it about? Who's Guy?"

Gwyn forced a smile onto her face. "Guy? I've no idea." *I must have been yelling for Gaius.* "I can't even remember it now—don't you hate how dreams do that? Go back to sleep. I'm sorry I woke you both."

Naomi stood there a moment longer, then retreated to her bunk. Gwyn closed her eyes and feigned sleep, but she could hear the twins.

"That's the third night in a row," Justin hissed. "She's getting louder."

"I know—that's why I woke her. Wish she'd tell us what the dream was. It'd probably help."

"I don't know if I want to know—sounded like she was being tortured. Did she do this before we came away?"

"No, only since we left Israel."

They both went quiet, and Gwyn was left alone in her thoughts.

Great. Three nights? I don't remember waking up before tonight. I should have known it was just a dream. She shuddered and rolled onto her side, hugging her arms around her chest, tucking her knees up. Despite the knowledge it wasn't real, the nightmare still coursed through her. She couldn't rid herself of the devastation she felt upon seeing her friends in the pile of the dead, and the paralysing terror of thinking Joshua had come to seek his revenge for the part she had played in his death.

I can't forget about it. The pocket watch lodged in her left palm reminded her that she had experienced weeks of harrowing and difficult experiences, while mere minutes had passed for her family. She sighed and clenched her eyes shut, willing sleep upon herself. Whether it was fear of the nightmare returning or an overactive brain churning the thoughts through her head, sleep did not come.

* * *

Hours later, she tagged along behind her parents as they toured the Palace of Parliament in central Bucharest.

"Ceauşescu, like many infamous dictators, was not the tallest man." Their English-speaking guide paused at the bottom of a grand staircase. "However, he was obsessed with his public image and ordered this staircase to be rebuilt three times so that each step was neither too tall nor too shallow. That way, when he used it, his height was not accentuated."

"Just like Tom Cruise standing on a box in Top Gun," Gwyn overheard her dad whisper to her mom, who giggled.

"Was this where he was shot?" Justin asked.

The guide shook her head with a smile.

"No. Nicolai and Elena fled Bucharest to Târgovişte, where they were captured, trialled and executed by firing squad. Târgovişte is also famous for being the capital of Vlad Dracula, or, as you might know in English, Vlad the Impaler. You can visit the ruins of his castle there."

"Are we going there, Dad?" Justin asked excitedly.

"No." Their dad ruffled his son's hair, who shied away with annoyance. "We head north for Transylvania after this."

Justin's disappointment was so obvious the guide took pity on him. "You can probably find a guide at Ghencea Cemetery to show you Ceauşescu's grave—although he was exhumed last year and moved. Or if it's Dracula you are interested in, Bran Castle near Braşov is a popular tourist attraction for Dracula fans, even though Vlad's real castle was nowhere near there." The tour group trailed after her.

Naomi dropped back to walk beside Gwyn. She frowned but didn't say anything at first, her blonde bob swaying gently with her stride. Then, in a voice that belied her thirteen years with its seriousness, she asked, "Is everything alright, sis? You've been a bit funny since Israel."

Gwyn glanced at her, sighed, and said, "I'm fine, thanks—just all this traveling tiring me out, I guess."

It was plain to see Naomi wasn't convinced. "You've been so excited about coming away for months. It was all you talked about before we left. You even talked about, you know," her voice dropped, "asking Mom and Dad about staying on when we go home."

Gwyn felt a twinge of annoyance that she'd confided in her sister about that. "You better not have blabbed,' she warned.

"Of course I haven't!" Naomi's tone was indignant. Several people in the group turned to look. Gwyn frowned and made shushing motions with her hand. Their parents were up the front, quizzing the tour guide about the logistics of the building, but her mother had excellent hearing.

Facts, facts, facts, Gwyn thought gloomily. *Always about the facts with them.* She preferred the stories about the people who had built this monstrosity—forced labour, hidden bunkers, dramatic tales from the Communist Regime.

"So?" Her sister was still buzzing like an annoying fly. "What's wrong? You can tell me."

Her insistent tone was both an irritation and a temptation. *I just need to talk to someone about all this. Who knows how long it'll be before Michelle comes back for me? If she ever does.* Michelle had said several weeks. Originally Gwyn had been glad of the break, but that was before the nightmares, the daytime jitters and her lack of appetite. And it had only been three days. If she didn't get a grip, she'd lose her mind. The inability to vent about what she'd been through was eating her from the inside.

Oh, God damn it. "I'll tell you later, I promise," she muttered. Maybe her sister would think she was nuts, but if she didn't say something, Naomi might tell their parents about Gwyn wanting to stay on in Europe. She had that look on her face. They didn't often argue, but the younger teenager wasn't averse to fighting dirty to get her way.

Naomi started to protest, clearly unsatisfied.

Gwyn simply nudged her way politely through to the front of the tour group to join their parents, and they continued on through the Palace of Parliament.

TWO

PRESENT DAY

Gwyn stared out of the window as the train drew slowly out of Gara du Nord. Bucharest was not a pretty city. Too many decades of Communist rule had left dull grey blocks of housing throughout most of the city, save where the political elite had lived and worked. The ornate architecture of the city centre and tree-lined avenues in suburbs such as Primaverii were left behind as the train rattled north out of the capital through grimy industrial estates and semi-slum areas.

The Turners were heading north to Brașov, gateway to the Carpathians. The six a.m. departure time was no hardship to Gwyn, who had been woken by her alarm before her nightmare reached its horrific conclusion. Leaving the hostel also made her happy—she missed the luxurious Crowne Plaza hotel, though she struggled to sleep on a soft bed after so many weeks on the ground or a rough pallet. Now that they traveled on their own budget, not their company's, Stephen and Danielle were frugal in their accommodation choices for the family. But Gwyn still knew she was experiencing far greater comfort than anyone had at Masada, so a weird sense of guilt left her surly.

"Just got my period," she lied to her mother when quizzed about her dark mood. *That's another thing I never asked about. Stupid time device.* It annoyed her that the pocket watch actively deterred her curiosity about the Time Space Agent, conveniently forgetting that this feature had saved Gwyn multiple times in Ancient Judea. She was jotting down a list of questions to put to Michelle the next time she saw her, determined not to be put off by the device again.

"Gwyn, can you come with me to the toilet?" Naomi asked, rousing

Gwyn from her self-absorbed sulk. The five of them took up the entire train compartment, with backpacks and their parents' suitcases balanced precariously above on the luggage racks, and day packs stashed on the sixth seat. Any other traveler looking for a seat would likely take one glance at the group and pass by. The train was not particularly busy— Gwyn had already considered retreating to another compartment, but Naomi pre-empted her.

Her mother glanced up and nodded, "Yes please, Gwyn. I'd prefer it that no one wanders off alone, even on the train."

Sighing, Gwyn shoved her half-drawn earphones away and pulled at the compartment door. It stuck, old brown fittings jamming in the runners. She pulled harder, jerking it open, muttering under her breath. *Piece of shite.*

The train was old; worn carpet and faded paint flaking off the walls, and a faint musty smell that permeated both corridor and compartment did nothing to improve her mood. Naomi rolled her eyes as she stepped over her father's legs and led the way down to the back end of the carriage. The hydraulics of the doors hissed and clunked as the sisters crossed the coupling into the carriage with the ladies toilet. They were perturbed to see the external door on the side of the train was open— some mechanism appeared to have failed, though the click-hiss made it sound like it was trying to close.

"Go on." Gwyn ushered her sister into the loo and stood guard outside. *I suppose I'll get in trouble if I scoot off.* The landscape rushed by; Bucharest's outer suburbs gave way to countryside and the first hints of autumn colouring in the leaves.

Lost in her thoughts, Gwyn leant against the rattling corridor wall while she waited for Naomi. The train's brakes whined as it entered a curve, then a violent lurch shook the whole carriage. Before she had time to react, Gwyn was launched out of the open door.

Her arm shot out and fingers wrapped around the edge of the door frame, anchoring her just enough to turn her straight fall into an arc. Her body slammed onto the outside of the train with one foot hooked inside the carriage. She struggled to drag herself back in, but the continued rattling along the tracks and the tilt of the carriage around the curve meant that it was all she could do to hold on as the wind buffeted her violently, screaming death in her ears.

She couldn't hold on for much longer. Fingertips burned from holding her weight. Each little bump from the train edged her further out the carriage door.

Help! She felt the panic rise like bile in her throat, and with a last desperate attempt she used a microsecond of weightlessness that came from the train's motion and hoicked herself back—

Just as a hand grabbed her forearm and jerked her inwards. Tumbling onto Naomi in a heap, her sister grabbed her in a hug and they rolled against the toilet door. Gasping and shuddering, it was all Gwyn could do to catch her breath in the sudden quiet. The funky odour and hard metal door of the bathroom was a welcome assault after the whistling, fresh air that a moment ago had spelt her fate as a gory smear on the train tracks of Romania.

"Are you okay?" Naomi stared, panting and wide-eyed.

Gwyn managed to nod, then shook her head and trembled as the realisation of what had just happened hit her.

"Come on," her sister urged her into a crawl and they moved down the corridor, pulling themselves into an empty compartment. The insulated walls deadened the sound from outside, especially once Naomi hauled the door shut.

Gwyn dragged herself onto the seat, head in her hands, elbows on her knees. *It's okay, you're alright. You're alive.* Her breathing calmed as her little sister put an arm around her shoulders and spoke Gwyn's thoughts out loud.

"You're okay, it's alright. Sheesh, that was close. What happened? I'd just finished washing my hands when the train lurched and I looked out and all I could see was your foot and I thought you'd died and I was so scared!" Her words tumbled out.

"You were scared?" Gwyn almost laughed. "I was fu—, freaking terrified!"

"Freaking?"

This time, she did laugh. "Fucking terrified."

Naomi joined her with nervous laughter, until both girls were in hysterics, shaken and relieved at the close call.

Finally, they calmed down. "Mom and Dad will wonder where we are," Gwyn said, making to rise.

"No, they won't, you weren't listening when we left; they were discussing pollution in the Danube. Justin was playing games on his phone. None of them will notice if we're gone for a while.'"

Gwyn had to concede the point, taking another relieved breath. Her sister fixed her with a pointed look.

"Now, will you tell me what's the deal with you? You've been super weird since Israel."

Guess I can't wiggle out of it. She'll think I'm nuts, but it'll be worth it to get it off my chest.

"When did you get so grown up?" she smiled lopsidedly at her younger sister. Taking a deep breath, Gwyn looked up and froze.

Michelle was standing outside the compartment door.

AUTHOR'S NOTE

When I was fourteen, my father worked in Israel for a month, seconded to a company to help deal with managing crops in such an arid environment. We joined him for a week at the end of his secondment, and were toured all about the country, including Masada. Ironically, I sulked a good part of that day, finding the heat unbearable, and not appreciating the incredible opportunity and gift of travel and history that I had been given.

But the memory of the place stayed with me, enough so that when I was twenty-seven, and was prompted by a colleague into writing a book, it was Masada that spoke to me as a setting for the story I wanted to write.

I've always found history fascinating—it is so rich with incredible people and places, and served to inspire me to write this particular story. I feel that while certain social, political and economic trends cause history to trundle along in a cyclical fashion (empires rise and fall, people migrate and mingle, war both decimates and drives change), I love the idea that perhaps there are turning points where things could have gone quite differently, and those turning points may have been influenced by quite subtle factors.

This is the driving idea behind *The Siege of Masada*—that despite inertia, the right pebble in the right stream might be enough to make a difference to the course of the river. For the sake of the story I have taken liberties with historical facts, timeframes, and locations, but I tried to capture the essence of the event, and of course any inaccuracies and mistakes are my own.

This version of Masada has been somewhat edited and rewritten compared to the original book I released, but the original thanks remain: to my family for never doubting that I could write a book, to my original beta-readers and the ones I've acquired since, and of course, to Trevor, for embarrassing me into starting in the first place. You made me realise that dreaming of being a writer is not enough—if you want to be a writer, you have to write!

ABOUT THE AUTHOR

Jodie Lane is an avid amateur historian, combining her love of travel and adventure with fascinating stories from the past. Brisbane based, she studied a variety of modern history at the University of Queensland, and loves to read a wide range of historical and science fiction.

Her travels have taken her all over the world: she has lived and taught English in China and Romania, backpacked through Europe and South America, and holidayed in the Middle East, Central and North America, South East Asia, New Zealand and South Africa. She speaks basic Spanish as a second language and her sport of choice is wing chun (kung fu).

Transylvanian Knight is the sequel to *The Siege of Masada* in "Turning Points"—a time travel adventures series visiting pivotal historical events and exploring an exciting new future for humanity. You can find out more via www.jodielane.com

BIBLIOGRAPHY

I am indebted to the following books and websites for providing information and background about the era and region:

Blech, Rabbi Benjamin. *Eyewitness to Jewish History.* John Wiley and Sons, Inc. Hokoben, New Jersey, 2004.

Dougherty, Martin J, Haskew, Michael E, Jestice, Phyllis G and Rice, Rob S. *Battles of the Bible 1400 BC – AD 73: From Ai to Masada.* London, Amber Books Ltd, 2008.

Jewish Virtual Library: Archaeology in Israel: Masada Desert Fortress. http://www.jewishvirtuallibrary.org/jsource/Archaeology/Masada1.html

Josephus. *The Jewish War.* Translated by G. A. Williamson. London, Penguin Books, 1959.

Magness, Jodi. Masada: From Jewish Revolt to Modern Myth. Princeton, New Jersey, Princeton University Press, 2019.

Like time-travel?

Check out the Turning Points series
at jodielane.com

The Siege of Masada
Transylvanian Knight
To Kill An Emperor
Renaissance Woman
Heart and Stomach of a Queen

Turning Points Short Stories:

Siege of the Heart
The Time-Traveller's Date
A Soldier's Love
A Soldier's Honour

www.ingramcontent.com/pod-product-compliance
Lightning Source LLC
Chambersburg PA
CBHW030623120726
47904CB00006B/2015